DANCING
THE CODE

DOCTOR WHO – THE MISSING ADVENTURES

DANCING THE CODE

Paul Leonard

First published in Great Britain in 1995 by
Doctor Who Books
an imprint of Virgin Publishing Ltd
332 Ladbroke Grove
London W10 5AH

ISBN 0 426 20441 7

Cover illustration by Paul Campbell
Xarax helicopter based on a sketch by Jim Mortimore

Typeset by Galleon Typesetting, Ipswich
Printed and bound in Great Britain by
Cox & Wyman Ltd, Reading, Berks

Acknowledgements

First and foremost thanks must go to Jim Mortimore for:
1. getting me involved in Doctor Who books in the first
place; 2. loan of videos and books; 3. sketches of Xarax
(see front cover); 4. editing, plot suggestions; 5. moral
support. At least three-fifths of the enjoyment you may
get out of this book is due to Jim. Secondly, thanks to
Barb Drummond for sterling efforts in reading through
the text and correcting innumerable bits of unworkable
prose (any that remain are strictly my fault!). Two-fifths of
your enjoyment is due to Barb – and watch out for her
novel, it's going to be good. Then there's Craig, who
once again made many useful suggestions on Doctor
Who continuity. One-fifth of your reading pleasure is
down to the eponymous Mr Hinton, I believe. And
one-fifth to be split between: my mother, for use of telly
and much needed moral support; Bex and Andy at
Virgin, for editorial support and general chumminess;
Chris Lake, Nick Walters and Mark Leyland of the
writer's circle (comments, suggestions and encouragement); Dr Richard Spence (telling me I wasn't going to
die just yet); Peter-Fred, Richard, Tim, Matthew and
Steve of the Bristol SF group (enthusiasm); Pat and
Martine, Anita and Joe, Anna, Ann H, Helen, Nadia
(friendship and support).

And if anyone noticed that without all those people, their
reading pleasure would have been minus two-fifths –
well, that just about says it all, doesn't it?

For Anna and Philip

may you travel far together

Prologue

– sweet sweet honey honey –

– sweet sweet good good honey dancing to be dancing honey –

Can you speak?

– sweet dancing honey dancing good good sweet sweet –

Do you understand me?

– dancing understanding honey dancing sweet sweet sweet honey to be understanding to be dancing –

I am human. What are you?

– human dancing honey dancing to be sweet sweet honey to be dancing human to be honey –

I came here to help to find peace. Tell me, how do I find peace?

– peace to be dancing peace to be honey peace to be good good honey sweet to be making nest to be good sweet honey dancing –

They told me you could bring peace!

– peace to be human to be honey dancing peace to be honey dancing –

I might be able to bring more humans to you –

– more humans to be dancing to be sweet sweet honey honey –

– *but first there are some things you have to do for me.*

– dancing to be human to be honey to be –

Do you understand? I'm making a bargain. I bring you people – humans. You bring me peace. YOU BRING ME PEACE, YOU UNDERSTAND?

– peace to be dancing honey to be dancing peace to be

dancing the code –
   Yes. Peace. At last.
   – honey dancing sweet sweet peace honey honey –
   – dancing the code dancing the code –
   – dancing the code –

Book One

War Dancing

URGENT MEMORANDUM

FROM: R.COM Z OFFICE

TO: R.COM C-IN-C

SECURITY CLASSIFICATION: R.COM STAFF ONLY

RE: DANCERS

PROJECT NOW READY TO PROCEED. NEED 1000 REPEAT 1000 PERSONNEL **URGENT** TO SUPPLY DANCERS. SCHEDULE OPERATION COUNTERSTRIKE FOR 1230 TUESDAY REPEAT 1230 TUESDAY. I WILL BE READY.

One

The fire was almost out, no more than a pile of ashes and softly glowing charcoal. Its dim red light gleamed on the enamel teapot that stood warming on the brazier, shone more faintly on the guns stacked by the closed flap of the tent. Catriona Talliser closed her eyes for a moment, let herself feel the warmth and comfort, the spice and smoke-laden smell of the air.

'You are tired? We could speak in the morning, if you prefer it.'

Catriona opened her eyes again, fixed them on the shadowy shape of her host, the gleaming eyes in the dark, fire-lit face, the grey, pointed beard. The white shirt and Levis he was wearing seemed somehow out of place on him; he looked as if he should have been wearing a traditional burnous, like Omar Sharif in *Lawrence of Arabia*. He probably had done, she thought, when he was younger.

'I have to leave early in the morning,' she said. 'I need –' I need to be back in Kebir City by two-thirty tomorrow, to interview Khalil Benari, the leader of your enemies. But she couldn't very well say that. 'My editor needs my story in before eleven,' she lied.

The *Sakir* Mohammad nodded. 'More tea, then?'

Catriona almost said no – she found the strong, sweet, minty tea of the Giltaz all but undrinkable – but she knew it would help her stay awake, so she nodded.

The *Sakir* clapped his hands. 'Tahir! Light the torch!'

There was a movement in the near-darkness. For a moment, Catriona imagined that Mohammad's son was going to light a real torch, a wooden brand dipped in sheep's fat, like the ones she'd seen in the flicks when she was a kid. But there was a disappointing metallic click, and ordinary electric light filled the tent, throwing sharp, swiftly moving shadows against the grimy camel-wool walls. She saw that there were more guns than she had noticed at first: as well as the Kalashnikovs stacked by the entrance, the light caught a rack of hand guns, and a leather belt hung with small, black grenades.

She made a mental note for her report: 'The Giltean Separatists are well armed, and their equipment is modern.'

Tahir put the torch down, and Catriona saw that it was in fact a battered bicycle lamp, emblazoned with the logo 'EVER READY'.

Tahir sat cross-legged in front of the fire, poured the tea from the enamel pot into the tiny glasses; poured it back again, and out again, then examined the decanted fluid by the light of the torch. He added some sugar to the glasses, some tea to the pot, poured back and forth a few more times, examined the results once more, then, satisfied, passed one of the glasses to Catriona.

She sipped the tea – too sweet, too strong, too hot – and smiled.

'It's wonderful.' She was conscious of her own awkward, English politeness.

Tahir drank his own tea in one gulp, said nothing.

Catriona looked at him: broad nose and lips, narrow black moustache, dark, watchful eyes. She wondered for a moment if it was Tahir that she should be interviewing, rather than his father. The young man of action, rather than the Old Man of the Desert.

Tahir caught her eye and smiled slightly. Catriona had the unnerving sensation that he knew exactly what she had been thinking. She turned her gaze quickly back to Mohammad.

'*Sakir*,' she said, 'may we begin now? I'll use the cassette recorder if you don't mind.'

The old man waved a hand, murmured, 'Of course, Monsieur.'

Catriona frowned at the 'monsieur', then remembered the little ceremony Mohammad had insisted on making before she could enter the tent with them, when he had declared her to be an honorary man. That had happened to her before in her dealings with desert Arabs; but she hadn't expected Mohammad to take it literally, to the extent of calling her 'monsieur'. The feminist in her – the woman who had quite literally burned her bra, on a hot day in London in the crazy summer of '69 – resented it bitterly. Why couldn't the Giltaz let her into their tents as a *woman*? Why couldn't they treat her as what she was – a human being, who happened to be female?

With an effort she suppressed her annoyance, turned away and unshipped the cassette recorder from her rucksack. She held the microphone a foot from her lips, and rather self-consciously tested the level. The miniature VU meter flicked back and forth with a series of faint clicks.

'Three – two – one – go.' She took a breath. 'I'm in the secret desert headquarters of the Giltean Separatist movement, the FLNG. With me are the *Sakir* Mohammad Al-Naemi, acknowledged leader of the resistance movement, and his son Tahir.' There would be no audience for the recording except herself, when she typed up her story in Kebir City tomorrow, but Catriona liked to keep her tapes clearly labelled.

She paused, then looked the old man in the eye and began.

'*Sakir*. You were known as the leader of the political opposition in Kebiria for many years. You participated in debates with Khalil Benari in the National Assembly. Why do you feel it necessary now to take up arms against the government?'

She knew what the answer would be, of course: and it came immediately, well-rehearsed.

7

'Mr Benari began this struggle. He imprisoned my son; he executed my friends. Now he bombs our children, the children of the Giltaz. What choice do we have but to fight back?'

There was a hollow sadness in his voice, an emptiness in his eyes as he spoke. Catriona wished she could capture it for her report. She decided to try moving away from her planned line of questioning.

'But you aren't happy with having to fight?'

The *Sakir* glanced at his son, a sharp, sidelong glance. Catriona risked following it, saw that the tense, watchful look on the younger man's face had intensified.

But it was Mohammad who spoke. 'We do what we need to do.'

Back to the interview plan then, thought Catriona. She took another sip of the tea. It was cooler, but didn't taste any better.

'But surely you must know that you can't hope to force the Kebirian government to grant independence to Giltea? They have a large modern army and an air force; you have a few hundred soldiers in the desert.'

There was a short pause. The electric torch dimmed, then brightened again.

'Our cause is just,' said Mohammad simply. 'Allah Himself fights with us.' Again he glanced at his son. This time the young man frowned, looked away.

He doesn't believe in Allah, Catriona decided. She wondered what he did believe in. Marx? Mao? The power of the gun?

Tahir caught her glance, and his lips curled into a slight smile. Mohammad rubbed his hands together above the fire, as if warming them.

'You see,' he went on, 'we intend to set up a democratic state – a Muslim state – whereas Mr Benari runs a dictatorship. Furthermore, we make no claim to the territory of the Kebiriz. We merely wish for the Giltaz to have self-government in their traditional lands.' He paused, still rubbing his hands together; Catriona

8

wondered if he really felt cold. The tent was warm, stuffy. 'I cannot understand,' the old man said, with a note of genuine puzzlement in his voice, 'why the people of England, and France and America, do not support us, when our cause is just.'

He fell silent, closed his eyes. Catriona hesitated, unsure as to whether she should ask the next question. Perhaps the old man had fallen asleep. From the corner of her eye, she noticed that Tahir's smile had broadened. He was drumming his fingers on the camel-wool matting that covered the floor of the tent.

Suddenly he leaned forward.

' "Monsieur" Talliser,' he said quietly. 'Would you like to have a talk with me — "off the record", as you say? Outside? Man to — "man"?'

She glanced at him sharply, was met by cool, amused eyes. *Let's try your courage, then*, they seemed to say.

Okay, thought Catriona. Let's.

She nodded at Mohammad. 'If the *Sakir* permits —'

The old man opened his eyes, frowned, looked from one to the other of them. Catriona had the impression that he really had been asleep.

'Very well,' he said, waving a hand.

Tahir turned without a word, grabbed his boots and dived out through the flap of the tent. Catriona followed, stopping only to pull on her own boots and lace them, and check that her cassette recorder was still running. She didn't want to miss anything, 'off the record' or not; and she couldn't risk fiddling with the microphone switch when Tahir was within earshot. She clipped the microphone to her pocket, and hoped that he wouldn't hear the motor running.

Outside, it was cold. The air was brittle and still, the stars overbright. There was no moon, the landscape around was little more than shadow, broken by the dim lights from within the tents of the encampment. Tahir was just visible, his face a pale shape in the faint light from the tent behind them. A star burned near his lips; he was

9

smoking a cigarette. Silently, he offered Catriona one. She shook her head.

'I've given up. Smoking's bad for you.'

Tahir said nothing for a while, then suddenly set off at a fast walk. Catriona followed, tripping once or twice on the rocky, uneven ground. After a while, her eyes adjusted, and she could make out ahead of them the dim shape of the Hatar Massif, the mountain range which divided the desert – and the territory of the FLNG – from the scrublands held by the Kebirian government.

Tahir stopped walking, as suddenly as he had started. Catriona almost collided with him. He turned, took the cigarette from his mouth, blew smoke. There was a silence, in which she could hear his breathing, and her own.

'Miss Talliser, will you tell the truth about us?' he said at last.

Catriona just managed to suppress a smile. All this, for such an obvious question! But then, she told herself, Tahir wasn't a reporter. He didn't need to be sophisticated, he was just asking what he needed to know.

She thought for a moment, remembering the road that afternoon, the two bodies hanging from the dead cypress tree, 'traitors' to the Giltaz, executed without trial; but remembering also the prison camp in Giltat, the government jets screaming low over the city in triumph. Khalil Benari's cold, smiling face on the grimy black-and-white TV above the bar in Burrous Asi: 'The revolt has been crushed.'

And the broken bodies on the road outside the town. The children, flies crawling over their wounds.

She looked up at Tahir. 'The whole truth, and nothing but the truth,' she said quietly.

Their eyes met. Tahir smiled.

'In the name of Allah?'

Catriona, surprised, made a solemn nod; she knew that it would be inappropriate and stupid at this moment to tell Tahir that she didn't believe in God. Or that she didn't think he did either.

Tahir smiled again, then turned away from her, pointed up at the Hatar Massif. 'Benari lost a thousand men up there yesterday. Men, equipment, armour, artillery. They were sent after us, to "flush the rats out of their nests". They never got here.'

Catriona gathered that she was meant to sound impressed, so she whistled softly. 'That's a pretty significant victory.'

Tahir puffed on his cigarette. 'Yes, and we will be claiming it as such. Perhaps you would like to report it – an "exclusive" for your paper.'

Catriona nodded, though she knew that a story as big as this would hardly stay under wraps for a whole day – it must have broken in Kebir City even as she'd left in the afternoon.

'But what you will not report –' Tahir stepped forward in the darkness, reached out and pulled the microphone from her pocket, switched it off, put it back again '– what I could not possibly let you report is that we did not do it.'

Catriona stared into his eyes, now only a couple of feet from hers. 'What do you mean?'

'I mean that they vanished.' He paused, took a step back. 'My father says that Allah took them. Most of the men think they crossed the border and sought asylum in Morocco. You and I know that this is not possible.'

Catriona nodded. It was certainly improbable. Even assuming that a force so large would defect wholesale, the Moroccans were sympathetic to the Kebirian government and were quite likely to ship them back for punishment. Could they have made a break for the Atlantic, through Moroccan territory? But who would pick them up? The Russians? The Chinese? It sounded even more improbable.

'Could they have – got lost, or something?'

Tahir laughed. 'One man might get lost, if he is stupid

11

enough. But not a thousand at one time, with radios, jeeps, tanks. No, some other thing happened to them. Something you cannot explain in the ordinary way of things.'

Catriona had a sudden sinking sensation. Had Tahir brought her out here to tell her that he thought the enemy were being captured by ghosts or demons? She could just see Mike Timms's reaction when she sent in her story – 'Kebirian Army kidnapped by demons – leader of resistance movement claims divine intervention'.

'Have you any ideas?'

The question startled Catriona. Whatever else she had expected of Tahir, she certainly hadn't expected him to be asking her for advice. She took a few steps away from him, looked back at the faint lights of the encampment. Shook her head.

'You know the desert much better than I do.'

'That's true. I know the desert: I know it well enough to tell you that a thousand men do not disappear into a hole in the ground.'

Catriona thought for a moment. 'Are you sure they have disappeared? Where does your information come from?'

Tahir laughed, said quietly, 'Spies.'

'Maybe your spies have been misinformed.'

Tahir laughed again. 'Maybe so. Maybe one of them has been – how do the American films put it? – "turned". In which case –'

He stopped speaking, sucked in a breath, turned away from her, his boots scuffing on the loose stones.

Catriona frowned. 'You mean they might still be –'

'Quiet!' hissed Tahir.

Then she could hear it, echoing through the cold night air: the sound of engines, the bump of tyres moving on the stony surface of the desert. She swung her head round, trying to locate the source of the sound, saw a moving, silvery light reflected off a nearby cliff.

12

'Get down!' whispered Tahir.

Catriona crouched, then lay flat. The sound grew louder, a pair of headlamps appeared, lighting up a silver swathe of rocks and sand. Catriona felt her heart thumping against her ribs.

She pulled the microphone of the cassette recorder from her pocket, flicked the ON switch. 'I'm in the Giltean Separatist base in the desert, and it appears that we're under attack.'

She cautiously raised her head, saw a single jeep bouncing down the slope. It suddenly occurred to her that it was unlikely anyone would be attacking in one jeep, with the headlamps on full beam. It was more likely that it was some Western visitor — perhaps her photographer had turned up at last —

Tahir shouted something, pulled at her shoulders. With a jolt of shock, Catriona realized that the jeep was out of control, and heading straight towards them. She half rolled, half jumped to one side, saw the jeep rush past. There was something huge and black crammed into the driving seat, but before she could register what it was, the jeep had ploughed into a tent and rolled onto its side. It slithered across the rough stone for a few yards, stopped with a sickening crunch of metal.

Catriona took a step forward but Tahir grabbed her arm.

'It could be a bomb!' he shouted. 'A suicide attack!'

Catriona hesitated for a moment, then shook off his grip and ran towards the crash. Ran because she'd seen a human face above the huge black round thing, could still see something that looked like flesh in the reflected light of the one remaining headlamp. As she got closer, she saw the treacly fluid oozing out of the driver's door, smelled petrol and a perfumed, spicy smell.

Roses and cloves, she thought. Odd. Did he bring a suitcase full of perfume? She saw the letters UNIT emblazoned across the crumpled bonnet of the jeep. United Nations Intelligence —?

13

She quickened her pace, her reporter's instinct for a story thoroughly aroused.

Then she got close enough to see properly. To see the human face, stretched until the skin broke open, and weeping blood from the huge cracks. To see the translucent body beneath, covered with the shreds of clothing, with dark half-shadows that might have been bones or organs inside it. To see the staring blue eyes, shot with blood and twitching with pain.

I will not be sick, she thought. I will *not* be sick. She searched the body for clues, saw the pocket of a uniform jacket, the words 'Capt. A. Deveraux' sewn on to it.

Then she heard a whisper, coming from a throat buried in the mass of blood-sticky honey, chitin and bone that had once been a human body.

'Tell them – tell them honey – sweet sweet honey –'

Instinctively, Catriona pushed the microphone forward, near to the grey, desiccated lips.

'– sweet sweet to be honey – tell them – human to be honey to be dancing –'

The voice wavered, faded; for a moment was nothing but an empty rattle.

'What dancing?' asked Catriona, her own voice no more than a choked whisper.

The eyes found Catriona's, stared.

'– dancing the code –'

Then there was a sucking sound. A bubble blew out from the lips, then air rushed out as the entire bloated body sagged. Honey-like fluid, streaked with muddy brown, ran out across her boots. With a horrible shock Catriona realized that the brown streaks were human blood. She stepped back; her boots made sucking noises as she lifted them from the ground.

She looked around, saw Tahir and the others approaching. They seemed to be moving in slow motion, as if wading through deep water. She lifted the microphone but her hands were shaking so much that she couldn't work the 'off' switch.

14

'He's dead,' she said. 'I've just interviewed a dead man.'

Then she was sick. Violently, and at some length, all over the stony ground.

When she was finished, she straightened up, found a handkerchief in her pocket and wiped her face. She heard a whisper of breathing, turned and saw the *Sakir* Mohammad standing by her side.

'Don't move,' he said quietly.

Catriona frowned. 'Why not?'

But the old man had turned, was talking to Tahir. 'Bring all the petrol we can spare.'

Then he turned back to Catriona, pulled the sleeves of his shirt down over his hands, bent down to her feet and pulled at her boots.

'What are you doing?' Catriona tried to step back, but strong hands took hold of her arms.

'I'm sorry,' said the *Sakir*. 'But you will lose your boots.'

The first boot slipped off, hurting her foot as it went because the old man hadn't unlaced it.

'I can get my own bloody boots off!' shouted Catriona.

But the *Sakir* only heaved at her other boot. It came away, taking the sock with it.

'I'm sorry,' he muttered. He stood up, threw her boots into the sticky pool surrounding the crashed jeep. Then he took his shirt off and threw it after them.

To prevent infection, thought Catriona, understanding it at last. Of course.

'You could have told me what you were doing,' she said. 'I'm not stupid you know.'

Mohammad shook his head, clutching his arms around his thin chest. He told his men to let her go. Catriona winced as her bare foot took her weight on the sharp stones. She heard footsteps approaching, turned and saw Tahir with a couple of his men returning with drums of petrol. Mohammad gestured at

15

the crashed jeep and the bloated body.

'Burn them,' he said.

'Wait a minute!' said Catriona. The thought of just burning a human being's body without any kind of ceremony felt wrong to her at some basic, almost instinctive, level. '*Sakir*, don't you think we should say some words –'

Mohammad shrugged. 'If he was a good man, he will go to Allah or whatever God he believed in. If not, then –' he shrugged again '– he will not. What else is there to say?'

Quite a lot, thought Catriona. She could hear the metallic scraping sound of the cap of the petrol drum being removed, hear the liquid splashing as they poured it out.

Mohammad pulled at her arm. 'Come with me. Let me tell you how the Giltaz fell from the favour of Allah.'

There was a shout from behind her, an explosion of flame.

'I still don't agree –' Catriona began again, but Mohammad interrupted her, his voice taking on a story-telling lilt.

'Seven hundred years ago, in the time of the Ba'ira Caliphs, there came an earthquake in the lands of the Giltaz. In the Hul-al-Hatar, the mountains glowed at night, and the sky filled with smoke. You would say a volcanic eruption –'

Catriona nodded.

But the *Sakir* was shaking his head again. The roaring flames from the burning jeep made the shadows jump and shift on his face. 'It was a visitation of Allah. On the fourth day after the earthquake, a merchant named Ibrahim visited the Hul-al-Hatar. He returned to the Caliph at Giltat with the news that there were magical creatures roaming the mountains: men with horse's heads, grey lions with metal jaws. And there were men – or things that looked like men. They walked in the cold of night, and they smelled of roses and cloves, and their

16

skins were as hard as stone.

'Ibrahim said that the creatures, whom he called *Al Harwaz*, had offered him many things – gold, spices, slave women. He said that they could imitate anything made by men. And all these things could be had for no payment; *Al Harwaz* wanted nothing in return, except that the men and women of the Giltaz should learn a dance. They called it *dancing the code*.'

Catriona felt a cold shock in her belly. Mohammad couldn't have heard those whispered words – he had been nowhere near the jeep when Deveraux had died –

'In the next months, the Giltaz became rich. *Al Harwaz* supplied them with spices for themselves and to trade, and gold and silver and fine hardwoods, and beautiful women who sold for a high price in the market. They prospered, and it seemed likely they would continue to prosper in the years to come.

'But the Caliph wanted more. He wanted *Al Harwaz* to assist him in his endless battle with his enemies, the Kebiriz of the northern marshes – just the same people who are our enemies today. The Caliph asked Ibrahim to tell *Al Harwaz* to make weapons: swords, and spears, and Greek fire. Ibrahim supplied the weapons, and also a thousand stone warriors in the shape of men. The stone warriors of *Al Harwaz* went into battle with the Giltaz against the Kebiriz, and the Kebiriz were massacred and their city razed to the ground.

'On the morning after news of the victory reached Giltat, Ibrahim brought *Al Harwaz* to the Caliph's palace. They showed him the dance, the dance that they wanted the Caliph and his people to learn as a price for all that they had given. They shook their arms and legs as fast as an insect beats its wings – so fast that there was a sound, and the sound snuffed out the lamps in the Caliph's palace, and cracked the tiles of the roof. Ibrahim said that they wanted everyone to dance the code, always, and that if they did there would be no more war, and many opportunities for trade.' He stopped, made a rueful grin. 'The Caliph didn't believe them, of course. He was afraid of this strange dance, and if the truth be known, he was afraid of *Al Harwaz*, despite all that they had given him.

'Now that they had brought him victory, he thought he needed them no more, so he threw the visitors from the walls of Giltat. Their bodies broke like clay dolls, and honey spilled out of them, and the honey smelled of roses and cloves.

'In the morning, there came the punishment for the Caliph's action. The air filled with vast hordes of flying monsters, circling the bodies of the dead *Al Harwaz*. And the strumming of their wings brought all the city of Al Giltaz to ruin, and they took all the people there. It is said that they walk in the desert, looking for their souls –' He broke off, looked at the ground, spat onto the dry stones. When he spoke again his voice had returned to normal. 'But I don't believe that. I think they were lost for ever. Certainly it was the end of the Ba'ira Caliphs, and the end of the great days of the Giltaz. We have been nothing more than tribesmen since.'

Catriona bit her lip, glanced at the burning jeep. The flames were slowly dying down; the jeep was only twisted metal, the body seemed to have vanished without trace.

'These *Al Harwaz*,' she asked at last. 'Have they been seen again?'

Tahir answered, from somewhere behind her. 'Of course not! They were never there in the first place. That's just an old fairy tale – and this is all some trick of Benari's people.'

Catriona nodded. Tahir's voice had broken the spell, brought some sense of reality back into her head. 'What your son says is a lot more likely, I'm afraid, *Sakir*,' she said.

Mohammad turned away from her, spat onto the ground again.

'It is not a fairy tale,' he said, looking from one to the other of them. 'And I only hope that neither of you will have the misfortune to find out that you are wrong.'

He walked away towards the tents, leaving Tahir and Catriona staring at each other in the light of the dying fire.

Two

'Well,' said Mike Yates. 'How do you like my new office?'

Jo Grant looked around her. The office was tiny, even for UNIT HQ. A lightweight desk, four feet by three, with a chair behind it; another chair in front of it – which barely left enough room for the door to open; a single filing cabinet crammed against the wall, with a card index perched on top. A small window showed a clump of ragged daffodils twitching in the March wind.

But still, it was nice to be home, Jo decided. She'd had enough alien planets to last her a lifetime.

'It's lovely!' she said. 'I'll bet you're pleased with it!'

'Well – yes,' said Mike. 'It almost feels like promotion.' He smiled for a moment, then sat down behind the desk. 'Actually –' He paused, his voice a little uncertain.

Jo glanced at him in surprise.

'Actually, the Brig asked me to have a word with you about the Doctor.'

'The Doctor?' Jo frowned. What had he done to offend the Brigadier now? They were always arguing, and she didn't seem to be able to stop them.

Mike picked up a pen and began flicking it from hand to hand. 'You see, I'm not sure – the Brig's not sure – whether he's really working for us any more.'

Jo stared. 'But of course he is! He's here, isn't he? Really, Mike, how could you possibly think that he would leave?'

Mike shrugged. 'Since he got the dematerialization circuit back you two have spent more time away from UNIT than you've spent here. The Brig says you've only been on the premises for about five days out of the last two months.' He paused. 'Let's face it, Jo. The Doctor's free to go anywhere he pleases now. And that's exactly what he's going to do.'

There was a short silence. Jo stared down at the desk top, saw a large, glossy black and white photograph, with a travel guide to Kebiria on top of it.

It was true, she realized. With his temporal powers returned to him, the Doctor could go anywhere – anywhen – he wanted to. He didn't have to answer to the Brigadier, or anyone else.

But she didn't want it to be true.

'The Doctor's in the lab now,' she said. 'He's working on something.'

'An improved navigation system for the TARDIS, I gather,' Mike rapped out. He sounded quite angry. 'Using our facilities.'

'He's got every right to use your facilities! Just look what he's done for you! Really, Mike –' Jo could feel her cheeks flushing with anger.

Mike dropped the pen on the desk, looked up at her. 'I know that, Jo, but it's just that – well, I don't think the Brigadier would admit this, but we felt a bit defenceless while you two were away.'

'Defenceless?' asked Jo, bemused. She sat down in the chair opposite Mike. 'I don't understand.'

He picked up the guide to Kebiria, began tapping the photographs with it. Jo noticed that, even though it seemed to be a perfectly ordinary Collins' guide, someone had stamped the words 'TOP SECRET' on it. The photograph was similarly stamped, and showed a rocky surface, grey on grey. A red circle had been drawn around a large dark shape near one of the corners.

'If anything like the Nestenes or the Axons came again,' Mike was saying, 'we'd need the Doctor's special skills.' He grinned at her suddenly. 'At any rate, that's the way the Brigadier puts it. "Need him to save our bacon" might be more like it.'

Jo nodded, stood up, began pacing the small space between the filing cabinet and the far wall.

She knew that Mike was right. The Doctor *was* going to wander in space and time, now that he could – he was still talking about going to Metebelis 3, even after all their adventures failing to get there over the past few weeks – and, just as surely, he *was* needed on Earth. There had to be a compromise. Something that would keep everyone happy.

She looked around the tiny office, hoping for inspiration. The metal filing cabinet – the card index, open at the letter 'D' – the strip lamp overhead –

She bit her lip.

The phone rang.

Mike picked it up. 'Captain Yates speaking.'

Yes! That was it!

'A phone!' she said aloud. 'If he put some kind of phone in the TARDIS – or some way of leaving a message –'

'Who is this?' Mike was asking.

'Even if he didn't get the message straight away,' Jo went on, half to herself, 'he could travel back in time to answer it.'

'I'm afraid I can't speak to reporters, Miss Talliser. How did you get this number?'

'Or, at least, I think he could,' mused Jo quietly. Surely the Doctor could do anything now that the Time Lords had unblocked his mind. She perched herself on the edge of Mike's desk, tried to get his attention. The phone conversation didn't seem to be very important.

'Captain Deveraux has no authority to reveal –' Mike was saying.

A loud objection crackled from the receiver.

Mike's face changed. 'Oh. I see. How –?' He picked

up the pen from the desk top, pulled a notepad towards him. Jo stared, transfixed by the expression on his face; he looked ten years older, almost middle-aged.

'I see. Yes. Gilf Hatar.' He began scribbling notes on the pad. 'Looked like −?' There was a long pause. 'Yes, I'm sure they were. It must have been −' He began sketching something on the pad; it looked like a football with arms. The voice at the other end talked rapidly, loud.

'Of course. We'll send a team at once,' said Mike Yates at last. 'Look, I'd appreciate it if in the meantime you could keep this off the record. I can guarantee you an exclusive when it breaks. Is there a number ?' He scribbled something on the pad, then put the phone down.

Jo slipped off the desk, sat down in the chair again. 'What's wrong?'

Mike didn't reply directly, instead stood up and walked around the desk to the filing cabinet.

'His wife's name is Heléne,' he said, and walked back to the desk with a card in his hand.

'Mike −?' said Jo.

He looked up at her. 'I've just lost one of my men,' he said quietly.

Jo looked away. 'Oh.'

'I'd tell his wife personally, if I could, but she lives in Geneva. I've got to get on to our people there, have them send someone round.' He paused. 'There are two children.'

'That's awful.' She looked up at Mike, put a hand over one of his. 'I'm sure he died bravely.'

It was Mike's turn to look away. 'I don't suppose he had much choice, Jo,' he said, still quietly.

Jo removed her hand, stood up. 'Look, I'll talk to the Doctor about what you said. I'm sure I can get him to carry on helping you.'

'Thanks, Jo.'

She turned to go.

'Oh, and Jo –' She turned back, saw Mike holding out the guide to Kebiria and the photograph. 'When you see him, get him to have a look at these, and –' he opened a drawer, pulled out some more photographs '– these, too. See if he can make anything of them.'

Jo took the sheaf of documents, left the office. As she closed the door she heard Mike asking the switchboard operator to get an international line. She wondered what it was like to have to tell someone that their husband had been killed in action. She wondered how many times Mike had had to do it.

Then shook her head. No use getting morbid. She set off down the corridor towards the lab, holding the photographs under her arm.

On the way she flicked open the guide to Kebiria, ignoring the 'TOP SECRET' stamp reiterated on the flyleaf and title page. By the time she'd reached the lab, she'd learned that Kebiria was a former French colony given independence in 1956; that two thirds of the population were Muslims and the rest Christians, the latter mostly Catholic and French-speaking; that the country was divided into a fertile strip of Mediterranean coast, and a thinly populated 'desert hinterland'. She'd also collided with the wall at least once, and almost knocked over Sergeant Osgood as he emerged from one of the offices.

The lab door was open, so she walked in. She saw the Doctor, standing near one of the benches with a strange expression on his face. Almost as if he were frightened –

'What's wrong, Doctor?' she asked.

But he ignored her, didn't seem to see her, just kept staring at a corner of the lab near the TARDIS. Jo turned, saw the Brigadier –

The Brigadier, with a gun in his hand –

The Brigadier, pulling the trigger –

The gun flashed, bucked in his hand.

Jo opened her mouth to speak, but no words came out.

24

She saw the Doctor stagger, blood staining the pale green frills of his shirt. In the corner of her eye, the gun flashed again –

– silently –

– and the Doctor fell, fresh blood running down his velvet jacket, more blood jerking from his mouth. He twitched a few times and was still.

'Doctor!' shrieked Jo, running forward. She saw the Brigadier walking past her, pushing his gun back into its holster. 'Brigadier!'

But he ignored her, stepped out of the lab door. In the doorway, Jo saw something –

Someone – a girl –

A girl's body, with blood leaking over the straw-blonde hair, staining the blue T-shirt –

Her T-shirt –

Her body –

She started screaming.

'Jo!'

The Doctor's voice. She looked up, saw him striding across the lab, clean of blood, wearing his purple velvet jacket and magenta shirt. He reached down, put both arms around her.

'Jo! It's all right! It's only an image!'

She looked down, saw the Doctor's body once more, blood pooling on the floor. It still looked real, but as she watched, it blurred, lost its colour and depth, became more like a projection. Static washed over it and it vanished.

'But Doctor, I was so frightened and I thought it was real and you were dead and the Brigadier had killed you and –'

The Doctor patted her back.

'All right, Jo, all right. We're not in any immediate danger, I can assure you.'

'I should hope not, Doctor.' The Brigadier's voice. Jo jumped, twisted her head around. He was standing by the TARDIS, swagger stick under his arm. Jo noticed that he

25

wasn't wearing his gun holster. 'I certainly don't have any intention of shooting either you or Miss Grant, now or at any time in the future.'

'Of course not!' said Jo, detaching herself from the Doctor. Her heartbeat was beginning to return to normal. 'What was it, Doctor – a sort of 3-D television?'

The Doctor shook his head. 'No, Jo, I'm afraid it's a lot more serious than that.'

She frowned. 'But then –'

'It's something that's actually going to happen to you and me, at some time in the next few weeks.' He strode across the lab, bent over a collection of flickering lights on the far end of the bench.

'But Doctor –' began Jo.

'Doctor, it's quite ridiculous –' said the Brigadier at the same time.

The Doctor ignored them, prodded at the apparatus. 'Unfortunately, it doesn't look as if I'm going to be able to get a fix.'

He turned a dial. The apparatus bleeped a few times, with a steadily rising pitch, then gave a loud *pop* and issued a cloud of smoke and sparks.

The Doctor retreated, coughing.

Jo and the Brigadier glanced at each other.

'Look, Doctor,' Jo began again. 'Don't you think it's more likely that there's something wrong with that – that device, whatever it was, than that the Brigadier's going to shoot us?'

The Doctor stared at Jo, then at the Brigadier, slowly shook his head.

'That "device",' he said, 'is a Personal Time-line Prognosticator. The projection is based on a formula given to me by a friend of mine on Venus, many years ago. It's always worked before – there's no possibility of error. What we saw, however improbable it might seem, actually has a probability considerably greater than ninety-nine per cent. The Brigadier is going to shoot you, Jo, and then he's going to shoot me. Both of us are

26

going to die.' He turned on his heel, opened the TARDIS door. 'Now, if you'll excuse me, I'm going to try and find out why.'

He stepped into the TARDIS and closed the door behind him.

Three

The press conference was crowded – but then it would be, thought Catriona. It's not every day that a country loses half its army in the desert. She peered around the big, white-roofed hall of the Ministry of Information Press Room, saw only a crush of heads and jackets and shirts. Somewhere in the middle of it loomed the tall frame and sticky-out ears of Gordon Hamill, the *Scottish Daily Record* correspondent. He was already waving his press pass in the air even though no one had appeared on the platform as yet, let alone said they were ready for questions.

She pressed herself further into the sweaty crush, was rewarded by not being able to see at all. She cursed herself for being late, but she hadn't had much choice. It had taken over two hours to set up the call to UNIT, being passed from one operator to another, waiting to be phoned back, finally shouting at that poor English captain, 'Captain Deveraux is *dead* and this is a bloody emergency!' But at least once he'd realized what the situation was he'd seemed to know what he was doing. She hadn't meant to shout at him, but she was still shaken up by the events of the previous night. Christ, anyone would be, she thought. She remembered the smell of roses and cloves, felt her stomach heave.

Someone tapped her on the shoulder. She turned, rather faster than was necessary, smiled when she saw the broad, reassuring figure of Bernard Silvers. The BBC's Man On The Spot smiled back, put a steering hand on her arm.

'Saved you a seat,' he said. 'Thought you looked a bit harassed.'

'Harassed wasn't half of it,' said Catriona, making a conscious decision as she spoke not to mention Anton Deveraux or UNIT. 'Benari cancelled my bloody interview, of course; and then my revered Editor was out to lunch when I rang and the only person in the office was Andy Skeonard, who left school about last month and probably thinks Kebiria is a sort of Greek salad dressing. God help him if he gets my story wrong.'

They began to edge around the crowd. To Catriona's amusement, Bernard said 'excuse me' to every person they came within about three feet of, instead of just using his elbows like everyone else. Amazingly, it worked. It must be the BBC manner, she thought; I'd never get away with it in a million years.

Bernard's reserved seats were at the front. His cameraman and sound tech were occupying them, but got up when Bernard and Catriona arrived, muttering something about exterior shots.

'Won't let them film in the building,' explained Bernard. 'Suppose they think we might point the camera to the right, or something.'

Catriona decided that this was supposed to be a joke; the Kebirian government was, theoretically at least, left-wing. She managed a slightly forced grin.

Above them, a figure had walked on to the platform and was fiddling with the microphone. A dull booming sounded from the speakers at the back of the room. The man nodded to himself and walked off again.

There was a long interval, during which Catriona checked out her cassette recorder for the fourth or fifth time. It seemed to be okay.

Voices rose once more behind her, then abruptly fell silent. Catriona looked up, saw a man in a suit standing on the platform. His face – smooth, round, with large round spectacles – looked vaguely familiar, but she couldn't immediately put a name to it. She glanced at Bernard, frowned.

'Sadeq Zalloua,' he muttered. 'Benari's science man.'

Zalloua stood there, biting at his fingers like a nervous child. Then he nodded suddenly, half sat in a chair, then got up again, glancing into the wings. Catriona followed his glance, saw the Information Minister Seeman Al-Azzem and the Prime Minister's spokesman Abdallah Haj walking on to the stage to join Zalloua. All three of them remained standing, which was odd.

Then Catriona saw the familiar stern face and thin black moustache of Khalil Benari, the Prime Minister himself. He glanced around the hall, his expression impassive, his eyes sharp, then stepped on to the platform. A speculative whisper ran through the gathered reporters. Catriona felt her own heart quickening; Benari's presence meant that there might be some real news, not just Al-Azzem's standard evasions.

But the Prime Minister only walked slowly to a chair and sat down. Haj and Zalloua sat down beside their Prime Minister, but Al-Azzem remained standing, arms folded, until there was silence in the hall. When he was satisfied, he began speaking into the microphone.

'Many of you will have heard rumours of a grave defeat by our forces in the Hatar-Sud district yesterday.' He paused, grinned widely, showing white, even teeth. 'Well, it is not true.'

There were some snorts of derision in the hall; of course, no one had expected him to admit the full extent of the disaster, even though the Defence Ministry had as good as confirmed it that morning by admitting that several brigades were missing.

Al-Azzem held up his hand, still grinning. 'However, we have lost some men.' A pause: silence. 'It is *why* we lost the men that is important.' Another pause. 'The twenty-fifth brigade were engaged on anti-terrorist duty in the Hatar-Sud district yesterday when they were attacked and destroyed by an unknown weapon. We are reasonably sure that this weapon was provided by the

Libyans, since its capacities are clearly beyond those of anything possessed by the terrorists. The Libyan ambassador has been summoned —'

It went on, in a rather predictable fashion, but Catriona wasn't listening. The *Libyans*? It didn't make any sense. It was true that the Libyans gave some assistance to the Giltean Arab Front in the east, but that was pretty minimal and only in the hope that a GAF government would turn out to be pro-Libyan. The FLNG — the Al-Naemis' group — would have nothing to do with the Libyans, regarding them as even more anti-democratic than Benari.

And anyway, Catriona knew that the Al-Naemis knew nothing about the mysterious weapon. Unless —

Unless Mohammad had made up that legend on the spot, to cover the fact that he knew exactly what was happening to Anton Deveraux, and exactly why his body had to be burned.

Catriona remembered the honey-like substance, streaked with blood, flowing over her boots. Germ warfare, she thought. Or chemical. I nearly became a test case for the latest version of Agent Orange. Jesus, I could still be a test case if Mohammad's precautions didn't work.

Suddenly the air in the hall, which had seemed hotter than comfortable up till now, felt cold. Goose bumps rose on Catriona's skin. She looked around at the ranks of faces staring at the platform, the microphones on clips, the potted palms growing against the walls. I shouldn't even be here, she thought. I should be in a hospital being checked out, Christ why didn't I ask that UNIT guy something about it, why didn't I make him tell me what I should do —

She noticed that there was a silence on the platform. She knew she must have missed something, wasn't sure what, suddenly didn't care.

She got up. 'Talliser, the *Journal*, London. I have a question.'

Al-Azzem stared down at her. 'You always have questions, Miss Talliser. Go ahead.' He gave another of his broad grins. There was some laughter in the hall. Ordinarily Catriona would have been angry, because she knew that Al-Azzem was implying that she was curious because she was a woman, and that some of the male journalists in the hall agreed with that view. But at the moment she was too frightened to care.

She swallowed, made a conscious effort to control her panic. 'Is there any evidence that this unknown weapon may have been bacteriological or chemical in nature?'

There was a muttering in the hall. Catriona heard the word 'bacteriological' being echoed in whispers all around her.

Al-Azzem frowned, looked round at Zalloua. The science advisor bit at his fingers again, then leaned over to Benari and muttered something. The Prime Minister frowned, then got up and walked slowly to the microphone. His eyes flashed from the hall to his advisors, lingered on Zalloua.

Catriona tried to meet his eyes but Benari avoided her gaze, staring instead at some point in mid-air towards the back of the hall.

'Yes, Miss Talliser,' he said. 'There is a suggestion that such –' he hesitated '– unorthodox weapons have been used. We cannot say anything further at the moment, in the absence of any definite evidence.'

'You say you don't have any evidence? What about the report of the UNIT North Africa representative, Anton Deveraux?' It was a long shot; she had no idea whether such a report existed. But the Captain had to have been investigating something – and had been killed for his pains.

Benari frowned and glanced once more at Zalloua, who shook his head. 'No comment,' said the Prime Minister briskly.

They know something they don't want to tell us, thought Catriona. From the rising murmurs around her in the hall, she knew that she wasn't the only one who'd spotted that.

Benari stepped back from the microphone, gestured fiercely at Al-Azzem who shuffled forward and took his place, still smiling broadly.

There were shouts from the hall. Catriona heard the words 'cover up'.

Maybe, she thought.

'Yes, Mr Hamill?' said Al-Azzem at last.

Wrong reporter, thought Catriona. Gordon Hamill won't let it drop.

Sure enough, the Scotsman didn't.

'What precisely does Monsieur Benari mean when he says "a suggestion", Monsieur Al-Azzem? Either the weapons have been used or they haven't. Surely that's obvious.'

Al-Azzem glanced at Benari, gave his usual grin. 'We're really not ready to comment on that at the moment, Mr Hamill,' he said, politely enough – but Catriona could hear the edge of anger in his voice, and knew that this Press Conference was likely to be wrapped up quickly without any further revelations.

Right, she thought, let's really throw the pigeon amongst the cats.

She stood up, shouted over the growing uproar in the hall: 'Monsieur Zalloua – if I could ask you please –' She was gratified to see the science advisor jump nervously. '– I'd like to know if you know of anything that could kill someone by swelling their body to twice the normal size –' as the noise grew around her, she repeated the last words, at the top of her voice '– twice normal size, and turning their flesh into something like honey.'

Zalloua stood up. 'And where exactly have you heard of such an agent, Miss Talliser?' he asked. His voice was quavery, weak: he sounded genuinely worried, almost frightened.

'I saw Mr Deveraux killed by it last night!' bawled Catriona.

There was sudden, absolute silence in the hall. Into it, someone shouted, 'Deveraux –' Then silence again.

Zalloua glanced at Al-Azzem, got up and walked off the platform very quickly.

Al-Azzem forgot to grin this time. 'I don't think we can comment on that one.'

Uproar in the hall. Catriona heard fragments of shouted questions.

'But if they're using –'

'– Geneva convention –'

'– Libya would not countenance any such –'

Catriona saw Benari stand up, wave a hand dismissively at the audience.

'I'm afraid that's all for today.' Al-Azzem's voice boomed from the speakers: someone had clearly turned the volume up. 'We will give you more information as soon as we have it.'

Catriona knew that was it. She got up, turned and walked out of the hall. She was conscious of the hundreds of pairs of eyes on her, the shouted questions now directed at herself, of Bernard's hand on her arm. She ignored it all, shook Bernard off in the lobby, ran out through the huge brass doors, across the wide lawns and into the street.

She took three deep breaths, looked from side to side. People were going about their ordinary business, hurrying up and down the pavement under the orange trees. A big car with CD plates and darkened windows swished past her. Bernard's film crew were chatting to a French crew in a mixture of languages beneath the marble statue of Khalil Benari that stood in the middle of the lawn. Catriona took a good look at it, at all of it, at the grey sky, and wondered if she were seeing it for the last time. If she had unwittingly killed everyone in the Press Room, was infecting everyone here in the street, in the city, just by breathing –

Hospital, she thought. I need to get to a hospital. But what will they know about germ warfare? I'd only be putting them at risk. Perhaps I could contact specialists –

but who the hell would know anything about it? The MoD in London? I should get to the embassy, explain the situation –

But she did nothing, just walked on, following the long curve of the boulevard as the sun gradually broke through the clouds. Slowly, her panic subsided.

That stuff killed a thousand men and it must have killed them quickly, she thought. If I'm still standing twelve hours on, I'm okay. I've got to be bloody okay. Besides, Tahir didn't look too worried. Not as if he thought I was going to die – certainly not as if he thought that he was going to die. And he knew all about it. He must have done.

She was sure of that much: the more she thought about it, the more it made sense. Tahir's elaborate denial that the FLNG had anything to do with the missing men. Mohammad's 'legend', so contrived, so improbable. The Kebirian government's evident confusion at being struck from so unexpected a quarter.

'– *dancing the code* –'

She remembered the voice as she had heard it on the cassette recorder, played back several times in her hotel room that afternoon. Faint, scratchy, almost inaudible under the tape hiss.

Anton Deveraux couldn't have known what Mohammad was going to say. Which meant that –

Catriona shook her head. She couldn't work out what it meant, except that it was all more complicated than she'd first imagined. Perhaps the UN were in on it. Perhaps the man hadn't been Deveraux at all, but had been wearing his uniform. Perhaps he had been a spy for Benari's government. Or for someone else. Pieces of theories chased each other round in her head, argued with each other.

With a start she realized that she'd walked all the way back to the concrete tower of the Hotel du Capital, where most of the press corps in Kebir City stayed. Rather to her surprise there was no one outside the porch except a company of Kebirian soldiers. A gold-braided

35

captain stood in front of them, looking around him as if he owned the place. She walked up to him, past him –

'Catriona Talliser?'

Catriona turned, found herself facing the Captain. His men, she noticed, had formed a ring around her.

'Yes?' Catriona tried to sound only irritated, tried to ignore the tension in her stomach, the thumping of her heart.

'I must ask you to come with me.'

'Why?'

'You are under arrest.'

Catriona felt a shock go right through her. She became aware of the captain's hand on his gun in its leather holster, of the other men staring at her, their fingers hooked over the triggers of their guns.

The captain reached out and took her arm, pulled her towards an Army truck parked by the side of the road. Catriona tried to pull back, but one of the soldiers caught her other arm and she was dragged towards the truck.

'What's the charge?' she shouted, beginning to struggle. 'What's the bloody charge?'

'I must ask you to come with me,' repeated the officer. Catriona wondered if perhaps that was all the English he knew.

'I said, what – is – the – charge?' she repeated, slowly. But the soldiers only dragged her onwards. Catriona saw a couple of pedestrians standing, staring. She felt like shouting for help, but knew it would be no use.

This is what 'police state' means, she thought. Jesus *Christ*.

Someone was pulling her arms behind her back, clipping something cold and metallic around her wrists. Then they hauled her up into the back of the truck.

'You can't bloody arrest me like this!' She was shouting now, her voice echoing from the metal of the truck. She became aware that her body was shaking. 'I'm a reporter,' she shouted. 'I'm accredited by the government. Your bloody government. They can't do this.'

The captain climbed up into the truck with her. Behind him, the doors slammed. The truck pulled away, the motion throwing Catriona against the hard metal.

Slowly, her eyes adjusted to the dim light seeping in through the barred window in the door; she saw the captain, with one hand braced against the side of the truck, staring at her hard-eyed.

She tried again. 'You can't arrest me without charge. You have to tell me —'

'We don't have to tell you anything!' shouted the captain. 'You have committed treason!'

'Treason? What —'

But the captain interrupted again, leaning down so that his face was only inches from Catriona's.

'Save your breath,' he said. 'You are as good as dead already.'

Four

Jo hesitated, glanced around the empty lab, then knocked on the door of the TARDIS.

There was no reply.

She knocked harder. 'Come on, Doctor, I know you're in there.'

Silence.

He had to be in there. Didn't he?

'Doctor! Please! I need to talk to you!'

She pushed at the door; to her surprise, it swung open. The Doctor was standing at the console, his head bowed. A single yellow light flashed under his right hand. Jo ran up to him, put a hand on his arm.

'You're still worried about the Brigadier shooting us, aren't you?'

'Aren't you, Jo?' The Doctor had not responded to her touch, was not even looking at her.

Jo let go, then thought about it for a moment. 'No,' she said finally. 'I'm not. I just don't believe the Brigadier would do it.'

The Doctor turned round. Jo heard the TARDIS door shut behind her.

'Jo,' he said softly. 'The Brigadier is a soldier. He obeys orders. If his commanding officer – or the Secretary-General of the United Nations – ordered him to shoot us, he wouldn't have much choice but to obey, now would he?'

Jo, stubborn, shook her head. 'He wouldn't do it, Doctor. And anyway, an order like that would be illegal. He wouldn't have to obey it.'

The Doctor began pacing up and down in front of the console. 'All right, Jo. Suppose we both became infected with an alien virus, and our continued existence threatened the lives of everyone on Earth. Suppose the virus made us act irrationally – dangerously. What then?'

Jo bit her lip, stared around her at the white walls of the console room, the familiar yet alien roundels, the blank screen of the scanner that showed a view of nothing. She felt a cold, hard, knot form in her stomach. The Doctor sounded so sure – and if he was right –

She'd been fourteen when her Aunt May had been given three months to live. She remembered her dad telling her about it, remembered running into the garden, crying with disbelief. Kicking apples on the wet grass, staring at big white clouds in a blue sky. Not believing it. Refusing to accept it.

But Aunt May had died anyway.

'What can we do, Doctor?' she whispered. 'There must be something we can do.'

The Doctor walked up to her, took her hands, gave her his most reassuring smile. 'Well, the first thing we have to do is split up. Whatever is going to happen to us, it will almost certainly happen when we're together. So as long as we stay apart, we're fairly safe.'

Jo thought about this for a moment, frowned.

'But surely we're safe as long as we stay out of the laboratory? That's where it happened – where it's going to happen, I mean.' She felt her stomach lurch as the meaning of the 'it' she was talking about came home to her again.

'Not necessarily, Jo. Have you ever heard of a bell distribution?'

Jo frowned. 'It's something to do with statistics, isn't it?'

The Doctor smiled. 'That's right. Well, what the Prognosticator shows is the middle part of the distribution – the most probable sequence of actions, if you like.

39

Around that are a lot of less probable sequences it doesn't show –'

'Like where the Brigadier misses us, or doesn't shoot us at all?' asked Jo excitedly.

But the Doctor shook his head. 'No, Jo. Like where he shoots us in the car park, or in the radio room. Or where he uses a different gun, or it happens a day later or a day earlier. The probabilities you're talking about – where the key event is different – are very small ones indeed. That's why it's more than ninety-nine per cent certain that something very like what we saw will happen.'

'But we can make it less likely?' Jo couldn't quite squash the feeling of hope growing inside her.

'It should be possible, in theory,' said the Doctor. 'The trouble is, I don't know how at the moment. If I'd managed to get a fix before the tri-capacitance circuit shorted we'd have known more, but as it is the best thing you and I can do is to keep away from each other as far as possible.' He walked over to the lockers, opened a door and took out a device the size and shape of a transistor radio, with an odd pattern of coloured buttons on its surface. He pressed one of the buttons with his thumb, said, 'Say something, Jo.'

'Anything?' she said doubtfully.

The Doctor smiled again. 'Yes, "anything" will do nicely.' He pushed another couple of buttons and handed the device to her. 'Now that I've set it up, this device will only respond to your voice, Jo. What you should do is find out what's happening around the HQ – anything strange, anything at all – and then record a message for me, telling me about it. You need to press the blue button – this one – to record. I suggest that after –' he glanced at his watch '– two hours you leave the device on the lab bench, where I will pick it up. Then leave the area of the lab. After another hour, come back to the lab and pick up any instructions I leave you – you'll have to say "recall" into the device, and press the yellow button. Is that clear?'

Jo looked at her own watch. It was three o'clock.

'Five o'clock. "Recall". Yellow button. Okay, Doctor.'

The Doctor half-turned to the console, then turned back to face her.

'Oh, and Jo –'

'Yes?'

'Good luck.'

He extended his hands, and Jo rushed forward, hugged him, her head against his chest. She knew that they might not meet again, or that if they did they might only have a few minutes left to live. She wanted to say a lot of things. She wanted to say that being his assistant was better than being a spy. She wanted to say that he was like a second father to her. She wanted to say that he had shown her the wonders of the Universe, and that there weren't the words to tell how she felt. But she didn't say anything much in the end, only a muffled, 'Goodbye, Doctor.'

Then, quickly, before she could panic or change her mind, stepped out of the TARDIS and into the lab. It felt strange, somehow, almost as if it were another alien planet. As the door shut behind her, she saw the pile of photos and the guide to Kebiria that Mike Yates had given her, lying on the lab bench where she'd left them. She turned back to the TARDIS.

'Doctor –'

But the whistling, roaring sound of dematerialization had begun.

'Doctor!'

The TARDIS faded from view. Jo looked around her, looked over at the doorway. She remembered the image of her own body slumped by the door, remembered the blood staining her T-shirt.

She pressed the blue button on the recording device.

'Well, Doctor,' she said. 'At four-oh-two the TARDIS dematerialized, with you in it.' She paused, looked at the doorway again. 'I hope you're coming back,' she said.

Brigadier Alistair Lethbridge-Stewart thought about killing people, and decided that he didn't like it very much.

He thought about killing the Doctor and Jo, and shook his head.

'Impossible,' he muttered. 'Quite impossible.'

But on the other hand –

He tried not to think of the circumstances in which he would have to shoot them. He knew there were such circumstances. They were conceivable.

'But the Doctor's wrong,' he muttered. He imagined the Doctor standing in front of him, immaculate in his peculiar costume of velvet and lace. 'No. This time, Doctor, you're wrong.'

There was a knock at the door.

The Brigadier looked down at the paperwork he was supposed to be doing, sighed. 'Come in.'

The door opened and Captain Yates stepped in, saluted casually. 'I need your approval for an ENA team, sir,' he said without preamble. 'We need to look at the Gilf Hatar anomaly.'

The Brigadier raised his eyebrows. 'The *what* anomaly?'

'Kebiria, sir.'

'Kebiria? Isn't that Captain Deveraux's patch?'

Yates looked down at the carpet.

'We've lost Deveraux, sir. He's been missing for a couple of days and –' He told the Brigadier about Catriona Talliser's telephone call. Lethbridge-Stewart felt his heart sink. Another one gone.

'This – reporter person,' he said, when Yates had finished. 'Is she sure about the ID? I mean, have we got any corroboration for this?'

Yates nodded.

'She saw his uniform ID, and he was driving a UNIT jeep.' He paused. 'I've put someone on to the family.'

'I'm sorry. Deveraux was a good man.' The Brigadier stood up, walked past Captain Yates and looked at the map on the wall. Kebiria was there, stretched out between the Mediterranean and the Sahel, coloured in the pale green reserved for Francophone countries. Giltat was a tiny dot on the map, not even rating the square-with-a-dot accorded to 'major population centres'; Gilf Hatar wasn't marked. The Brigadier hadn't expected it to be. An unmarked grave. Again.

He turned back to the captain. 'Look, Yates, are you certain this justifies sending in a whole team? The Kebirian situation's pretty unstable you know. We have to stay inside our mandate – no provocation, no incidents. And for that, the fewer people we send, the better.'

'The satellite photos indicate that the anomaly is a fair size, sir. We may need the back up.'

The captain's voice had an edge of impatience in it. The Brigadier realized he was sounding bureaucratic, officious, restrictive. He remembered what it had been like when he'd been a captain – when he hadn't been responsible for things like budgets, when he hadn't had ministers peering over one shoulder, accountants peering over the other, civil servants expecting him to dance like a puppet between them.

'How many were you thinking of?'

'Myself and Benton; Benton's squad. And the Doctor. Eleven altogether, twelve if Miss Grant comes with us.' He paused. 'Though I'd rather she didn't, in the circumstances.'

The Brigadier glanced sharply at Yates. 'The Doctor, eh? That's if you can find him. If he hasn't gone flitting off in that contraption of his.' He walked back to his desk, sat down, unlocked a drawer and pulled out a grey form marked EXTRA-NATIONAL AUTHORITY – C/O ONLY. He filled it in with the details of Yates's request, signed it, stamped it, handed it over.

'By the way, did you speak to Miss Grant?'

Yates nodded. 'She said she'd have a word with the Doctor. I gave her the Kebirian stuff too – the photos and so on. She was going to show them to him.'

There was a knock at the door. The Brigadier nodded at Yates, who opened it, revealing Jo Grant herself. She stepped inside, glanced at Yates, stepped back.

'Sorry, Brigadier, I didn't realize you were busy –'

'That's all right, Miss Grant, we were just talking about you,' said the Brigadier. 'Yates needs the Doctor's help with an investigation.'

Jo hesitated, her face colouring. The Brigadier had a sudden vision of her body lying by the lab door, of himself calmly, coldly, turning the gun on the Doctor.

It was the *coldness* of his own expression that had got to him. He would never kill Jo Grant with a look like that on his face.

Would he?

Captain Yates was talking. 'What's the matter, Jo?'

'The Doctor's gone off in the TARDIS somewhere.'

But she sounded a good deal more upset than that fact alone could explain. The Brigadier half-rose from his seat, frowned. 'Gone off, Miss Grant? Gone off to where?'

Jo shrugged, glanced at Mike Yates. 'He didn't say.'

'I hope he's coming back again.'

'Of course he'll be back.'

But the Brigadier noticed the catch in her voice, and knew that she wasn't sure either. He remembered again the Prognosticator's images, decided that he didn't really blame the Doctor. In the circumstances he'd probably have beaten a hasty retreat himself.

'Well, I'd better make some arrangements for the transport –' began Yates, turning to leave.

'Transport?' asked Jo. 'Where are you going?'

'Kebiria.'

The Brigadier listened whilst the captain again explained the circumstances of Anton Deveraux's death.

'That's why I was hoping the Doctor would be able to help,' he finished. 'But if he's gone –'

Jo bounced forward, took his hands, her face suddenly a picture of eagerness. 'I could still come with you, couldn't I?'

Mike Yates shook his head. 'No, Jo. It's too dangerous.'

Jo directed an appealing look in the Brigadier's direction, as he had known she would. He sighed. Jo had no business going anywhere without the Doctor – and he ought to keep her here in case the Doctor showed up – but –

'Please,' said Jo. 'I've never been to Africa.'

It occurred to the Brigadier that if he sent Jo away, then she was safe from him. He wouldn't shoot her, with that cold expression on his face. She would be somewhere else. It wouldn't be possible.

'Well, I suppose Captain Yates could do with someone to stay in Kebir City, for liaison with the local UN team. Couldn't you, Yates?'

The captain looked from Jo to the Brigadier and back again.

'Yates?' said the Brigadier again.

'Well, it wouldn't do any harm, sir.' He turned to Jo. 'If you really want to go, that is.'

'Big game, rolling savannah and all the sun a girl could want!' Jo grinned. 'When do we start?'

But the Brigadier noticed the nervous little glance in his direction and knew that he wasn't the only one who thought that a visit to Kebiria might break the Prognosticator's spell.

'I'll go and tell Benton to get his men together,' Yates was saying.

The Brigadier nodded. Yates and Jo left, Jo chattering loudly, eagerly.

He ought to make some phone calls, he realized. Make sure the Secretariat was informed. And the Defence Ministry in London, who would have to bill the UN for the job.

But he just stared blankly at the telephone, tapping his pen on the desk blotter. After a while he unlocked a drawer on the right-hand side of his desk and pulled out the spare .38 revolver he kept there. He looked at the gun for a long time, checked it was loaded, then carefully put it away again and relocked the drawer.

Then he spent some time pulling the key off his ring. Holding it in his hand, he walked out of the building, past the salute of the desk sergeant, into the dull grey light of a spring evening. He found the kitchen waste bin – which he knew was collected daily, and wouldn't be checked – and dumped the key in it.

It didn't make much difference. The drawer could be forced. He could collect a weapon from the armoury any time he liked.

But he was fairly sure it had been that weapon – his own, slightly outdated .38 – which had been in his hand in the Prognosticator image. Which meant that he might have gained himself a few minutes. A few minutes in which to think. Remember. Realize. Whatever.

'Just in case,' he muttered, looking around in the fading light at the parked cars, the high fence with its barbed wire, the scudding clouds above. 'Just in case it's true.'

Jo stood in the empty laboratory, looked around her, looked down at the small recording device on the bench.

'I don't know when I'm going to be back from Kebiria,' she said to it. 'But whenever it is, I'll come to the lab at six o'clock and leave a message. If the machine's still here. If not, I'll leave a note. I hope you're all right. I hope I'm doing the right thing.'

She became aware that her voice was quavering a little. She swallowed, with an effort, then said, 'Goodbye, Doctor.'

Perhaps he won't be back, she thought. Perhaps I won't see him ever again.

She picked up the photographs and the guide to Kebiria from the bench and left the lab, locking the door behind her.

Five

'The number – where did you obtain it?' asked the interrogator in her strangely accented French.

Catriona looked around the whitewashed walls of the interrogation room, her eyes involuntarily stopping at the pockmarks that might be bullet holes, the faint brownish stains that might once have been blood.

'Answer me!' The interrogator was a woman, but she would have passed for a man at a distance. Her shoulders were broad, her arms thick and heavy. Her face was hard, leathery, deeply lined. Her eyes had less sympathy than a hawk's. And there was a gun in her hand, pointing at Catriona across the wooden surface of the table.

So much for Arab countries being backward in matters of women's liberation, thought Catriona. Not true: they were bang up to date here. In all the ways that mattered to them.

She licked her lips, tried to swallow; but her mouth was too dry. Finally she croaked, 'He was a United Nations officer on United Nations business. It took me over two hours to get through to his superiors. I didn't have time to inform the authorities here before I went to the press conference.'

'So you informed foreigners before informing us. Why?'

The screaming started again as the interrogator spoke: a horrible, insane, panicky howling, mixed with gabbled pleas for mercy in Arabic. It had been going on at intervals ever since she had arrived. Neither the guards nor the interrogator had explained it, indeed they didn't

47

even appear to notice it. Catriona wondered how many others were being 'interrogated'. Wondered what they were doing to the woman who was howling. What they would do to her if she didn't cooperate.

She tried desperately not to think about it.

'Why?' repeated the woman, emphasizing the question with little jolts of the gun in her hand.

'I've told you,' said Catriona. Her throat was dry to the point of soreness, and it was an effort to keep her voice audible. 'I wasn't thinking clearly. I was in shock. The thing was horrible. It wasn't— it isn't anything to do with the terrorists.' She'd learned better than to call them 'Giltaz' or even 'separatists'. 'They're just as frightened of it as you are. Anyway,' she added desperately, 'until he cancelled on me, I thought I was going to interview the Prime Minister at two-thirty.'

'You were not! Monsieur Benari is seeing no press reporters today! You will tell the truth or it will be worse for you!' She jolted the gun again, moved the lamp by her left hand so that it shone directly in Catriona's face. 'You will tell me how the United Nations people and the terrorists destroyed our army. You will tell me within one minute or I will kill you.'

The woman looked at her watch: a man's watch, huge and gold-plated. She isn't going to kill you, Catriona told herself. She's probably got strict instructions not to lay a finger on you. You're a bloody *reporter*, for Christ's sake. They *can't* hurt you. But somehow the argument didn't feel as convincing as it had an hour ago.

The screaming was still going on outside, but it was a little fainter now.

With difficulty, Catriona controlled a mounting feeling of panic. She said, 'Look, can't we just stop this rubbish and talk some sense? I don't know anything about the Gi — about the terrorists, except where they were camped last night and that won't do you any good because they've moved. I know damn all about this whatever-it-is that turns people into smudges of sweet-smelling goo except that it's probably done it to half your Army already and if you're not careful it'll probably do it to the rest of you. Now I've told you everything I know so will you bloody well let me out of here!' By the last sentence her voice was shaking with hysteria. She bit her lip, aware of the sound of her own breathing, of the interrogator's hard, brown eyes looking into hers.

The lamp snapped off. For a moment Catriona, dazzled, could scarcely see anything; then the walls of the room slowly became distinct again. She stared for a moment at the grey paint on the steel door, at the tiny, barred window in the top part of it, then returned her gaze to the heavy, sweat-stained uniform of the figure sitting opposite her.

The interrogator put her gun away, settled forward on her elbows, pushing her face to within six inches of Catriona's. Her breath smelled of mint tea and chewing gum.

'Very well,' she said, in her low, hoarse voice. 'We will talk sense. We will let you go, if you tell us everything about your connections with the English MI5, this so-called UNIT organization, and the Giltaz terrorists.'

Catriona closed her eyes, near to despair. For a moment she'd really thought that the woman was going to start acting like a normal human being. But evidently that behaviour wasn't in her repertoire. Not when she was on duty anyway.

'I will help you to help us,' the woman was saying. 'According to our telephone operator, you requested Captain Yates to send in a team. How many will be in this team? What are their objectives? What excuse will they make for entering our country?'

'How many times have I got to tell you, I don't know? I'm a reporter. I don't order in troops.' The hawk-like eyes watched her steadily. Catriona felt her voice quavering as she spoke again. 'All I know is that they'll be investigating this – incident, that I've reported. They're bound to ask your government for permission anyway, so

I don't know what all the fuss is about. You've only got to say no and they won't bother you.'

The woman nodded, smiled. 'So you say.'

A pause. The screaming had stopped. Something scraped against the outside of the metal door. Catriona had the bizarre notion that it was Anton Deveraux, enormous and sweet-smelling, come to rescue her by turning the entire staff of the prison into globes of honey. Then they would float away, oozing out into the streets –

A fist crashed down on the table in front of her, jolting her back to reality.

'Now! You will tell us their secret entry route into our country!'

Outside, the screaming started again, turned into a horrible gurgling sound. There was a thud, and silence.

Jesus *Christ*, they've cut her throat, thought Catriona.

'NOW!'

The interrogator's hand rose from the table, the fist unfolded inches from her face. Catriona's head was jolted back, her cheek stung.

She stared at the hand, still only inches from her face, felt a sudden surge of anger. Then she did something that, even as she was doing it, seemed to her the stupidest thing she had ever done in her life. She reached forward, grabbed the woman's wrist, and bit the extended finger as hard as she could.

She remembered Tahir's smiling eyes: *Let's try your courage.*

Her head was jolted back again, this time with enough force to send a stab of pain through her neck, but Catriona didn't let go. She seemed to feel, rather than see, the heavy hand coming towards her face. There was another jolt, and the world spun. Something snapped in her mouth, and then she was sitting on the floor, pain shooting down her back and along her jaw, and her mouth full of blood.

The interrogator was standing, a gun in one hand, the other dripping blood. Catriona raised her eyes to the other woman's, wiped a hand across her lips.

Slowly, the big woman put the gun away. Catriona became aware of blood trickling down her neck from her chin, of a ringing in her head. The left side of her face throbbed with a gradually increasing intensity.

'Your friends will be here later tonight,' said the interrogator at last. 'We will see what happens then.'

'My friends?' said Catriona thickly, swallowing blood. The woman could only mean the UNIT team. 'You mean you're letting them into the country?'

The interrogator smiled.

'Of course we are. They will be arrested at the airport.' She rapped on the steel door: it opened, with much clattering of bolts and keys. 'I will leave you to think about that.' She walked out through the door, then looked round; the corridor and the gun-toting guards behind her. 'Maybe I will have you beaten properly later.'

Two female guards strode into the room, hauled Catriona to her feet, dragged her out into a grey, neon-lit corridor.

'Let me go!' protested Catriona. 'Let me go, I can walk!'

One of the guards wrenched at her arm. 'Maybe we can fix that,' she said. She let go of Catriona for a moment, kicked her leg, hard, just below the kneecap. Catriona just managed to suppress a cry of pain. The guard laughed.

By the time the mist had cleared from her eyes, she was inside a tiny, windowless cell. The door slammed shut behind her, the locks clattered back into place. Catriona stared at the door for a moment, then slowly, carefully, stood up. She swayed; her head throbbed; the ringing in her ears got louder. But she managed to stay upright. She touched the left side of her face; the hand came away without blood on it.

Only a bruise.

She became aware that she badly needed to pee. There

51

was a bucket in the corner of the cell; she used that, then, since there was no furniture in the room, lay down on the floor. It wasn't comfortable — it was bare stone, hard and gritty — but it was slightly cooler than the air in the cell.

'They won't torture you,' she told herself, aloud, staring at her stockinged feet, the dirty and scuffed cloth of her trousers. 'That woman only hit you because you bit her. She knew she couldn't go on after that. She knew she'd disobeyed her orders, and couldn't risk any more of it. So what's going to happen now is that the British government will contact the Kebirians and tell them to bloody well let me go. I'll be out of here in the morning.'

By the time she got to the last sentence, her voice wasn't shaking any more.

Good.

She stared at the ceiling, at the flies orbiting the solitary light bulb in its steel cage. She tried to think of how she would start her report on this incident for the *Journal*. It should run to a whole feature, she reckoned. Three columns. Might even make the weekend magazine.

'The worst thing about prison isn't the fear, it's the humiliation —' she began, absurdly wishing that she had her cassette recorder.

Abruptly, the screaming started again, right outside her cell. Catriona heard a sickening crunch that sounded like bones being broken, and the screaming peaked, slowly faded away into meaningless babbling. She got up, walked unsteadily to the door, banged on it.

'Stop that!' she shouted. 'Stop doing that to her!'

There was a moment's silence, then a woman laughed and the screams started again.

Play-acting, thought Catriona. It's got to be play-acting. They're just trying to scare me. I'm not going to let them succeed. I'm not going to believe that it's real.

She lay down again and closed her eyes.

The screams went on, and on, and on.

* * *

52

Jo was disappointed by the flight. The transport plane might be as big as a 747, but it was noisy, the passenger compartment had no windows, and there wasn't anything to read. Mike Yates wasn't very communicative – he disappeared at an early stage to chat to the pilot, an old school friend of his. Sergeant Benton had taken the guide to Kebiria away from her and was reading it, propped up against the metal side of the plane. His men were similarly propped up, reading magazines or asleep. Some of them were smoking, which they probably shouldn't have been.

Jo sat cross-legged in the middle of the floor, trying to control a feeling of airsickness and wondered why on Earth military aircraft couldn't have proper seats. From time to time she found herself wishing that the Doctor was with her, then remembered why he wasn't, and then wished she hadn't thought about it in the first place.

Abruptly the engine note changed, and the plane tilted slightly.

'That's it,' said Benton, folding up the guide and returning it to Jo. 'Coming in to land. Put the fags out, lads, and check your straps.'

Jo wondered how he could be so sure what was happening, but nonetheless scrambled to her position and strapped herself in. She glanced at her watch: nearly midnight. She yawned. The first thing she was going to do when they landed, she decided, was find a hot bath and a cup of tea, and then she was going to bed.

Mike Yates appeared on the cockpit steps, jumped down. He leaned over and muttered something to Benton before strapping himself in next to Jo. He looked worried, she thought. She wondered if she should ask him what the problem was, but decided it would wait till they landed.

The engines throttled back, and Jo's stomach lurched as the plane began to lose height. There were several jolts as they hit air pockets on the way down, and Jo began to feel sick in earnest. She was greatly relieved when, with a barely perceptible bump, the wheels hit tarmac.

But, feeling sick or no, she was unbuckling her harness before they'd stopped rolling.

Mike put a hand on her arm. 'Hold on, Jo. We might have a bit of a problem.'

She froze, her hand on the buckle. 'What's wrong?'

'We've been diverted to a military airfield – and there was a fighter escort, just to make sure we stayed diverted. I'd better get out first and see what's going on.'

The aircraft shuddered slightly as the engines were throttled back; as soon as they were silent, Jo could hear the scream of jets, close by and getting closer. Mike stood up, went to the main hatch and opened it. Warm, dry air blew in, smelling strongly of jet fuel.

'You have to what?' shouted Mike from the hatchway, evidently addressing someone outside. A bright light shone in through the doorway. The scream of jets increased, then abruptly diminished as the engines throttled back.

'But this is a United Nations plane!' Mike shouted. 'We have permission from your government –'

The other speaker interrupted. Jo could hear the voice now, heavily accented, apologetic. 'My orders . . . little choice . . . weapons . . .'

Mike looked over his shoulder at Sergeant Benton, an expression of incredulity on his face. 'They're putting us under arrest!'

One of the men said, 'Oh, no. Here we go.'

Jo unbuckled her harness, stood up. 'But that's illegal!' she said. 'What are they arresting us for?'

Mike shrugged. 'He just says it's orders. Could be anything. They want all our weapons and they're going to impound the plane.' He paused. 'The Brig will be furious. We've got his helicopter in the hold.'

There was a clatter of metal on metal. Jo ran up to the hatchway and looked out. A searchlight shone in her face, almost blinding her. She couldn't see the man that Mike was talking to, though after a moment she made out the form of the jet fighter she'd heard. The suited and helmeted pilot sat in the cockpit, his figure picked out sharply by the bright light. Beyond the plane, Jo could see the low brick fronts of some buildings and a pink-flowered bush that looked as if it were made of plastic. Beyond that, nothing but darkness. As well as the jet fuel she could smell dust, metal, the sea.

Jo heard the sound of a diesel engine, saw a small truck with a flight of steps on it moving slowly towards the plane. Trotting beside it were two soldiers, both armed with machine-guns. Jo saw more soldiers in the half-shadow around the base of the searchlights, also armed, their guns pointed casually at the plane.

She looked at Mike. 'We haven't got much choice but to go along with them, have we?'

Mike shook his head.

'Can't the pilot radio for assistance?'

'Too far – all our signals from here have to go through Kebir City. But the Brig's sure to find out, sooner or later. He'll get us out, don't worry. And they won't dare do much to us – UN personnel, and all that. It just means a night or two in the clink.' He grimaced. 'Sorry, Jo. It might not be very nice.'

The steps connected with the side of the plane; one of the soldiers trotted up them, gun at the ready. He was young, Jo noticed – younger than she was. He looked more nervous than anything else.

'*Allez!*' he shouted. '*Mediatement! Allez!*'

Mike looked at the sergeant. 'After you, Benton.'

But Benton only grinned. 'Rank Hath Its Privileges, sir.'

Jo looked from one to the other, wondered how they could make jokes at a time like this.

'*Allez!*' repeated the young soldier.

Mike started down the steps. The soldier frisked him, took his service pistol and the clip of ammunition that went with it.

Jo stepped forward into the light, ignoring Benton's

muttered, 'Be careful, miss.' The young soldier caught sight of her, turned and shouted something in Arabic to his invisible superior.

There was a pause. A fat man in a gold-braided uniform stepped into view, stared at Jo for a moment, then shouted something in rapid Arabic.

The young man turned back to her, grinned broadly. '*Ma'moiselle*,' he said. '*Vous* – uh – you go Kebir City, yes please? We – uh – accommodate you?'

'I prefer to stay with my friends,' replied Jo, speaking French. Her tutor had always told her that her accent was atrocious, but it couldn't be worse than the young man's English.

Another consultation in Arabic and French followed. Mike joined in from the bottom of the steps, where he was standing between two armed guards. Finally he shouted up at her, 'It's no use, Jo. You've got to go to Kebir City. I'm sure you'll be all right. They won't hurt you. They seem just as confused by their orders as we are.'

'I will *not* be all right!' Jo began to feel panic take hold. She tried to tell herself that being arrested on Earth, even in a strange country, was hardly likely to be as dangerous as Spiridon under the Daleks, or Solos. Somehow it didn't seem very convincing. 'Tell them I've got to stay with you!' she yelled.

The fat man said something, and Jo heard a brisk voice speaking in English: 'The girl has to go to the *Moussadou*.'

The young soldier was still standing on the narrow steel platform at the top of the steps. Jo turned and smiled at him. 'Please,' she said in French. 'I would like to stay with the Captain.'

But the young man only beckoned her to follow him.

Her shoulders slumped. So much for seeing Africa. She let herself be led down the steps. Mike Yates had disappeared. Behind her, she heard Sergeant Benton mutter, 'Don't worry, miss. It'll all be sorted out in the morning.' He didn't sound convinced. Jo tried to turn to smile at him, but he was being led away. His men were trailing down the steps behind him, dumping their guns in a pile on the tarmac.

'*Où est cette "Moussadou"?*' asked Jo of the young man.

He looked at her sorrowfully.

'Is – political prison,' he said. 'For enemies of the people.'

He led Jo across the tarmac towards the buildings, the sorrowful expression still on his face. Jo began to wonder if going to Africa had been such a good idea after all.

Six

When Catriona Talliser woke up, she hadn't forgotten where she was. She hadn't slept much; she was surprised that she'd slept at all. The stone floor hurt her back if she stayed still for too long, and the glaring light bulb and the flies constantly crawling over her skin hadn't helped. When she had slept, there had been disturbed dreams – she remembered one where she was being interrogated by the dying Anton Deveraux, who was screaming at her, and was somehow carrying a Kalashnikov and a belt of small black grenades. More than once she had woken with a grunt of fear, drenched in sweat.

This time, it was the door that woke her. The lock was being worked, the bolts drawn. Catriona sat up, sweating, her heart thumping. She glanced at her wrist, but they'd taken her watch away from her.

The door opened. Catriona composed a stony face, an angry stare. But it wasn't her interrogator: it was one of the other female, pistol-toting guards. She wondered in passing whether this was an all-female prison, or whether it was a women's wing of your ordinary hell-hole where they kept political prisoners.

'*Allez!*' said the guard, looking over her shoulder. The door opened wider, and another guard pushed forward a small, young, blonde woman wearing a blue T-shirt and brown flared trousers.

'You can't *do* this to me!' she was protesting. 'I'm from the United Nations!'

Catriona would have laughed, but it didn't seem polite.

'At least give me my shoes back!' the young woman shouted at the closing door. She tried beating at the door as the locks were turned and the bolts were pushed home on the other side. Then she stopped, shrugged and began running her hands over the metal, prodding at the lock with her fingers, feeling the edges of the door for – Catriona supposed – gaps or hinges. Finally, she turned round to look at the cell.

'Hello,' said Catriona quietly.

The girl – *woman*, Catriona corrected herself with an effort – stepped away from the door and managed a quick grin.

'Er – hello,' she said, then marched across the narrow cell with her hand extended. 'I'm Jo Grant.'

'Catriona Talliser.' Catriona pushed herself upright, shook hands.

'Er – what are you – in for?'

Catriona grinned. 'I'm a reporter.'

'What happened to your face?'

Catriona felt at the bruise, winced, then managed another grin. 'I bit the interrogator. I think I'd got slightly bored with the interrogation.' She paused, swallowed. Time for a bit of honesty. 'I'm glad to see you, Miss Grant.'

'Jo.' The young woman met her eyes and smiled. 'And I'm glad to see you, Catriona. Do you know anything useful? Why they've arrested us, for instance?'

Catriona shook her head. 'All they've done is ask a lot of very stupid questions and threatened to kill me a few times.'

'Oh.' Jo sat down on the cell floor, cross-legged. She didn't look at all unnerved by the prospect of death threats; she seemed to be thinking. Catriona decided that she wasn't either as young or as inexperienced as her manner suggested.

'You're the one that rang Captain Yates, aren't you?' said Jo at last. 'About Captain Deveraux.'

Catriona nodded. 'And you're attached to UNIT, the

United Nations top secret intelligence taskforce against alien and other unclassifiable threats, which, by the way, the entire press corps knows all about, so I wouldn't worry about the Official Secrets Act too much if I were you.'

Jo glanced at her, not particularly surprised. 'Oh, well, I suppose after that stuff with Sir Reginald Styles's conference quite a lot of people got to hear about us.'

'The cybermen?' hazarded Catriona.

'Oh, no. They were Daleks. Well, Daleks and Ogrons. You see there was this alternative future, and the Doctor –' She stopped abruptly, put a hand in front of her mouth. Her face went an interesting shade of red.

Catriona grinned again, sat herself down on the cold floor next to Jo.

'It's okay, I know what's off the record. And you can't get more off the record than locked up in a cell in a Kebirian People's Prison awaiting possible execution.' She paused, realized what she'd just said. 'I don't suppose they sent you on your own?'

The young woman shook her head. 'Mike Yates came with me. And Sergeant Benton, and a team of – well, back-up people. But they arrested all of them. I'm – well, just an assistant, really.'

It figures, thought Catriona. Whilst they're defeating the latest threat to the Earth, they need someone glamorous to make the coffee.

She almost said it out loud, bit her tongue just in time. It wasn't fair, and it wasn't accurate. Jo wasn't glamorous: she had the kind of robust innocence that entirely precluded glamour. And she wasn't stupid – she looked as if she could do a lot more than make coffee if she put her mind to it.

As if to prove this, Jo suddenly leaned forward and said, 'Do you think we could escape from here? I can pick locks.'

Her large brown eyes radiated an impossible sincerity.

'And can you run two or three miles barefoot?' asked Catriona.

The young woman looked at her feet, already grubby from the prison's none-too-clean floors. She shrugged, jumped up, began to pace to and fro in the tiny space.

'We've got to do *something*. We can't just sit here.'

'Why not? They're bound to let us go sooner or later – they can't hold foreign nationals indefinitely. Especially not United Nations people. They'd lose every trade concession in the book.'

It didn't sound convincing, even to Catriona's own ears. She became aware that her back was still hurting, that clumps of pain and tension were forming at the base of her neck.

Jo bit at a fingernail. 'What if they're not Kebirians?'

Catriona frowned.

Jo stopped in front of her, knelt down so that their faces were level. 'They could be aliens. Some of the aliens I've seen could make themselves look like people. Or could make duplicates of people – the Axons could do that. And that thing you saw sounded like it was an alien.'

'How many sorts of aliens have you seen?' Catriona asked.

To her amazement, Jo began counting on her fingers. 'Well, first there were the Nestenes, and their plastic things, the Autons. Then there were the Axons, the Daemons, Ogrons, Daleks, Methaji, Arcturians, Sea Devils, Ice Warriors, Draconians, Hoveet, Skraals, Solonians – and – umm – Kalckani and Venusians, though I've never really met the Venusians but the Doctor talks about them all the time – and then if you count things like the Drashigs – oh, and the Spiridons of course, that was only last week, except that you can't actually see them because they're invisible –'

The earnest, innocent expression in the big brown eyes didn't falter once. Catriona began to experience a strange emotion, for the circumstances: envy. This young woman had seen things that would win her a whole lifetime's worth of Pulitzer Prizes.

'Over a dozen, I should think,' Jo concluded. 'The Doctor says the Daleks are the worst but I was terrified by the Autons.' She paused. 'They could look like people, too. If they had masks on.'

She sprang up, paced over to the door, pressed her ear against it for a moment, then began examining the lock. 'Have you got a nail file?' she asked suddenly. 'They took my bag away.'

Catriona stared at the younger woman. There were a hundred things she wanted to ask, from UNIT policy to what the aliens looked like to had all these aliens been to Earth or had she been to other planets –

Jo was stepping carefully around the room, examining the walls as if she were looking for a hole in them.

'I need a piece of metal about two inches long and thin enough to be flexible,' she said, adding, 'At least, that's what they said on the training course.'

Catriona decided not to think about why this 'innocent young woman' might have been on a lock-picking course. She just said, 'Jo, there are two bolts on the outside of the door. I've heard them drawn across several times now.'

'Yes, that's what I need the nail – the piece of metal for. The lock I can do with a hairpin.'

'I haven't got a hairpin either.'

Jo smiled. 'That's okay. I've got several in my –' She stopped suddenly, and her face fell. 'Oh.'

Catriona tried very hard to suppress a grin, and didn't quite succeed. Fortunately Jo was lost in thought and seemed not to notice.

'The other thing I've done when I've been locked up in places –' Catriona decided not to ask how many times Jo had been locked up in places '– is to call for the guard, then when he turns up, one of us stands by the door and bashes him over the head with – with –' she scanned the room for a moment, then saw the bucket in the corner, which was a heavy, iron affair. She went over, picked it up, then seemed to realize what was in it. She put it down, rather suddenly, and again went an interesting shade of red. 'Sorry.'

This time, Catriona didn't bother to suppress her grin. Jo looked at the floor, then giggled a little. Wearily, Catriona got up, walked over to the girl, took her arms.

'Look, Jo, if we do something crazy like that the best thing that could possibly happen is we get chucked back in here, painfully, and maybe kicked about a little before they lock us in again. The worst –' she paused, to make the younger woman meet her eyes, then repeated it '– the worst result, if the guard panics, is that we could be shot.'

Jo looked down, bit her lip. Catriona let her go.

'We've got to do something,' she said eventually, stubbornly.

Catriona began to wonder if this young woman was as stubborn – and therefore as dangerous – as the Kebirian interrogator.

'We can't do anything!' she shouted. 'This is a prison, for Heaven's sake. There are armed guards all over the place, several locked doors between us and the street, barbed wire, watchtowers and we haven't even got any shoes on!' She suddenly became aware of how loudly she was shouting, turned away and sat down, breathing hard. 'We'll have to wait until the morning. It's all we can do.'

'And what if they're aliens? All of them? What then?' Jo was angry too: she was staring at Catriona, her fists clenched by her sides.

With an effort, Catriona controlled her voice. She pretended she was talking to Bernard Silvers, that she was on camera.

'I respect your experience with aliens, Jo, and I know after what I've seen that something pretty strange is going on, but I don't believe that the entire population of Kebiria is under alien control. Not even the entire army.'

'It wouldn't have to be all of them,' said Jo. 'Just the leaders. I've seen them do that, too. Or try to.'

Catriona put her head in her hands. If only the woman would shut up for a minute and let her think.

'We've got to do *something*.'

Catriona gave one of the theatrical sighs that she was famous for in the newsroom of the *Journal*. It was going to be a long night.

The phone was ringing.

The confounded phone was always ringing, thought the Brigadier, struggling reluctantly back to consciousness. Did it have to ring at – his sleep-numbed fingers found the bedside lamp, switched it on – half-past four in the morning? He had been having a nice dream. It had been about – about –

Well, something nice. And now the phone –

Was still ringing. With a groan of dismay, he pushed himself upright, pulled the receiver towards him.

'Lethbridge-Stewart here.'

It was Osgood, the duty Sergeant. 'Sorry to disturb you, sir, but Captain Yates and his team have been arrested.'

'Been *what*?'

The Brigadier's body, long trained in middle-of-the-night crises, was already rolling out of the bed, finding the trousers of his uniform, which were neatly folded over a handy chair, and stepping into them, even as his mind took in the details of the Kebirian situation as relayed by Osgood on the phone.

'I'll be right over,' he said, already buckling his belt. 'Oh, and see if you can find the Doctor. I'll bet he's still working on that contraption of his. He never seems to sleep.'

'Right-o, sir.'

It was only after the Brigadier had hung up that he remembered that the Doctor and the TARDIS were gone, and might not be coming back. That the Doctor thought he was going to shoot him. Thought that he was going to shoot Jo.

64

He shook his head, quickly finished dressing; then glanced at himself in the mirror. Crisis or no crisis, he decided, there was time for him to shave.

Catriona was half-asleep again when she heard the footsteps approaching the cell. She jolted awake. Jo had already grabbed the bucket, was positioning herself by the door.

I don't believe she's doing this, thought Catriona.

Jo seemed to read her thoughts. 'It's all right,' she said. 'I've done it loads of times.'

Catriona looked up at her. 'What, hit someone over the head with a bucket full of piss?'

Jo blushed. 'You know what I mean.'

Outside, voices spoke in Arabic, not quite loud enough for Catriona to make out any of the words. Then the bolts drew back, the key rattled into the lock. Jo gave her a confident grin.

Catriona swallowed. This wasn't funny. The woman was mad. She was going to get them both killed. United Nations or no, Catriona should stop her before –

The door swung open, and a guard stepped inside. 'You are to come with me for further –'

She stopped talking as her eyes flicked across to Jo. The pistol seemed to spring out of its holster of its own accord, was in her hand. Then the bucket crashed down over her head. Drops of liquid spattered over the uniform, over the stone floor. The woman dropped to her knees, and Jo hit her again, then pushed the bucket down over her head.

The gun crashed, bucked in the woman's hand. Catriona thought she heard a bullet whistle past her ear, certainly heard a dull crack of broken plaster.

There was an instant's absolute, terrifying, silence. Then, slowly, the woman collapsed. Her gun landed on the concrete floor with a clatter of metal.

Jo vaulted over the body, ran through the door. Shaking a little, Catriona gingerly picked the gun up and looked out through the doorway. Jo was standing in the middle of the corridor, staring at her. There were two more guards racing towards her, pistols in their hands. Without thinking, Catriona raised her own gun. They both saw her at the same time, stopped, turned to aim at her –

– there's no need to shoot them no need to shoot anyone just tell them to drop their guns –

But Catriona's finger curled on the trigger.

The gun seemed to explode in her hand and she almost dropped it. One of the women staggered slowly backwards, a startled expression on her face. She aimed the pistol, but her hand started to shake. She dropped it, fell sideways, her entire body twitching as if there were a damaged motor in it.

– Jesus Christ I've killed her I've bloody killed her –

She turned to the other guard, half expecting to see the gun aimed at her, half expecting the force of a bullet to knock her back against the wall. But the woman was stepping back, her hands shakily raised, her head turning from side to side in terror. Suddenly she turned and ran, her footsteps echoing on the stone.

Catriona turned to Jo, who had picked up the dead guard's pistol and was holding it out towards Catriona.

'You'd better have this – I mean – you seem to know how to –'

Of course I don't know how to, thought Catriona. I don't even know why I picked the thing up, I just pulled the bloody trigger by accident, I didn't even know it was happening and *Jesus Christ I killed her* and I don't want to have to do it again, not ever, not under any circumstances, so just take that thing away from me –

But she said nothing, just held her hand out. Jo plonked the gun in it, managed a shaky grin as Catriona took a grip on the weapon.

'We'll need the keys,' she said, looking over Catriona's shoulder. Catriona turned, saw the bunch of keys still hanging from the door where the first guard had opened it. She stepped over, took them.

Shoes. They had to have shoes.

She looked down at the second guard, who was lying still in the corridor, with more blood than Catriona would have believed possible pooling around her chest.

'Bloody hell,' she muttered, then closed her eyes for a moment. She found herself wondering if perhaps there was a God after all, and if so what He would have to say to her about this.

She opened her eyes, put the gun down. Her fingers shaking a little, she began fumbling with the laces on the dead woman's shoes. They were shiny, black, flat-heeled. Policewoman's shoes. Surprisingly, they were too small for her. She flung them across to Jo, who stared at them for a moment, then slowly began to put them on.

Someone was shouting in the distance.

Quickly, she turned to the first guard. She was lying still in the doorway, with the bucket over her face. Catriona suddenly realized that she might be dead too, or dying. She had an absurd impulse to check the woman's pulse. Instead she pulled off the woman's shoes, pushed them on to her feet. They were too big, but she laced them tight.

Footsteps were racing across stone, doors clattered, more shouts.

'Shouldn't we take their uniforms?' said Jo. 'Then we could –'

'No time,' said Catriona. She started running, the loose shoes flopping on her feet so much that she began to wonder if she'd have been better off without them. They ran past a line of cell doors, towards a barred door. Catriona looked at Jo.

The younger woman tried several of the keys, finally found one that fitted. As the door opened an alarm bell started to ring. Catriona stepped through the door, found herself in another corridor with barred cell doors. She swore, glanced at Jo.

'Left or right?'

Jo hesitated. A guard appeared at the end of the

corridor to the right, shouted something which was inaudible over the bell. Jo ran: Catriona followed her, expecting at any moment to feel a bullet shatter her shoulder blades.

'Halt!' A man's voice. 'Halt now or we will shoot you!'

Jo stopped, looked around wildly, dived to one side. Catriona saw a cell door set into the wall, the young woman wrestling with the bunch of keys. She wondered why on Earth Jo was trying to get *in* to a cell, but before she could catch up with her and ask there was an explosion of gunfire. Catriona tried to drop flat, only got as far as her knees. Then her body seemed to freeze. Behind her, over the sound of the bell and the humming in her ears, she heard booted footsteps approaching, echoing off the steel doors of the corridor.

'Put your hands up!' said the voice.

Catriona tried to move, couldn't. With an effort, she managed to lower the hand carrying the machine pistol so that the weapon pointed at the ground.

'Throw the gun down! NOW!'

She tried, but she couldn't let go. Her fingers wouldn't respond to the commands from her brain. She tried to speak, to say she couldn't move, couldn't let go of the gun, but her mouth only produced a faint croak, like someone moaning in their sleep. Cold metal touched the back of her neck.

She tried to think, a last thought, a last story, anything that would make sense of her dying, but all she could come up with was *I killed her. I killed her. And now I'm going to pay.*

Seven

With a final thud, the TARDIS materialized in the darkened laboratory. After a moment, the door opened, and the Doctor stepped out. He switched the lights on, then sat down in a chair, facing the door, with a slight, confident smile on his face.

Thirty seconds later, the Brigadier came in.

'Right on time, old chap,' said the Doctor.

The Brigadier stared at him.

'Osgood said the place was empty.'

'That's because it was, until a few minutes ago.' The Doctor stood up and put his hands behind his back: his 'lecturing position', the Brigadier sometimes called it. 'I've repaired and calibrated the Personal Time-line Prognosticator. It predicted that you would be here at 4.42 a.m. It's now 4.43 and you arrived about half a minute ago. That's a fairly low margin of error, wouldn't you agree, Brigadier?'

The Brigadier stared at him.

'Doctor, you don't *want* it to be true, do you? You don't want me to gun down you and Jo, here in the laboratory?'

The Doctor shook his head. 'It doesn't have to be in the laboratory. As I told Jo, it could be anywhere, anywhen. And no, of course I don't want it to happen. There is even a small chance that it won't happen. I just want to make you aware of the facts.'

The Brigadier looked uncomfortably away. 'I am aware of them, thank you, Doctor. And I have taken what steps I can. Now, can we deal with more immediate matters?'

'Jo has been arrested in Kebiria,' said the Doctor.

'How on Earth do you know that?'

'My dear fellow, you don't think I haven't used the Prognosticator to track Jo's movements as well? Last time I checked on her she was in a prison cell in Kebir City with another woman and as far as I could tell from reading their lips they're planning an escape.'

The Brigadier considered this for a moment. 'I don't think that's wise. I've already got somebody from the Secretariat on to this, they should be in touch with the Kebirian government first thing in the morning.'

'Yes, but Jo doesn't know that. I think it would be easier if I went and collected her, don't you?'

The Brigadier stared at him. 'Collected her? In that thing?' He gestured with his swagger-stick at the TARDIS. 'I thought you never knew where you were going to end up?'

The Doctor frowned severely. 'It's not quite that bad, Brigadier. I've just had a little difficulty getting used to the navigational systems again.' He paused, glanced down at a key that he was holding in his hand, frowned. 'Anyway, this should be easy enough. I've linked the Prognosticator to the primary space-time orientation circuits. All I have to do is work out where Jo will be in – say – ten minutes, and the TARDIS will take me there. Then, if you'll be kind enough to sit here for the next twenty minutes, I can use a fix on you to return here.'

He started towards the TARDIS, the key in his hand.

'Just a minute, Doctor,' said the Brigadier. 'Are you telling me I've got to sit here for the next twenty minutes whilst you swan off to Kebiria in that thing?'

'That's right, Brigadier,' said the Doctor over his shoulder, opening the TARDIS door. 'Twenty minutes.'

The door closed.

'But Doctor –'

The TARDIS began to issue the wheezing, grating noise which the Brigadier recognized as being a prelude to dematerialization. The light on the top flashed. The wall became visible beyond the machine.

It had almost vanished when there was a muffled thud, like distant thunder. The TARDIS winked in and out of existence, appeared, wraith-like, in several different parts of the room at once. Then there was another much louder thud and a gust of wind hit the Brigadier in the face as if something had exploded. Automatically he threw himself flat on the floor, covered his eyes. There was another loud bang, followed by a strangulated trumpeting noise: the Brigadier looked up, saw the TARDIS back in place. Before he could react, the door flew open and the Doctor emerged in a cloud of smoke, coughing. From within the TARDIS there was a hissing sound, and the smoke issuing from the door thinned and then stopped.

Too late. Quite a lot of it had accumulated under the lab ceiling.

A bell began ringing, painfully loud in the small room. A red light flashed. Somewhere in the distance, a siren started to blare. Cold water began showering down over the lab, and the lights went out.

The Doctor ignored all of this, just looked around, then down to where the Brigadier was slowly picking himself up, trying not to think about the dry-cleaning bill for his uniform.

'On the other hand, Brigadier,' he said sheepishly, 'perhaps we should take a plane, if you would be good enough to arrange one.'

Jo stared at the man, and the man stared back at her. He was an Arab, tall and lanky, his face burned and wrinkled by the desert. He was wearing a frayed denim jacket and loose jeans; his feet were bare.

'Are you a prisoner?' asked Jo, feeling that it was a silly question even as she asked it. She looked at the bunch of keys in her hand. She had a ridiculous notion that she ought to apologize to the man for barging into his cell without knocking.

71

'I have that misfortune,' said the Arab, in slow, careful English. 'Can I help you?'

'We're — trying to escape,' said Jo, glancing over her shoulder at the corridor outside. She heard a man shouting.

The man got up, walked swiftly past her to the cell door, peered out. Jo started to follow, but he held up a hand, shook his head.

Suddenly, he was gone.

There was a scuffle, a crash of gunfire. Jo ran forward, saw Catriona standing over the body of the guard, splashes of blood staining her shirt. More blood leaked from a neat line of holes in the man's back. The prisoner was looking up and down the corridor, holding the guard's machine pistol.

He turned, smiled at Jo.

'My name is Abdelsalam,' he said. 'Follow me.' He began to run lightly down the corridor.

Jo looked at Catriona, who shrugged. 'No choice, I suppose,' she said. Her voice was shaking.

They set off after Abdelsalam, caught up with him by a locked door. 'Come on Jo, do your stuff,' said Catriona.

Jo swallowed, worked the lock. Catriona pushed the heavy door open. Abdelsalam jumped through, gun at the ready, but there was no one there. An empty corridor faced them, of the familiar design.

Abdelsalam ran down it, shouting, 'Vincent! Belquassim!'

There were shouts from several cells. Abdelsalam listened, then ran to one and beat on the door. Jo joined him, frantically examining the keys. The wailing of sirens drifted in through the door, accompanying the continuing clamour of the alarm bell in the women's block.

'Quickly!' said Abdelsalam.

The first key Jo tried didn't work. The second jammed in the lock. Jo looked around frantically.

Abdelsalam put the muzzle of the gun against the lock. 'Stand back,' he said quietly. 'And pray to Allah.'

He fired, twice.

The door opened.

Inside the cell, a short, dark-haired man with startling green eyes glanced at her briefly, then turned his gaze to look over her shoulder at Catriona. A strange expression, half-frown, half-smile, crossed his face.

'Miss Talliser! So you have decided on direct action at last!'

Jo looked round, saw Catriona wiping blood from her chin with one hand, pushing back the messy hair from her forehead with the other.

'Vincent bloody Tayid,' she said. 'I might have known it would be you. And no, I haven't decided anything. I just didn't have much choice.'

Vincent grinned. 'Nevertheless I am pleased to see you.' He stepped forward, held his hands out. Catriona threw him the pistol that she was still holding.

'You should be careful with these things, my friend,' said Vincent, hefting the gun, clicking something into place. 'They're killing machines, eh?'

Light blazed into the corridor. Vincent pushed Jo sideways into his cell, so that she fell onto the floor. There was a crash of gunfire. Jo saw Catriona crawling towards her across the floor, heard a man scream.

Catriona rolled into the cell, winced.

'Are you all right?' shouted Jo.

Catriona winced again. 'My neck hurts,' she said. 'But I'll live.'

Outside, the gunfire stopped. In the silence, Jo muttered, 'Who is Vincent? Can we trust him?'

'An old friend,' said Catriona. 'And absolutely yes.' She paused, bit her lip. 'I think.'

Footsteps sounded in the corridor, stopped outside the door.

'Are you all right, ladies?' Vincent's voice.

There was a moment's silence. Catriona didn't seem to be going to say anything, so Jo spoke up. 'We're okay. What do we do now?'

The door swung open, and Vincent beckoned to them.

'We get Belquassim,' he said. 'Then we get out of here.' He indicated a cell door. 'That one.'

Jo managed to unlock the cell this time: Belquassim turned out to be a younger version of Abdelsalam, with — Jo thought — a nicer smile. He greeted Abdelsalam and Vincent with a brief embrace, bowed to Catriona and Jo.

'Come on,' said Vincent.

They ran.

A guard lay dead at a junction in the corridor, blood pumping from his head. Jo stopped, stared. For the first time it really came home to her: these were people, *people*, not Autons or Daleks or Ogrons. And they would still be alive if she hadn't insisted on escaping from that cell —

Someone grabbed at her arm, pulled her along. Jo looked up, saw Catriona. Their eyes met for a moment.

'Time for regrets later,' said the older woman quietly.

Jo swallowed, nodded. They ran on.

Vincent seemed to know the layout of the prison well. They descended some steps, came to a locked door. Jo got her bunch of keys ready, but Vincent didn't wait for that. He pushed his gun up to the lock, fired. It took several seconds for Jo's ears to recover sufficiently to realize that another alarm had gone off. By then they were running along a darkened passage past something that looked like an office.

They came to another door, this one protected by a coded lock.

'Only trusted prisoners in here,' said Vincent, looking round with a grin. 'We're all trustworthy, aren't we?'

Belquassim laughed.

Vincent punched in the code and opened the door, gun at the ready.

'Empty,' he said, beckoning them forward. 'It shouldn't be. We get lucky. Which one of you is it has the luck, eh?'

Jo stepped through, found herself in a large room lined with books, evidently the prison library. Vincent was already clambering up a set of steps intended to fetch down books from the shelves. When he reached the top, he jumped, hung by his hands from something on the ceiling.

Jo heard the sound of a bolt sliding back. Then a second bolt. By this time, Belquassim had climbed the steps, grasped hold of Vincent's legs. He pushed, and Vincent disappeared into a hole in the ceiling.

Abdelsalam now climbed the steps, was lifted by Belquassim. The steps tottered dangerously, and Abdelsalam was gone. Catriona glanced at Jo.

'Go on.'

Jo clambered up, felt Belquassim grasp her under the arms. He almost threw her up. Someone caught her hands. She thought her arms would pop out of their sockets, but within a moment she was scrambling out into the open.

She found herself on a low, flat roof. Rather to her surprise, it was raining: big, isolated drops. The sky glowed with the reflection of street lights. Vincent and Abdelsalam helped Catriona up, then Belquassim jumped, gripped the edge of the trapdoor and was hauled to safety. A loud crash from below told Jo that the ladder had fallen down. She slammed the trapdoor, then looked up, saw Vincent peering over the edge of the roof. Catriona was by his side. 'Come on!' he called, in a stage whisper.

Jo realized that Belquassim was already gone, that Abdelsalam was in the act of lowering Catriona over the edge. She trotted up, saw Belquassim standing on a wide pavement ten feet below, saw Catriona drop into his arms. He swung her round like a partner in a waltz. Catriona winced, and gave him a nasty glance.

Jo grinned to herself, took a couple of steps sideways and jumped on her own. Ten feet was no worse than landing with a parachute, and she'd done that loads of times.

75

She landed easily, rolled, jumped up, and grinned at Belquassim from a safe distance. He smiled broadly in return, and winked.

Vincent landed behind her, patted her on the shoulder.

'You know how to jump, eh? As well as having the luck. You are good to have around.'

A siren began to sound, horrifyingly loud, from the direction of the prison. Vincent ran down the street like a sprinter. Jo and the others followed, but only Belquassim could keep up with him. After a moment she saw what he had been running towards: the dark blob of a car parked against the side of the road.

'Can you break into this?' asked Vincent, as they approached it.

'Got a piece of wire?' asked Jo.

'No need,' said Belquassim from the passenger side. 'They left the window down.'

There was a click, and after a moment the driver's door swung open. Abdelsalam – still out of breath from the run – got in.

Vincent opened the back door, ushered Jo and Catriona in, then got in himself. In front of them Abdelsalam was fiddling with the wires beneath the dash. Abruptly the engine fired, and Jo was jolted back in her seat as they accelerated wildly along the road.

'Where are we going?' she asked.

They took a corner, bearing right, tyres screeching.

'Vincent?' asked Catriona. 'Where *are* we going?'

Vincent laughed, and said something in Arabic. Abdelsalam laughed. Belquassim looked over his shoulder and winked at Catriona.

'He says we ought to blindfold you,' said Belquassim. 'We are taking you to our safe house.'

Vincent laughed again. 'Which only the entire Kebirian Secret Police, and the Army, Air Force and probably the Navy too know about!' He looked across at Jo. 'You know who I am, eh? Vincent Tayid, world-famous Arab

76

campaigner for revolutionary justice? You have heard of me?' The last question had an almost pleading note.

Jo opened her mouth to say, *No, you must be kidding* – then closed it again. Now that he mentioned it, the name did seem awfully familiar. She just hadn't had a chance to think about it in the last ten minutes or so.

She looked at Catriona. The older woman glanced at her sidelong; her lips curled in a small, ironic smile. 'Sorry, Jo,' she said. 'But you make the strangest friends when you're a foreign correspondent.'

Eight

When the Brigadier got to the hangar, the Super-hawks were ready to go. The first plane was already hitched to the guide truck, its RAF roundels standing out clearly in the glare of the floodlights. The pilot, his helmet on, was in his seat in the open cockpit. The Brigadier strode across the concrete floor, feeling slightly embarrassed and more than slightly hot in his flight suit, hastily put on over a still-damp uniform. He wondered where the Doctor was.

The pilot stood up, waved, pulled off his helmet, thus revealing himself to be the Doctor. The Brigadier noticed for the first time another man in a flight suit standing under the wing of the plane, inspecting one of the engines.

'Hurry up, man,' shouted the Doctor. 'There's not a moment to lose!'

The Brigadier shook his head. 'We still haven't got permission from the Kebirians. I don't know about this, Doctor. We might have to turn back, you know.'

'Nonsense, Brigadier. This young man says the Super-hawk can outpace anything that the Kebirians have got.'

The Brigadier felt the familiar impatience growing inside him. 'It can't outpace a missile, Doctor. And we're not going in there armed.' This wasn't, strictly speaking, true: the bomb bays were empty, but the Brigadier had made sure that the wing guns were loaded.

'Brigadier, I really must insist that we leave as soon as possible. If I'm right, Jo and the others could be in considerable danger.'

The Brigadier ignored him, instead walked up to the flight-suited young man and tapped him on the shoulder. 'Flight-Lieutenant Butler, isn't it?'

The young man ducked out from under the wing and saluted. 'Sir.'

'You'll be taking your orders from me, young man. I'll be in the rear plane, but I'll contact you by radio if there are any developments. If I say turn back, we turn back. Don't take any notice of the Doctor, whatever he says.'

About half way through this speech, an expression of consternation crossed Butler's face. When the Brigadier had finished, he said: 'But I'm not going, sir! My orders were to show the Doctor the route and set up the flight directory, then leave him to it.'

'Leave him to it?' The Brigadier shot a suspicious glance up at the Doctor, who was putting his helmet back on. 'You mean he's going to fly the thing?'

'With you as passenger, sir.'

'But what about –?' the Brigadier gestured at the second plane.

'Not going, sir. Air Vice-Marshal's orders.'

'Look, Butler, I spoke to the Air Vice-Marshal not half an hour ago. He assured me that there would be two planes, and two pilots.'

'Sorry, sir, but the Air Vice-Marshal has been in touch with the Ministry. As soon as they found out that the Doctor was a qualified pilot, they ordered –' The young man looked at his boots. 'Well, they said it was a lot cheaper to send one plane, sir.'

The Brigadier swallowed hard, looked hard at the Doctor, who was flicking switches on the control panel, smiling brightly like a child with a new toy.

'Doctor? Can you really fly this thing?'

The Doctor looked up, pushed his visor up. 'Of course I can, Brigadier. I did over seventy thousand hours on a Martian Exploder a couple of centuries ago. This plane is practically the same apart from the radar and Flight Lieutenant Butler has very kindly briefed me on that.

Now will you please get in? We're supposed to be taking off in three minutes' time. You know, I really can't imagine why it's taken you nearly an hour to get all this ready. It would have been quicker to replace the TARDIS navigational circuits altogether than wait for your people to come up with the goods.'

The Brigadier swallowed again, muttered a dismissal to the Flight Lieutenant, and climbed the cockpit steps. He got into the back seat, fastened his helmet, heard the Doctor's voice talking to ground control. The plane began to move as the guide truck revved up.

'Doctor,' said the Brigadier quietly. 'You will remember that as pilot of this aircraft you're under my orders, won't you? If I say we turn back, we turn back, is that clear?'

'Perfectly clear, thank you, Brigadier,' said the Doctor. 'Now hush up, there's a good chap, I have to concentrate on this.'

There was a click and the channel went dead. A whirring of pumps announced the first stage in starting the Superhawk's twin jets; at the same moment, they cleared the hangar door into a grey, half-lit dawn. Rain spattered on the canopy.

'I wonder what a Martian Exploder is,' muttered the Brigadier to himself.

The jets began to rumble, and, detached from the guide truck, the Superhawk began to trundle across the tarmac. As they paused at the end of the runway, the Brigadier thought about the gun holstered inside his flight suit. It was a .35, nothing like the one in the Prognosticator sequence.

The jets throttled up, the airframe began to shudder. The Superhawk accelerated down the runway through the rain.

Everything's under control, thought the Brigadier. I hope.

The Sahara desert wasn't very interesting, Jo decided. So far, it seemed to consist of mile after mile of dusty emptiness, broken by the occasional stunted tree. It hadn't even been sunny at first, although as they drove south the sun had slowly broken through the clouds and it had begun to get hot.

Abdelsalam had driven them at breakneck pace to what Vincent described as a 'safe house'. To Jo's surprise it had been in the French quarter, amidst tall white colonial houses, above a street café. There had been much shouting and rejoicing at their return, then the distant wailing of police sirens had sent them through a back alley to a garage where they picked up a Land Rover – old and battered, but ready-filled with petrol, water drums, and a couple of Kalashnikovs in the back. Camouflage jackets were found for Vincent and Catriona. Jo was given a yellow cotton headscarf to wear, and false papers saying she was the café owner's wife. Abdelsalam and Belquassim – whom they had left behind somewhere in the café – reappeared in full Kebirian Army uniform, complete with French-made machine guns. Abdelsalam got in the driver's seat, Belquassim had the other. Vincent, Catriona and Jo rode in the back on the bare metal platform. They heard sirens frequently and once Abdelsalam turned down an alley to avoid a traffic queue which might have led to a roadblock, but otherwise there had been no incidents.

Jo looked up at Catriona, but the reporter was asleep, her head lolling on her shoulder, her mouth half open. Jo saw that Vincent had placed a piece of cloth behind her head for a bolster, and was holding it in place with one hand.

He seemed so kind, she thought. And yet –

It didn't seem possible that this was *Al Tayid*.

'Vincent,' she whispered.

The green eyes looked round, fixed on hers.

'Are you really a terrorist? I mean, I've seen your name in the papers, but –'

Vincent grinned. 'Stick to "revolutionary freedom fighter", eh?'

81

Jo blushed. 'Sorry. But –' she hesitated. 'Is that why you were in prison?'

Vincent looked away, said nothing. The Land Rover swung around a curve in the road, pushing them all to one side. Catriona woke up, rubbing her eyes.

Vincent glanced at her, at last returned his gaze to Jo.

'I killed a little girl,' he said quietly.

Catriona, still rubbing her eyes, said, 'Vincent, you swore to me – off the record –'

'I killed her,' interrupted Vincent. 'It was an accident. I was aiming at her father.' He made a brief half-smile. 'I killed him too.'

Catriona had a hand over her mouth. She turned her head to Vincent. 'But Vincent, we had a campaign going, a petition for your release. Mike Timms was going to get Leo to raise it in Parliament. Paul Vishnya was going to write an open letter to the Secretary-General. And now you're saying you did it all along?'

Vincent looked away. 'I did it. It was a mistake, I tell you.'

'Like the bombing of the Cairo Hilton?'

'I tell you I will not go into that again!' snapped Vincent.

Jo remembered the Cairo bombing, it had happened in her first year at UNIT. She couldn't recall the exact death toll, but she knew it had been in double figures. She stared hard at Vincent, who was looking out over the tailgate.

'I don't think it's right to kill innocent people, whatever you believe in.'

Vincent swung around, his face tight with fury, his eyes staring. 'And you think that governments don't kill innocent people? You think it is okay, when soldiers walk into the camps of the Giltaz, murder the men, women and children? Or steal the children and make them slaves? You think that is "legitimate political action"? Your "United Nations", your UNITs and UNICEFs and UNHCR, they are all a sham if they do not stop these things. Your politicians, your peacekeepers, they're just to make fat westerners feel good, to let you play games with our countries, with our lives. It is all a waste of time, a joke, a farce.'

Jo swallowed, looked at the yellow cloth of the headscarf, which had come loose and was trailing over her arms.

'I still don't think you should kill civilians,' she said. 'That's just dropping to your enemy's level.'

'Jo –' said Catriona in a warning voice.

But Vincent's anger seemed spent. 'We have no choice,' he said wearily. 'We've tried everything else. It is the only way, if there is ever going to be justice in the world.'

Jo looked up at him. 'But if you want justice, why don't you give the UN a chance? I don't think it's really fair what you said about them.'

She braced herself for another blast of anger, but to her surprise, Vincent laughed. 'We give them a chance. We write to them frequently. We have friends –' he clapped Catriona gently on the shoulder '– who speak for us. But it is the United *Nations*, you see. It is governments. They are not interested in people who are not governments.'

'That's not quite fair, Vincent,' said Catriona. 'There are a lot of people at the UN who would like to change things, and you know it. You also know that killing tourists in a hotel lobby doesn't help their cause or yours.'

'That was two years ago,' growled Vincent.

He did look a little ashamed now, thought Jo.

'So you admit it was wrong?' she asked.

'It happened.' Vincent shrugged. 'Right or wrong won't change that. What I do not admit is that it was not justified.'

Jo felt herself getting angry. 'But you can't justify killing people who have never done anything to you!'

Vincent's eyes flashed.

'They are part of the conspiracy against the oppressed

83

people of the world. They are part of the silence that allows it to happen. That is justification enough.'

Jo looked down at her knees again, then back up at Vincent. 'Then you should kill me,' she said. 'I've been silent. I haven't supported your party. So I'm conspiring against you. You should pick up one of those guns and shoot me now.' She gestured at the spare Kalashnikovs under their cover of tarpaulin.

Out of the corner of her eye, she saw that a broad grin had formed on Catriona's face. The reporter's gaze shifted from her to Vincent, in anticipation of his reply.

Vincent had obviously noticed this expression. 'You can't understand, either of you,' he said in a disgusted tone. 'You live in the West, you played with dolls when you were children, now you play politics and you think it is the same. You have never had to kill anyone.'

'That's not the —' began Jo, but Catriona interrupted her.

'I've killed someone.'

Jo and Vincent both turned to stare at her. Her face had gone pale, making the bruise stand out sharply on her cheek.

'What, today?' said Vincent. 'But you didn't tell me!'

'I wasn't proud of it!' snapped Catriona. She was almost shouting. 'I shot one of the guards outside our cell.'

Jo remembered the shot, the woman falling. Remembered Catriona throwing a pair of shoes to her — the shoes she was wearing now. *Dead woman's shoes.*

She swallowed, hard.

Catriona was still talking. 'I'd forgotten about it, when we were talking just now. Jesus *Christ*, Vincent, I killed another human being! How could I forget about it? Even for five minutes?' She put her head in her hands.

'You didn't have any choice,' said Jo. 'We had to get out of there.'

But Catriona only repeated, 'How could I forget it, Vincent? How is it possible to forget?' Her voice through her hands was muffled, almost choking.

Vincent reached out and took one of Catriona's hands, held it tightly.

'There are things you have to forget, sometimes,' he said. 'If you are to live at all.'

A single flat-topped thundercloud hung over the Mediterranean, capped with gold by the morning sun. From the forty-thousand-foot altitude of the Superhawk, the Brigadier could see over the top of the cloud to the receding brown-and-green mass that was Mallorca. Another, even more foreshortened smudge of rock and mist near the eastern horizon might have been Sicily or Sardinia. On the other side of the plane, a brown wedge of land projected into the clear blue sea: Kebiria. If he looked over the Doctor's shoulder through the front of the cockpit, the Brigadier could see more: a white sheet of cloud covering the Kebiriz coast, and dim shadows of mountains behind it, like frozen waves on a choppy sea.

The Brigadier fingered the talk button on the intercom. 'Any luck raising Rabat?'

As navigator/bombardier, the Brigadier had a complete duplicate set of controls for the radio system, but after three failed attempts at raising UNIT's North West Africa control he'd asked the Doctor to give it a try.

'Nothing there at all, Brigadier.' The Doctor's voice was crackling on the intercom, which was odd since he was only about four feet away. The Brigadier wondered for a moment whether the plane's radio systems might have developed a fault. 'I've tried Cagliari, too,' added the Doctor. 'But I can't get a clear signal from them either. It might be that storm, you know.' He gestured at the cloud, now falling behind them.

The Brigadier grimaced. He was beginning to smell a rat; the Doctor was being altogether too helpful. He glanced at the navigation radar. 'Doctor, we enter Kebirian air space in three minutes. You should start to turn now – west, I would suggest, so that we can make a landing at Cagliari.'

'Turn, Brigadier?'

I knew it! thought the Brigadier. I should never have let him pilot this thing – I should have flown him out here trussed and bound –

Aloud he said: 'Doctor, may I remind you that when we last spoke to UNIT control they had still not had permission from the Kebirian government for this mission to enter their national air space. You know perfectly well that if we don't turn round they're quite likely to shoot us down.'

'Oh, I expect they've given permission by now, Brigadier. And anyway if this plane is anything like a Martian Exploder we should be in there and down on the ground before they even know what's happening.'

The Brigadier took a deep breath. 'Doctor, as your commanding officer I order you to abort this mission and set a course for Cagliari.'

'Really, Brigadier! I am not a member of your brigade, nor even of HM armed forces. I am an independent advisor –'

'And you're flying an Air Force plane! I order you to turn back!'

There was a short silence. For a moment – just for a moment – the Brigadier contemplated pulling the Browning from his flight jacket and putting it to the Doctor's head.

Then he remembered.

'Well, I doubt it would do any good anyway,' he muttered.

'What was that, Brigadier?'

'We're entering Kebirian air space,' said the Brigadier. He looked at the main radar, which was showing two fast-approaching blips. 'And it looks like they're coming up to say hello.'

Nine

Jo hadn't expected Vincent's base to be a permanent settlement. But even from more than a mile away, it was apparent that it was in fact a full-sized town: a town of mud-brick houses, camel-wool tents and green, irrigated gardens. The largest building was draped with two huge canvases, bearing the shapes of the Red Cross and the Red Crescent. Men and women walked in the streets, and Jo saw a bicycle winding its way between the tents. The entire settlement was surrounded by a roughly lozenge-shaped wall and ditch; Jo saw sandbagged defensive positions set into the wall, men in khaki clothes and turbans crouching behind angular, canvas-shrouded objects which could only be weapons. Beyond the walls was flat shale desert, black as tar in the afternoon heat.

Belquassim came up beside her. 'Welcome to Free Giltea,' he said, his tobacco-stained teeth showing under his dark moustache. 'Do you like it?'

Jo blinked grit out of her eyes. 'It's pretty well organized,' she admitted. She glanced over her shoulder. Vincent and Catriona were sitting on the bonnet of the Land Rover, talking quietly. Abdelsalam was still in the driving seat, smoking a cigarette and reading a newspaper. Vincent had told them that the road was mined from here on; the only safe access to Free Giltea from the Kebirian side was on foot, a route through the minefield that Vincent and his fighters kept a strict secret. The aid workers and the civilians came in from the Algerian side. The settlement itself was technically in Algeria, but in practice the Algerians ignored it and had placed their border posts about five miles away.

'We have more than ten thousand people here,' said Belquassim proudly. 'And another three thousand fighting in the desert.'

'Why can't you beat the Kebirians then?'

Belquassim looked hurt. 'The Russians gave them planes, after the revolution. The Moroccans give them money and guns now, because they help against Polisario in the south. No one gives us anything, except the Libyans, a little. And we don't trust *them*.' He smiled again, suddenly. 'But we will win, one day, even so.'

'Why?'

'Because the land is ours.'

Jo realized that, as far as Belquassim was concerned, this was simple truth: victory depended not on guns or aircraft, but on who the land was supposed to belong to. She smiled at him. 'I think that's rather a nice way of looking at things.'

Belquassim's face softened. He reached out and pulled at her headscarf, which she had folded back over her shoulders.

'You should keep it over your head,' he said, gently pushing it back into place.

Jo giggled. 'Why? Because I'm supposed to be modest?'

'No. Because it keeps the dust out of your hair, and also the flies. So that it will be kept nice for your boyfriend.'

'I haven't got a boyfriend,' said Jo.

'That's a pity,' said Belquassim, but the expression on his face indicated that he didn't think it was a pity at all. Jo lowered her eyes and turned to face the Giltean settlement.

Something had changed, and after a moment Jo realized what it was. The canvas covering the weapons on the perimeter had been pulled back, revealing the gleaming metal teeth of anti-aircraft guns.

'What's happening, Belquassim?' she asked, but even as she said it there was a shout from behind, a clatter of gun metal, and the car door slammed.

Jo turned, saw Vincent running towards her, pulling Catriona after him.

'Down here! Quickly!'

'What's happening?' repeated Jo.

'The bastards have come after me!' He rushed past her. 'This way!'

Jo looked at Belquassim, who was scanning the sky with binoculars. He said, 'Jets. Three.'

Abdelsalam shouted something in Arabic. Vincent, already twenty yards down the rocky slope, shouted back. Abdelsalam shrugged, went to the back of the Land Rover and emerged with a Kalashnikov in each hand, and two belts of ammunition. He gave one to Belquassim and kept the other, so that they were each armed with two guns, the Kalashnikovs and the French machine guns that had been part of the uniform. Jo couldn't see the point of it.

'Jo!'

Catriona's voice.

'*Run!*'

The urgency in her voice convinced Jo to start down the slope, scrambling ahead of the two Gilteans. Vincent and Catriona were running ahead, dodging to the left now.

Belquassim shouted something, and a huge gust of hot air knocked Jo off her feet, sending her sliding amongst the hard pebbles. She saw something projecting ahead that might be a mine and struggled frantically to stop, scrabbling at the slope till her hands bled. She hit something soft: Catriona. For some reason the reporter was crouched with her hands over her head. Next to her Vincent was doing the same. Around them, pebbles were shattering and jumping into the air.

Something vast and silver thundered overhead, bringing an ear-hurting roar in its wake. Jo saw the white-hot exhaust at the rear of the jet as the plane sped away, barrelling over the Giltean settlement. The perimeter guns spat, but they were too slow to track the jet as it climbed away from them.

There was a flash of silver in the corner of Jo's eye. A fraction of a second later, one of the gun batteries exploded, pieces of metal and other debris scattering in a ball of flame. Another jet appeared over the slope, raced down across the settlement. Tents jerked as bullets hit them. A tiny figure with a gun fruitlessly fired at the tail of the plane.

Then an entire street exploded.

Over the confusion of sounds in Jo's ears, she heard Vincent screaming, 'No! They cannot do this! I should never have come here – they are doing this because they are angry with me –'

Catriona was shouting something too, pointing to the east.

Then Jo saw it: the first jet, rolling lazily back out of the sky, heading towards them.

Catriona dragged Vincent to his feet, and they started running. Jo looked over her shoulder for Belquassim and Abdelsalam, and to her horror saw only a scattering of burned and twisted metal where the Land Rover had been.

She stopped, stared, saw Abdelsalam lying on the slope, one leg buckled beneath him, his head twisted backwards, his eyes staring lifelessly at the sky.

Catriona caught at her arm, pulled her down.

'Where's Belquassim?' she asked the reporter.

Then she saw something burning near the remains of the Land Rover, saw the scorched pieces of clothing.

'Oh,' she said. She felt her stomach heave.

– but he was nice he was flirting with me we were having fun –

Catriona pulled harder at her arm. The jet roared overhead. Rocks exploded into fragments around them. A piece of stone hit Jo in the leg, making a rip in the

90

fabric of her trousers. Blood began to leak from the cut, but Jo didn't feel any pain. Somewhere on the other side of the road there was an explosion. A bullet must have hit a mine, Jo thought.

She began to run, following Vincent as he twisted and turned through the minefield, concentrating on putting her feet in the same spots as he did. The sounds of explosions from the settlement grew closer, but gradually diminished in frequency until all Jo could hear was a crackle of burning, the occasional crash of falling rubble and the constant sound of women wailing.

She could see very little ahead: the air was filled with dust and smoke. Vincent had tied a handkerchief over his mouth. Catriona was coughing, deep spasms that left her gasping for breath.

'Should we be going down there?' asked Jo. 'Won't they come back?'

Vincent shrugged. Jo realized that there wasn't really anywhere else for them to go. They could hardly walk back to Kebir City, or to Algiers.

They were walking across the black desert shale now. Ahead, through the thinning smoke, Jo saw a bank of loose rock and dirty sandbags. At first she thought it was rubble, then realized she was looking at the remains of the makeshift perimeter 'wall'. A piece of plastic pipe passed through the embankment. A man lay flat at the end of it, cradling a gun. After a few seconds Jo realized that he was dead.

Vincent advanced with caution, picking his way amongst the stones. The sun was shining through the smoke and dust now, dim and bloody.

Someone shouted from inside the embankment.

'*Al Tayid*,' said Vincent simply.

A gun emerged, followed by a man in khaki. He stared at Vincent, then stepped forward and embraced him. When he stepped back, he nodded at Catriona, then looked at Jo and shot Vincent an interrogative look.

'I'm Jo Grant,' said Jo, without waiting for Vincent's

91

explanation. 'From UNIT. The United Nations.'

The man gave her another appraising glance. 'Do you have any medicines?' he asked.

'Medicines?' said Jo blankly. 'No, we escaped with Vincent –' Then she broke off as it dawned on her why the man was so interested in medicines. She remembered the tents jolting under the bullets from the planes, thought about the people who had been in those tents. 'I do first aid,' she said.

The man glanced at Catriona, then turned back to Vincent.

'You'd better come through,' he said.

They crawled across the remains of the wall, into a scene worse than any possible nightmare. Two men in blackened uniforms were pulling a body out of a heap of dust and rubble that had once been a house. The street was already piled with bodies, some of them charred, others dismembered by the explosions. Several of the pieces were small enough to have come from children. Jo felt her stomach heave. She'd seen death before – too often – but this was the worst. Human beings had done this. Three human beings, she thought, remembering the number of planes. Just three people, in powerful machines. And just one decision, to send them, made in Kebir City.

What had Vincent said? *'You think that governments don't kill innocent people?'* The words seemed to echo in her head as she stared at the heap of bodies. Maybe people couldn't be trusted with power. Not any sort of power.

'Jo!' Catriona was beckoning from further up the street. 'They could do with a hand here.'

Jo ran up to her, saw an Arab woman with her head in her hands, sobbing. A turbaned man stood by her, a girl of about five in his arms. There was a piece of metal protruding from the little girl's chest.

Jo swallowed hard, made herself look closer. The metal was tubular, about two inches wide, and curved in an oddly familiar way – with a sudden shock she recognized the handlebars of a bicycle. The metal had entered the chest just above the bottom of the rib cage, to the left of the breastbone, pinning the little girl's bloodstained shirt to her skin. She touched the girl's neck, felt a weak pulse, bent down to listen to her breathing.

Saw the ragged end of the handlebars protruding from the girl's back.

Helplessly, she brushed away some of the grey flies that were crawling on the girl's face. Brown eyes opened, stared at her.

She looked up at the father, said quietly, 'She will have to go to the hospital.'

The man frowned.

Jo felt a hand touch her arm. 'That's the hospital, Jo. Over there.' Catriona's voice: she was pointing at a half-collapsed mud-brick building. The Red Crescent banner could be seen, scorched, torn, half-buried. Smoke rose from the only part of the building still standing, and Jo heard the distant sound of screams.

She opened her mouth to say something about the Geneva convention, then closed it again, realizing that there was no point.

The little girl gave a faint, whistling sigh. Jo looked down at her, saw that her breathing had become rapid, ragged. Her eyes locked on to Jo's, and a tiny hand reached out.

'You shouldn't move,' said Jo, though she doubted the girl understood English. She took the hand, squeezed it. The girl gave another faint sigh, and her breathing stopped. Slowly, the brown eyes glazed over.

Jo looked up at the father.

'I'm sorry.'

He touched her arm, gently, then turned and walked away, carrying the body of the child. His wife got up and followed, wailing softly. Jo stood there, feeling cool tears slowly run down her face. Flies tickled her cheeks, her nose, her lips, but she did nothing to brush them away.

Eventually she became aware of the sound of voices.

Vincent and Catriona were shouting, both at the same time.

Vincent: 'Promise me you will tell the world that the Kebiriz have tried to destroy these people. I want to see pictures on the front page of every newspaper.'

And Catriona: 'I haven't even got a camera, Vincent. You know I'll do my best but I haven't got a camera.'

Jo turned, saw Catriona holding Vincent's arms, almost shaking him. He was almost screaming now: 'The front page! Promise me!'

'Find a camera, Vincent,' said Catriona levelly. 'Find me a camera.'

Jo walked slowly away from them. She looked around at the burning hospital, at the heaps of bodies, at the ruins of the makeshift streets and gardens.

There must be something I can do, she thought. She looked at the hospital again, saw patients on stretchers being rushed out of the building, hastily set down in the street.

I could help with that, she thought. Perhaps that would help keep somebody alive.

She set off at a run.

The Brigadier's stomach lurched as for the fourth or fifth time the Doctor simply dropped the Superhawk out of the sky to avoid an incoming missile. This time when the dive bottomed out there was an ominous popping sound from somewhere in the aircraft. The plane flipped upside down, and the Brigadier had a dizzy view of a brown landscape flashing above his head – or was that below his head? – of trees –

Trees?

He glanced at the altimeter. They were flying at five hundred feet. Correction: flying upside down at five hundred feet. The air speed indicator showed Mach 2.4.

Ahead of them was a sheer escarpment, white rocks blazing in the morning sun.

'Doctor!' bawled the Brigadier. 'I don't think –'

He was unable to complete the sentence: the air was forced out of his lungs as the plane jerked upwards. There were more ominous pops from the body of the aircraft. He had a brief glimpse of a jagged edge flickering blurrily past the cockpit at a range he didn't care to think about, then the plane slowly rolled back upright.

Behind them the escarpment exploded. Twice. Two plumes of rock and dust, spreading out, but shrinking with incredible rapidity as the plane streaked away.

'Heat-seeking missiles,' said the Doctor's voice over the intercom. 'Clever, but not clever enough. You can always fool them with hot spots. A nice sunny cliff, for example.'

High, barren mountains rose ahead. The Brigadier tried again.

'Doctor, I don't see how we're going to clear —'

'Be quiet, Brigadier. I need to concentrate on this.'

A wall of rock was almost directly in front of them. For the second time in under a minute, the Brigadier made a closer acquaintance of a rock face than he would have cared to whilst flying at twice the speed of sound. There was a flicker of darkness: he could have sworn the Doctor actually flew *through* something — a cave, perhaps — then they were soaring out over a huge yellow-brown plain, with the mountains falling away behind them.

'Have we lost them?' asked the Brigadier.

'Have a look at the radar, man. You're the navigator.'

Sheepishly, the Brigadier examined the radar. A cluster of blurry, stationary reflections were the mountains; there was something to the west, but it wasn't moving; otherwise the scope was clear.

'I think so,' he said eventually. His head and limbs felt curiously wobbly, as if they weren't quite attached to his body properly any more. He'd been through centrifuge training when they'd set up UNIT, but he could swear that the last fifteen minutes had been worse.

'That's interesting,' said the Doctor suddenly. The plane swerved to the right, knocking the Brigadier's helmet against the padded side of the cockpit.

'What is?' The Brigadier could see nothing ahead but a wall of mountains.

'That black spire there – it seems to be made of something other than the local rock.'

The Brigadier craned his neck, was forced painfully against his flight harness as the plane suddenly started to decelerate. But he could see that there was indeed something dark amongst the rocks. 'I wonder if that's what was on Yates's satellite photos?' he said.

'What satellite photos?' asked the Doctor sharply.

'The ones that showed the anomaly. A black blob that had suddenly appeared in the mountains. That's what Anton Deveraux was looking into when he died.'

'Brigadier, you told me that Deveraux died of some mysterious disease and that Yates and his team had gone to Kebiria to investigate. You didn't mention anything about a construct of this sort.'

'I didn't know very much about it,' admitted the Brigadier. 'I didn't see the photographs. I'm a busy man, you know.'

'Good grief, man! Look at the thing! And you didn't think it was important?'

They were close enough now to see detail: a rough tower, several hundred metres high, tapering towards the end, and around it what looked like extensive excavations. As they passed overhead, the Brigadier thought he saw a helicopter on the ground.

'It's some kind of military base,' he said. 'Probably Kebirian government.'

'Maybe, Brigadier. But there are other possibilities. Let's take another look, shall we? I'll slow her down a bit more.'

There was a short silence. The mountains were getting dangerously close.

The Doctor pulled the plane up sharply, began to turn. There was a beeping noise, and a red light began to flash on the panel in front of them. The Brigadier looked at the readings, said, 'Doctor, we're almost out of fuel.'

'But that's impossible. Flight Lieutenant Butler told me that the wing tanks held enough fuel to get us all the way to Kebiria and back again if we had to.'

The beeping became a continuous angry note. With a sinking feeling, the Brigadier realized what the popping noises had been.

'The fuel lines to the wing tanks have broken on both sides, Doctor. All that manoeuvring must have been too much for the joints. We're spilling fuel like a leaky teapot.'

'We wouldn't have had this kind of trouble in a Martian Exploder,' said the Doctor irritably. The engine note changed as he throttled back. 'Hold on tight, Brigadier, this could be a rough landing.'

After that things happened very fast. A silver speck appeared in front of them, rushing along the curve of a mountain valley. It came closer with astonishing speed, until the Brigadier could recognize the tiny, clear shape of a Kebirian Air Force MiG. He saw a bloom of flame under each wing, and for an instant he thought it was on fire.

Then he saw the two missiles accelerating towards him.

His stomach lurched as the Superhawk dropped. The aircraft shuddered, then the roar of the engines faltered and died.

'Sorry, old chap,' said the Doctor. 'I think we're going to crash.'

Ten

Jo tightened the tourniquet around the young man's arm, then lifted the makeshift dressing from the wound. Some blood still leaked from it, but it didn't look too bad.

As long as it doesn't get infected, she thought.

The hospital's supply of antibiotics had been destroyed in the raid, and it was unlikely that more would arrive in time to save the young man. She tied a fresh dressing around the wound, then used some of the same clean, disinfectant-smelling cloth to wipe her hands, as the nurse had shown her.

The next patient was beyond help with the little they had left: a shrapnel wound in his stomach was still bleeding steadily. With every breath he clenched his fists and gave a little moan of pain.

Feeling sick, Jo dispensed another couple of aspirin, held his cold, sweaty hand for a moment. She tried not to think how many people she had seen die this afternoon.

There was a metallic click behind her, followed by a buzzing noise. Jo jumped, almost dropped the man's hand. Then she turned, saw Catriona. She managed a slight smile.

'Hello.'

The reporter was clutching a large camera and flash gun. She winked. 'I promised Vincent headlines, and headlines he's going to get.'

'Where did you get the camera?'

'One of the aid workers. She's got a broken arm, anyway, so she won't be using it for a while.'

The reporter seemed remarkably cheerful, considering what she must have been taking pictures of, Jo thought; but then she thought again, realized that Catriona had been doing her job. Getting the story out. That was bound to make her feel better. Jo wished she had a job that could be of some help in this situation. 'The Doctor's assistant' was all very well, when the Doctor was around. It wasn't a lot of use the rest of the time. Holding the hands of the dying and giving them aspirin felt so *useless*. Yet she knew it was all that she could do.

She wondered if she should have trained as a nurse instead of a spy. Not that it would have made much difference, in the present situation.

She realized that the man's hand was clutching hers tightly. She turned, stared as his breathing faltered and stopped, and his eyes glazed over.

'No,' she whimpered, tears streaming down her face. 'No, no, *no, no*!'

'I think you need a break.'

Jo felt Catriona's arm go around her shoulders. Every muscle shaking, she allowed herself to be hugged.

'Come on, we can go to Vincent's tent.'

They picked their way through the ruins with care: there were still unburied bodies around, and dark pits of shadow that might have hidden anything. As they approached Vincent's tent, they heard the sound of raised voices. Jo couldn't make out what was being said — she was fairly sure it was in Arabic — but the voices were angry.

She looked at Catriona. 'Perhaps we'd better not go in.'

The reporter nodded. 'He's having a discussion with the local Giltean commanders, I think. They don't like him very much.'

The voices were raised even further. Catriona took a step forward, then seemed to think better of it.

'Isn't Vincent a Giltean, then?' asked Jo, lowering her voice to a whisper.

'No. He's just a sort of — well, general-purpose international freedom fighter, really. He was Egyptian to start with, but he calls himself a Pan-Arabist. These people are supposed to be Pan-Arabists too — the Giltean Arab Front — but they're just Gilteans really. The GAF put up with Vincent because his name gets them money and weapons from the Libyans; they'd ditch him if they won, and probably the Libyans too. There's another group, the FLNG, who won't have anything to do with him at all, and just want autonomy for Giltea.'

Jo blinked. 'It all sounds a bit complicated.'

'Arab politics are complicated, Jo. There are hardly two people who want the same thing.' She paused, gestured at the tent where there was a renewed outbreak of shouting. 'They're probably blaming him for the raid.'

'And is it his fault?'

Catriona stared at the ground.

'I don't know,' she said at last. 'They might have been after him, they might have been after me; they might have been after you, for that matter. Or they might just have been angry and bloody-minded, or doing a bit of target practice. Who knows?' Her voice was shaking slightly.

Jo put a hand on her arm. 'It was their fault,' she said simply. 'The Kebirian government. They decided to do it. The reasons don't matter, do they?' Like Vincent and the Cairo bombing, she thought; but she didn't say it.

Ahead of them, a figure emerged from the tent. Jo recognized Vincent. She noted with relief that he didn't appear to be under arrest, in fact was carrying a gun.

He walked up to Catriona. 'They want to stage a reprisal raid on Kebir City! Tomorrow! In daylight!'

'They're mad,' said Catriona flatly.

'I know, but how do I stop them? They say I am not a Giltean, I do not understand. Of course I understand! I am as angry as they are — but this will not work!'

'What are they planning to do?'

Vincent glanced at Jo, seemed to see her properly for

100

the first time. He turned to her. 'I can't very well tell the United Nations that, eh? Sorry, Miss Grant.'

'I won't tell anyone!' protested Jo, but Catriona shook her head, led Vincent away.

Jo stared after them, baffled. Why was Vincent willing to discuss with a reporter what he wouldn't talk about in front of a member of UNIT?

Then she saw the way they were talking to each other, quietly, in the shadows near the tent, and realized that Vincent was appealing to Catriona as a friend – and was trusting the reporter in her to keep silence.

Jo looked away, let her eyes run along the intact part of the settlement, the mud-brick houses and the wall around them stained ochre by the setting sun. Suddenly she saw a familiar shape, black against the amber glare of the sunset, moving towards the settlement. Another behind it. And another.

She ran towards Vincent and Catriona, shouting. 'Helicopters!'

Vincent's head snapped round. He stared at the sky for a moment, then started swearing in a mixture of Arabic and French. He set off at a run for the boundary wall. 'I will kill them myself!'

Catriona started after him, shouted, 'Vincent! No! You'll get yourself killed!'

Jo hesitated, then followed them. The helicopters were already rushing towards the perimeter wall. Part of her mind told her that they would start firing at any moment, that she should take cover –

Then one of the 'helicopters' turned towards her, and she saw the scorpion-like sting on the end of the tail, the legs bunched under the body, the huge eyes staring at her.

'Oh-oh,' she muttered. She looked ahead, saw Catriona standing by the sandbags that ringed the one remaining anti-aircraft emplacement, staring upwards. Vincent had disappeared. Jo supposed he was inside, behind the guns.

'They're not helicopters!' she began shouting.

Catriona looked up, opened her mouth to say something, was drowned out by an explosion of gunfire from behind her.

Jo ran up, caught hold of the reporter, shouted in her ear. 'We've got to get him out of there! They're not helicopters! They're aliens of some sort – they could do anything!'

'What?' bawled Catriona. But the expression on the reporter's face told Jo that she hadn't heard enough to understand over the thunder of the guns.

'ALIENS!' screamed Jo. 'FROM ANOTHER PLANET!' But Catriona only stared at her.

Suddenly the guns stopped. There was a moment's silence, then something bellowed, an enormous, musical sound, like a discordant tuba. Jo saw something huge and dark fall across the road in front of them, the tail writhing like a wounded cobra. There was another tuba-like groan, an immense thud, the clatter of falling earth.

Silence. Jo's ears rang, but that false sound slowly faded and was replaced by the distant wails of women and a strange metallic ticking. Jo saw a second alien wavering across the roofs, its tail thrashing. As she watched, its body crumpled and it fell to the ground with a distant thud.

Then the guns started again. The ground trembled beneath Jo's feet.

Catriona was staring at the thing in front of them, shouting something. It sounded like 'perfume', but that didn't make any sense. Jo followed her gaze, hoping for a clue from the alien. On the ground, it didn't look much like a helicopter, more like a gigantic insect. The bulbous body was coloured an iridescent blue-black, as were the three pairs of legs and long, scissor-bladed arms. The tail was like a scorpion's: jointed, and tipped with a huge, deadly-looking sting. The eyes were closed, covered by shutters like Venetian blinds. Two 'rotors' were still intact: glimmering, almost transparent vanes about ten metres long. Jo noticed that they were much wider at the ends than at the roots, like an insect's wings. The creature leaked a honey-coloured fluid from numerous holes in its carapace and from a long gash along its side.

Suddenly, the sound of the guns stopped.

'Well, Miss Grant,' said Catriona. 'You're our resident expert on Things From Outer Space. What is it?'

She was trying to sound flippant, but her voice was hoarse and shaky. Jo glanced at her, realized that this time she was supposed to be the knowledgeable one. She swallowed, wished that the Doctor was with her. He would probably know what planet it came from, what species it was, and what you had to spray on it to make it go away. All she could think of was, 'I don't think it's entirely organic. At least, I've never seen anything organic that had rotor blades.' She swallowed, aware that she wasn't making much sense. 'It's certainly extraterrestrial in origin, though,' she concluded. 'No one on Earth could have made it or grown it.'

'What are you talking about?' Vincent's voice. Jo turned, saw him crouching on top of the sandbags. He was staring at the alien, his mouth open. Evidently he had been too concerned with destroying it to notice what it was until now. Jo wondered what the Doctor would have had to say about that.

'It's not from Earth,' said Catriona.

'What do you mean, not from Earth?' asked Vincent, still staring at it. 'You mean it came from Mars?'

'Probably much further than that,' said Jo.

Vincent started to laugh, was stopped by a sharp glance from Catriona. 'Jo knows what she's talking about.'

He stared at her for a moment, then looked up and scanned the sky, as if he were expecting to see a fleet of invading spaceships. Jo stifled a giggle; but Vincent noticed. He jumped down from the sandbags, grabbed her arms, started shaking her.

'What have my people done to deserve this, eh? First the Kebirians bomb us and do not care what the world thinks and now we are invaded from Mars! What is happening to us? Is this the luck that you have brought us, eh?'

'Vincent!' Catriona had a hand on his arm. 'Vincent! Stop it, it's not Jo's fault.'

Vincent stopped shaking Jo, but continued to stare, his green eyes bright, a fleck of foam at the corner of his mouth.

There was a splintering sound from the body of the alien. Vincent instantly let her go, swung his gun to cover the body. Jo heard the click of the safety catch. The splintering sounds continued and cracks began to appear in the blue-black carapace. Golden fluid bubbled out, and a sweet, pungent scent filled the air.

Catriona was staring at it, a frown on her face. 'It *is* the same smell,' she said. 'Roses and cloves.' She gripped Jo's arm. 'We need to burn the body. Now.'

'Burn it?' asked Vincent. 'Is it poisonous?' He still seemed bewildered.

Jo, alerted by a faint whickering sound, turned and looked at the sky behind them. Several dozen of the helicopter-like objects moved into view over the wall, long ropes trailing beneath them. 'More of them,' she said simply.

'Quickly!' yelled Vincent. 'Inside the gun turret!'

He pushed Jo up to the entrance; she almost fell inside. She collided with someone in the darkness, said, 'Sorry.'

Outside, there was a stutter of machine-gun fire. Catriona's voice screamed, 'Vincent!' Jo rushed to the doorway, saw Vincent entangled in rope-like tentacles, dangling several feet above her head. There was a gun in his hand. As Jo stared, he dropped it towards her. She caught it awkwardly, almost dropped it herself.

'Fire it!' he shouted. He was level with the top of the wall now. 'Quickly!'

Jo took aim at the back of the gaping mouth in the creature's belly, where most of the tentacles seemed to be anchored. Fired.

The gun almost jumped out of her hands. She saw Vincent drop past her, slowly, as if in a dream. Heard his body thump on to the sandbags. Then the tentacles lashed, caught on to her arms. The gun was snatched from her hands, flicked away. Jo felt her body being hauled upwards. Desperately, she tried to cling to the wooden lintel of the doorway, but her grip was broken by the overwhelming force of the tentacles. She saw Vincent sitting up, ten feet below her, looking half-stunned. Catriona climbed over him, almost dragged him to the door, flung him inside, then reached out for Jo.

'No!' yelled Jo. 'Get inside or it'll get you too!'

Catriona still reached upwards but Jo's body was jerked around so that she was looking up into the huge, tooth-filled maw of the alien. She had a brief glimpse across the settlement, saw two of the aliens with their webs of tentacles hovering over the hospital, saw patients, bodies, nurses, all entangled in the tentacles, all rising. Then a wall of teeth cut off her view.

– I did try to save those people please God I did try –

And then the teeth closed around her.

The night was silent: too silent for the Brigadier's liking. He looked at the sky, watched the slow movement of a satellite against the brilliant background of stars. Perhaps it was the one that had taken Mike Yates's photographs. Whatever. It was reassuring, somehow, that there was something man-made up there, even if there wasn't anything alive at ground level.

'Come along, Brigadier. We haven't got time for stargazing.'

The Doctor was striding ahead again, not waiting for a reply. The Brigadier set off after him, rubbing at his back, which he'd twisted slightly when his parachute landed.

The Doctor was carrying a small electronic device with a flickering purple light. He'd described it as an anti-electron something field something; when asked to clarify he'd started talking about probability waves, meson-electron whatchimacallits and an experiment with a dead cat; when the Brigadier had finally interrupted him and asked what the device actually *did*, in practical terms, the Doctor had said that it located living organisms.

'So we should be able to find an oasis?' he'd asked.

'We'll find,' the Doctor had replied, 'the nearest large concentration of living organisms.'

The Brigadier hadn't liked the sound of it, and he still didn't. The Doctor was being pedantic again and in the Brigadier's experience that always meant trouble. In this case, he suspected it meant that they were going to the black tower they'd seen before the plane crashed; a suspicion that was reinforced by the fact that they were now climbing a steep, rocky trail. True, it was too dark to see what lay ahead, but there was definitely something obscuring the stars in that part of the sky.

Well, he thought, I suppose it's what Anton Deveraux was sent to investigate in the first place. Then he remembered what had happened to Anton Deveraux, and his pulse quickened uncomfortably.

Suddenly he heard a sound above the regular crunching of their boots on the pebbly rock. A mechanical sound, a whickering sort of noise, like –

The Doctor stopped, held up his hand. The Brigadier heard it clearly then: helicopter rotors. He saw a chain of red lights, moving slowly out over the desert to the west.

'Helicopters!' he said aloud, immensely relieved. 'Well, Doctor, it looks like we're going to get a lift. The Kebirian government must have come to its senses at last.'

The Doctor shook his head, stepped quickly sideways, crouched down so that he disappeared from sight.

'I suggest you take cover, Brigadier.'

'Why? You don't think they're unfriendly?' He couldn't quite believe that the Kebirians would send a fleet of helicopters to find and kill UN personnel. The worst that could happen was that they'd be arrested and spend a few hours in a prison cell. It would all be sorted out in the morning. It certainly had to be better than wandering around in the desert, relying on one of the Doctor's erratic electrical devices to find a place that they might not want to find anyway.

'Get down, man!' hissed the Doctor.

The Brigadier stepped off the track, almost fell over a rock. He felt the Doctor's arm grab his, was steered into the shelter of a large boulder.

'Look, Doctor, I really don't think we have anything to be –'

'Listen!'

The Brigadier listened. The whickering noise was a little closer and louder: and, yes, there was something odd about it.

'No engines,' he said after a few moments.

The Doctor nodded, his face illuminated faintly by the glowing dial of the device he was carrying.

'That's because they're not mechanical devices, Brigadier. They're organic.' He gestured at the device: a bright purple arrow pointed in the direction from which the 'helicopters' were coming. He fiddled with something on the side of the box, and the arrow shifted slightly. 'Hmm. That's strange.'

'What's strange, Doctor?'

But the Doctor didn't reply, simply adjusted the box further. The arrow swung round and pointed at the Brigadier.

'They don't seem to be particularly intelligent. In fact they're considerably less intelligent than you are, which is somewhat surprising in the circumstances.'

The Brigadier blinked. 'Really, Doctor! I'm not as stupid as all that, you know.'

Again the Doctor didn't reply. He just pushed a switch on the side of the box and handed it to the Brigadier.

'Right, old chap. Just follow the arrow and you should be there by morning.'

The Brigadier looked at the box, frowned. 'Should be where, exactly?'

'That oasis you were talking about.' The Doctor

grinned, clapped him on the shoulder. 'It's only a couple of miles from here. Or at least, there are people there, so there ought to be some water.' He stood up, so that all but his boots disappeared from view.

The Brigadier stared up at him. 'And where are you going?'

'Oh, just going to have a look around, old chap.' He stepped away into the darkness. The sound of the 'helicopters' was quite loud now.

The Brigadier stood up too. 'Look, Doctor, I ought to come with you. As the officer responsible for this mission –'

'– you should be back in Kebir City as soon as possible, sorting out all those political complications you were so good as to explain to me earlier today. And no doubt getting Captain Yates and his men out of prison, too. Now get down out of sight before they realize that there are two of us.'

Before the Brigadier could reply, the Doctor sprinted away, his boots crunching on the loose rock. Beyond him, a line of red lights moved across the sky, dim shapes behind them. The Brigadier saw the eyes above the lights, and crouched down.

Within less than a minute the lights were near enough to cast a faint glow over the track. To his amazement, the Brigadier saw the Doctor jumping up and down on the track, waving his flight jacket at the approaching whatever-they-were as if he were a matador prancing in front of a bull. But the aliens took no notice, merely soared overhead and onward towards the dark shadow ahead of them.

In the last of the light, the Brigadier saw that the Doctor had set off after them at a run.

The tower was silent by the time the Doctor approached it, the flyers long since settled.

No doubt, thought the Doctor, they had disgorged their burdens already. All the more reason to hurry.

He approached the wall at a brisk trot. When there was a clattering noise to his left, he didn't worry about it too much: he had expected sentries. He didn't even flinch when a muscular arm wrapped itself around his neck and tried to throttle him. He simply broke the hold with a basic Venusian Aikido manoeuvre, then sprinted for the wall.

He almost made it. Just as he jumped up, his hands ready to grasp holds on the wall, a huge pair of mandibles closed heavily around his chest.

They squeezed, and the Doctor felt his ribs cracking.

'Now hold on old chap —' he managed to wheeze. He had expected them to try to communicate, not simply kill him.

But as the mandibles squeezed still harder, he began to realize that he might have made a serious miscalculation.

Book Two

Copy Dancing

Eleven

The dawn was clear and cold. Filaments of pink cloud streaked a dark blue sky, congregating in the north where they merged with a continuous sheet of white. To the west, the high peaks of the Hatar Massif were already bloodstained by the sun; to the south, the jumbled rocks fell away to the great stone plain of Al-Giltaz, which was still in darkness. Tahir Al-Naemi stared out over the plain, breathed deeply of the cool, dry air. Behind him, metallic ticks sounded from the engine of his jeep as it cooled. Faintly, beyond that, a clattering of pots and a murmuring of voices told him that everything in the encampment was well.

He looked up at the sky, wondering if he would see a falcon. When he had been a boy, he had dreamed of hunting with falcons. Every morning, just after dawn, he had sneaked out of his father's house and gone down to the market, where the birds waited to be sold. Tahir had admired their beautiful plumage, the fierce intelligence in their yellow or amber eyes, the clean fast death in their beaks and claws. He had envied the handlers, their heavy gloves, their weatherbeaten faces, their love of the birds.

Then had come the Revolution, and Tahir had learned that death is not fast and sharp and clean, but slow, messy, ugly. Gangrene in the wounds, flies in a pool of blood and shit. The falcons were replaced by vultures, and by bored French soldiers, leaning on their guns, waiting. When the French left, the Kebiriz came. For a time Tahir and his family had been favoured: whilst his father was the *Sakir* Mohammad in law as well as in name, whilst he

113

spoke in the parliament, at least they were not harassed in the streets.

But their friends died, or were murdered. Then the parliament was dissolved and Tahir's family were forced to leave Giltat, in one of the 'desert resettlement schemes' of which Khalil Benari was so proud. Within a year, his mother died of typhoid and his brother from a soldier's bullet. Tahir decided to fight back and, reluctantly, after much prayer, his father decided to help him.

So the killing began. And it was never clean, it was never perfect, it never came with the swiftness of the falcon. Tahir woke sometimes from dreams where he was swimming in blood, swimming without hope of reaching the shore. It was then that he knew he was lost, that the war could bring no victory that would give him back the better life, the life he had lived when he was a boy.

But then, on some mornings, mornings like this when the wind had been from the north and the sky was clear of dust, when the air was sharp and clean and smelled almost as it had when he was young, Tahir imagined he could hear the twitter of the birds again, imagined he could see them stretch their wings and fly far above the desert. He knew then that his dreams had not been lost, because they were still living in the hearts of the children: the scruffy, dirty children of Giltat and Burrous Asi were carrying his dreams. It was then that he swore he would fight on, that he would kill as many people as necessary, that he would drown the desert in blood if he had to – so that the dreams could come true, one day, for his people. So that they would not be wasted.

The sound of an engine close by startled him out of his reverie. Tahir swore, angry both at being disturbed and at having been so wrapped up in his thoughts that he had not noticed the sound earlier. If it had been an enemy, he could have been shot dead by now. He looked up the hillside, saw the sun glinting off the windscreen of a jeep. As the vehicle drew closer, he recognized his father's grey-bearded face in the passenger seat. There was a pair of binoculars in his hand.

He was shouting even before the jeep had stopped. 'Tahir! Tahir! We must leave at once!'

Tahir frowned. 'Leave?' he said, when the jeep had pulled up. Unconsciously, his hand moved to the safety catch of the Kalashnikov slung over his shoulder. He glanced at his father's driver, a tall, taciturn man named Yamin; but the man merely grinned at Tahir and shrugged. He hadn't stopped the engine.

His father reached over the door and gripped Tahir by the arm. '*Al Harwaz*. The dancers in the desert.'

Tahir felt his shoulders relax. He had imagined his father being pursued by the entire Kebirian Army.

'Oh, that old fairy tale,' he said, letting his annoyance at the interruption come to the surface now that it was clear there was no danger. He looked into the old man's worn, tired face, made an effort not to be too harsh.'You know, that reporter was quite angry with you for what you did. And I don't really blame her. It would have been better to at least let her take a sample from the body – what if the government are using chemicals against us? It is illegal – against the Geneva Convention. She might have been able to help.'

His father let him finish speaking, then said, 'Get in.'

Tahir blinked. It had been a long time since his father had spoken to him like this. He opened his mouth to object, but the old man got there first.

'There is something that you need to see.'

Tahir looked at Yamin, who shrugged again. He said, 'We should not leave my car unattended. I will follow you.'

The trail was long and narrow, barely navigable. Tahir was kept busy steering, avoiding rocks big enough to break an axle and treacherous stretches of scree which would have sent his jeep sliding to the bottom of the valley. It occurred to him that they could be ambushed very easily: it only needed a couple of snipers hidden in the jumble of boulders at the base of the cliffs, for instance.

His father's jeep stopped abruptly, and Tahir almost ran into the back of it. He got out, ran forward to catch up with his father who was already climbing a steep, rocky slope.

'Stay with the cars,' he said to Yamin, who nodded.

He started up the slope after his father. The sun was already hot on the back of his neck as he climbed; the top of the ridge above him shimmered slightly. He paused to draw his flask from his jacket and took a swig of the cold, metallic-tasting water.

His father also stopped to rest; with a few quick strides, Tahir caught up with him.

'What is there to see?' he asked, but the old man said nothing, only pointed out across the mountains, a surreal geometry of sunlit rock and grey-black shadow.

And something else.

A mound.

It was about half a mile away, standing at the base of one of the mountains, above a plain covered in jumbled rocks. It was about three hundred metres high, crudely shaped, tapering to a point, more like a stalagmite than anything else. It appeared to be made of dried mud, but Tahir knew that was impossible.

He stared, and stared, and stared. Words like 'rocket base' and 'watchtower' ran through his head, but they refused to make any sense of what he was seeing. The only thing the mound reminded him of was a termite nest, and that didn't make any sense at all.

His father handed him the binoculars. 'Look to the left of the tower, at the bottom,' he said.

Tahir looked, saw what he should have seen with his unaided eyes: a canvas shroud, hiding the unmistakable shapes of helicopters. And by the edge of the shroud, two tiny figures in Kebirian Army uniforms.

Tahir clenched a fist. So this was where Benari's people were hiding!

'The thing that puzzles me,' he said aloud, 'is why they have made it so obvious. Whatever that tower is hiding, it still attracts attention. Covering it in mud is no use.'

But the old man only gripped his arm. 'Watch the soldiers, Tahir. Watch them closely.'

Tahir watched. After a moment he realized that the soldiers were not standing still. Their bodies vibrated from time to time, their arms or legs or even their heads moving so fast that the motion was a blur.

'No human being could do that,' said Tahir. 'What are they?'

'They're dancing the code,' murmured his father. 'It is as that poor man said.'

Tahir took the binoculars from his eyes, looked at the old man. 'Whatever they're doing, there has to be an explanation. A rational explanation, father – not a fairy tale. Either they have been drugged, or they have built robots, or –'

He was interrupted by a shout from below: Yamin. He looked down, saw a uniformed figure approaching the jeep. As Tahir watched, Yamin shouted again. The figure stopped where he was and raised his hands. Tahir hurried down the ridge, his boots slipping on the loose rock. As he neared the bottom he heard the stranger talking:

'. . . from the United Nations. I request your hospitality until such time as I can contact my superiors.'

The United Nations, thought Tahir as he reached the jeeps. Maybe. Maybe not. He examined the stranger. His uniform wasn't Kebirian; it looked English, or Italian, perhaps. He carried a heavy leather flight jacket over his arm, and looked thirsty and dusty.

Tahir raised his own gun, spoke briskly to the stranger. 'Show us your identification,' he said, 'if you are from the UN.' He allowed a little sarcasm to creep into his voice.

The officer reached slowly into a pocket of his uniform, produced a small plastic card. He threw it towards Tahir: it landed on the bonnet of the jeep. Tahir picked it up, scanned it, checked the photograph against the face in front of him.

'Brigadier Lethbridge-Stewart,' he said slowly, but politely. The card looked genuine enough, and it would not do to offend the UN. 'You understand we will have to be careful –'

'No!' His father's voice, shouting from behind them. The old man had only just reached the bottom of the ridge. Tahir could hear the breath rasping in his lungs. 'No, Tahir! He is of the Dancers!'

Tahir turned, 'Father, I don't think –'

'Enough!' said the *Sakir*. 'There is only one way of dealing with this!'

And the old man drew his gun, the ancient British service revolver that he carried with him everywhere. As Tahir watched in consternation, he aimed it at the stranger and fired.

Catriona woke suddenly, as if someone had switched a light on. She looked around her, she saw the cramped concrete walls of the gun turret, the breech of the anti-aircraft weapon through the middle, the Arab gunner curled against the far wall, asleep.

Where am I this time? she wondered.

Then she remembered. Vincent's camp. The raid. The aliens. And Jo.

Poor little Jo. She had been such a *good* person.

Vincent was awake, crouched in the doorway. He looked back over his shoulder at her. 'They didn't come back,' he said simply.

Catriona nodded, crawled to the entrance, looked over Vincent's shoulder.

The sun was about an hour above the horizon, the sky blue. Everything in the settlement was sharp and still: the tumbled and scorched ruins of the houses, the battered jeeps parked anyhow over the dusty streets.

Nothing moved.

'There must be somebody else out there,' said Catriona.

'They're probably hiding, like us,' observed Vincent. He cupped his hands and shouted a greeting in Arabic.

A faint echo danced on the rocks for a moment, then

118

faded. Vincent slipped down from the doorway, set off along the street. His footsteps seemed oddly loud. He passed the remains of the creature he had shot down the previous night: it was formless now, a jumble of broken chitin embedded in a brown, tarry substance. He walked further up the street, called out again.

No response.

With an effort, Catriona forced her cramped muscles to propel her through the doorway, scrambled over the sandbags to the ground. After a moment she became aware of the sound of a woman shouting. She saw Vincent run forward, saw a figure in a chador emerge from behind one of the houses.

Good, thought Catriona absurdly. Now there'll be someone to cook my breakfast.

She set off down the road in the opposite direction to that which Vincent had taken. 'Hello,' she called. Then she shouted it, shouted words of greeting in every other language she could think of. Eventually a man and a small boy emerged from one of the houses. They were apparently uninjured but the boy had a strange, fixed stare on his face. Catriona tried to speak to the father, but he only shook his head.

'Kebiriz.' He spat at Catriona's feet. 'You help Kebiriz.' His English was thickly accented, barely comprehensible.

'No I don't,' said Catriona.

'You all help Kebiriz!' The man was shouting now. 'You are American whore!'

Catriona drew a breath to yell back at the man, then looked at the fixed, shell-shocked eyes of the child and thought better of it. The events of the night had been enough to unbalance anyone's judgement.

'I'm English and I'm a journalist,' she said quietly. 'I'm here to help you.'

But the man only swore in Arabic, the intent of his words clear enough even though Catriona didn't recognize all of them. Then he walked down the street, carrying his son in his arms.

Catriona started back along the street towards the hospital.

By the time she got there, a small crowd had gathered. Vincent was standing on the bonnet of a wrecked jeep. He appeared to be counting the survivors. He glanced down at her, nodded, carried on counting. Catriona sat down on the ground against the side of the jeep, suddenly very aware that she'd had two nights with little sleep. She closed her eyes, felt the growing heat of the sun on her face. Blurred thoughts began to chase themselves around her head. She saw Jo's face shouting something about the Doctor, bring the Doctor, but it was too late, the guard was dying, her eyes bulging with shock, the blood spreading on her chest. Slowly the woman fell to the ground, hit with the sound of a prison door slamming and a slight, terrifying moan.

— I took her shoes Jesus I took her shoes and she was dead I killed her and I stood over her unlacing her shoes and stole them —

The gun fired, jarring against her hand again and again and again.

Suddenly she was awake, dust stinging her face, the hard metal of the jeep digging into her back. She realized that Vincent was speaking.

'We cannot stay here,' he was saying. 'The Americans are certain to attack us again.'

The Americans? thought Catriona, struggling to clear her head. What was he talking about?

'Death to the Americans!' shouted someone, perhaps the man Catriona had spoken to earlier.

'Vincent?' asked Catriona, pushing herself upright; but he was ploughing on.

'I will send a message to our friends in Libya, asking for their help. They will send forces to avenge the crimes committed here. This wanton destruction of the free Arab people of Giltea will not go unavenged!'

A cluster of young men standing at the front of the small group jumped up, fists clenched. One fired a gun into the air. At the back of the crowd, Catriona noticed a woman wailing, beating the ground with her fists.

'Vincent!' called Catriona as he turned away from the crowd and walked up to her.

'I need a radio transmitter,' he said. 'There might be one in the garages.'

He gestured towards some tin shacks on the far side of the settlement and began striding towards them. Catriona stood up, hurried to catch him.

'You don't really believe the Americans were behind those – those things, do you?'

Vincent shrugged. 'Do you really believe they came from Mars?'

'Do you think they came from Earth?'

Vincent shrugged again. 'Does it matter?'

'Of course it matters! Jo –' She broke off, remembering again what had happened to Jo. She shook her head slowly, then went on in a quieter tone. 'Jo seemed to know what she was talking about. And she didn't say they were from Mars.'

'Mars, Jupiter, Saturn, Uranus, Neptune, Pluto,' said Vincent, then flashed her a grin. 'You see, I do know about the Solar System, I am not stupid. But does it matter where they come from? It is all the same. Only the Americans or the Russians could get them, and only the Americans would give them to Khalil Benari to use against us.'

'Don't be ridiculous! You know I agree with a lot of what you say about the Americans – but I don't believe they'd make an alliance with beings from another planet and press them into service as substitutes for the Marines!'

'Are you sure of that?'

Vincent was walking ahead of her now, climbing a slight incline covered with scattered rubble. Catriona saw a bloodstained fragment of clothing on the ground, shuddered.

'Benari lost a thousand men,' she pointed out.

'Lost?' said Vincent, his tone making it clear that the news was no surprise. 'Or temporarily mislaid? I would imagine these things need quite a bit of ground support, wouldn't you?'

Catriona remembered Mohammad Al-Naemi's words: '*They could imitate anything made by men . . . swords, and spears, and Greek fire . . .*'

She shook her head.

'You're wrong, Vincent. They've been here for hundreds of years.'

'What makes you think that?'

She told him about the *Sakir*'s story: the merchant Ibrahim, the *Al Harwaz*, Dancing the Code, the destruction of Giltat. Vincent snorted with disbelief.

'I didn't believe it at first,' said Catriona. 'I thought it was just a fairy tale. But it's beginning to seem like the simplest explanation. If they're aliens then they could easily have been here for five hundred years.'

Vincent snorted again. 'Those Al-Naemis are in the pay of the French and the Americans. You know that. They'd invent any story to make themselves seem more Western and "democratic". They're probably in it up to their necks.'

Catriona opened her mouth to object, then realized that she'd thought more or less the same thing less than forty-eight hours ago.

'And besides,' Vincent went on, 'even if the creatures have been here for so long, it doesn't mean that Benari or the Americans or the FLNG have not found them and decided to use them against us.'

Catriona took a deep breath. She was beginning to get exasperated by her friend's invincible paranoia. If you listened to him long enough, you'd think everyone in the world was against the Arabs, even other Arabs.

'Vincent,' she said at last. 'Even if it is the Americans, don't you think you ought to move your people from here? I mean, those things might come back; and the Libyans aren't going to help you, not straight away.'

Vincent didn't reply. They had reached the garages now. Though it was still only a couple of hours after sunrise, heat radiated from the metal surfaces as if from an oven. None of the garages had proper doors: some had sheets of metal propped up against the opening, others gaped wide open to the sun and the dust. Vincent pushed aside one of these makeshift barriers, looked inside and scowled.

'No radio,' he said. 'I thought this one had a radio.' He moved to the next garage.

Catriona tried again. 'I think it would be better if you evacuated everyone to Algiers. It's only two hundred miles – less than a day's drive. We could take some samples of the aliens' bodies; I could get them analysed.'

'And if the Algerians decided to hand us all over to the Americans?'

'Don't be ridiculous! You know as well as I do that the Algerians would never –'

'They may not have much choice. Besides, these are my people – I will decide what they need to do!'

Catriona felt her face redden with anger. 'They aren't "yours" at all! You don't own them! Let them decide what they want for themselves!'

'They are Arabs!' he shouted. 'They are of me and I am of them. You are from the country of the enemy – you know nothing about it.'

Suddenly Catriona had had enough. Enough of being called the enemy. Enough of being shouted at. Enough of Vincent.

'You've always got to be the bloody boss, haven't you?' she yelled. 'That whole Cairo business would never have happened if you hadn't –'

Vincent kicked viciously at one of the sheds: the metal rang.

'*Shut up!*'

He kicked the door again, began to swear incoherently in Arabic.

But Catriona knew better than to be intimidated by

Vincent's temper. She waited, breathing deeply, conscious of the blood pulsing in her temples. When he had finished, she said quietly, 'Vincent, we're not safe here. You know that.'

Vincent stared at her for a moment, breathing hard. His face was dark with anger and covered in sweat.

Catriona stared back, meeting his eyes.

'Oh, go to Algeria if you want to,' he said at last. 'And you are right – I will take my people to one of the oases.' He paused, looked away. 'I can't tell you which one; you know why.'

In case I get caught and interrogated, thought Catriona. Fair enough.

'I'll need a jeep and a couple of drums of petrol,' she said after a while. 'And some water.'

Vincent nodded. 'Take what you need. We are not short of supplies, at least.' He stalked off, presumably still looking for a radio to contact his Libyan allies.

Catriona turned to the nearest garage and began to inspect the dusty Land Rover parked inside it. She checked the tyres, the oil, the water, the petrol tank. She found the keys and a spare drum of petrol, drove the vehicle down to the hospital and got a barrel of drinking water from Jamil. A woman was cooking cous-cous; Catriona bolted down a little, burning her tongue in her hurry, then left.

It was only when she was on her way, on the road to the Algerian border posts, that she realized that there had been no need for such a hurry; that the reason she had hurried was because she was still angry with Vincent for being so *stupid*; and that she had left him, and left the settlement, without even saying goodbye.

Twelve

Jo's Aunt May was telling her how to make a duplicate key.

'It isn't difficult, Josie,' she said, picking up a metal tray indented with the shapes of hundreds of different keys. 'You just take the moulds, like this, and you pour your mixture in, like this.' The mixture was floury-white and sticky, but as Aunt May poured it in it hardened, turning ginger-brown. Aunt May drew the smiles on the faces of the little men, then put the currants in for their eyes. Jo giggled.

'It's fun,' she said, idiotically. 'It's fun, fun, fun.'

Aunt May smiled at her. But there was something funny about the smile, something fixed about her sky-blue eyes. Jo began to get frightened.

'No,' she said, as her aunt took one of the gingerbread men out of the tray, and turned to the heavy metal door behind her. 'No! No! No!' But it was too late: the key rattled in the lock, the door opened.

Jo screamed as the freezing, tooth-filled blast bowled her over, passed *through* her. Something else was screaming too: something chitinous, gigantic, impossible.

'*You have to get the key, Josie,*' Aunt May shouted. '*You have to get the key.*'

Jo tried to scream again, but her throat was dry and paralysed. She tried to open her eyes —

— and to her surprise they opened.

She could see a rough ceiling of dry earth, dimly illuminated and only a few inches above her face. Cold, dry air blew over her. Just for a moment she thought she might still be dreaming – she could still feel the cold sweat on her skin, could still hear echoes of her aunt's voice – but no, this was too real for that.

Get the key.

She sat up, banged her head against the ceiling. She couldn't see much: just something glowing, with gently waving antennae. Two huge, luminous eyes turned to look at her and a pair of open mandibles advanced through the narrow space.

Get the key.

Jo rolled sideways, collided with another body. A young man in camouflage fatigues. His eyes opened, stared blankly.

'– honey good good honey –' he muttered.

Jo heard a rustling, clacking sound behind her, felt something clutch at her leg. In desperation she rolled over the young man. She found herself at the top of a steep bank. A blast of cold air blew grit into her eyes.

A ventilation shaft, she thought. Well, the air had to come from somewhere. She scrambled down the slope, but as she did so the light grew steadily dimmer. Something greyish-white loomed ahead. Jo slithered to one side to avoid it, ran into a soft, smooth surface.

Slowly, her eyes picked out more detail. Faint greyish columns, perhaps twice as high as she was, and dark, umbrella-like caps above. 'Mushrooms,' she muttered. 'It's a forest of giant mushrooms.'

There was a rustling, clattering sound from the top of the slope, and the light behind her brightened. Moving as quietly as she could, Jo stepped into the forest.

After a moment her eyes adjusted and she realized that it wasn't completely dark. Small, luminous, wriggling things were chewing their way across the caps of the fungi. Looking up, she saw lights moving in the darkness above the caps, and heard a whisper of wings.

Then she heard a heavier tread, coming from somewhere in the shadows. Crouching down, she moved away from it. The ground grew softer under her feet,

126

then, quite suddenly, gave way altogether. Before she could react, she was up to her knees in dark, liquid mud. She tried to step back, fell on her face, felt the mud sucking at her body. With an effort she struggled upright, but she was up to her waist now and still sinking.

'Help,' she called out, shakily. She was pretty sure she didn't want help from the thing with mandibles and luminous eyes, but it was better than dying. 'Help,' she called, louder, as the mud rose around her stomach. '*Help me!*'

Mike Yates had been awake for some time when they came for him. He'd been lying on his back on the stone floor of his cell, his feet touching one wall and his head touching the other, wondering how much longer the Kebirians were going to keep him here. Whether they would let him see the other men. Whether they would let him see daylight. So far, he reckoned he'd been incarcerated for more than twenty-four hours – it was hard to tell for sure, because they'd taken away his watch. He'd been brought food three times, had been given a bucket for slops and a plastic jug of cold water to wash with. He'd tried tapping on the walls of the cell, to see if he could communicate with any other prisoners, but there had been no response. He'd even thought about trying to escape, but dismissed the notion as impossible.

When he heard the footsteps approaching, Mike hastily stood up. The door opened, and a man in the uniform of a Kebirian Army major stepped through. Mike saluted, automatically; the major saluted back, then smiled.

'I am Major Al-Raheb,' he said. 'Good morning.'

'Captain Yates,' said Mike, a little bewildered. Had this man come to interrogate him? Or had the Brigadier managed to get them released at last?

A guard standing behind Al-Raheb stepped forward: Mike's army boots were in his hand.

'Put them on,' said Al-Raheb. He pulled a clothes brush and a comb out of the pocket of his uniform jacket.

'And give your uniform a once over. You are going to meet the Prime Minister.'

Mike hurried to obey, immensely relieved. A meeting with the Prime Minister was hardly likely to amount to an interrogation; more likely a formal ticking-off, hard words to be passed on to his superiors when he was released. Not his problem.

'Will my men be released as well?' he asked, as he straightened his jacket.

Al-Raheb shrugged. 'It depends on the Prime Minister. My orders are only to bring you to him.'

Mike hadn't really expected a different reply. But it seemed promising that Al-Raheb gestured for him to leave the cell first.

They walked along the drab prison corridors until they came to a barred gate that Mike recognized from when he had been brought in. Outside was daylight: morning light. A large, black car was waiting in the street.

Al-Raheb stepped forward, held open the back door for him. Suddenly suspicious, Mike tried to hold back, but the guard pushed him forward. Crouching down, he saw that one of the back seats was already occupied, and that the person occupying it was the Prime Minister himself.

Mike stared in astonishment, wondering if he could be wrong: but the features were unmistakable, though the stern, square face had a few more lines etched into it than were shown in any photograph Mike had seen.

'Get in the car, please,' said Al-Raheb.

Mike got in. 'Monsieur Benari —' he began.

Benari smiled. 'Captain Yates. I'm pleased to meet you.'

The car door slammed shut, and they accelerated away along the narrow road.

Benari didn't speak until they reached the Boulevard Gamal Abdul Nasser, the wide dual carriageway that led past the People's Palace, the Prime Minister's official residence. Then he said, 'I'm sorry for the inconvenience

128

you have suffered. It was all the result of a misunderstanding, I can assure you.'

Mike nodded, wondered if the Prime Minister was telling the truth, or whether he was simply covering up the fact that he had been pressured into a reversal of policy. The expression on the deeply lined face was unreadable.

Well, he thought, never mind: as long as we're going to be released, I'll let someone else worry about whose fault it was.

'You must think our country very ill-run, that such misunderstandings can occur.'

'Oh – no, sir,' said Mike politely. 'I'm sure it happens in all countries. No one's perfect.'

They were passing the white onion-domes of the People's Palace. Mike expected the car to turn in at the gates, but it drove past. Benari must have noticed his puzzled glance, because he said, 'I'm sorry I could not see you in the Palace. But there are –' he hesitated '– alterations in progress. It would not be appropriate.' He paused. 'You will go straight to the airport: I have already arranged for your men to be released and taken there.' He paused again, looked at his watch. 'I must ask you to leave the country by noon at the latest. I have arranged for your plane to be transferred to the civilian airport and provided with fuel for the flight to England.'

Mike nodded again, stared at the tinted glass screen that separated Benari and himself from the driver.

'Naturally we'll leave as soon as we can, sir,' he said cautiously. He hesitated, then added, 'But I should point out that we were asked here to investigate a possible extraterrestrial incident. That incident –'

Benari raised a hand. 'It will be dealt with, Captain Yates. However, it is an internal matter, and we would appreciate your discretion.'

Mike frowned, decided to try one more time. 'With all due respect, Prime Minister, I don't think that a possible alien invasion can be described as an internal matter.'

Benari stared at him coldly.

'It is an internal matter, Mr Yates.' He seemed to have forgotten Mike's title. 'We are dealing with it, believe me.' He paused, smiled. 'Now, we will speak no more of it. Tell me, how did you find the famous Sandhurst College?'

Jo was almost up to her neck in the mud when something flicked across her face.

And someone was whispering: 'Pick it up. Pick up the turban.'

Jo saw a white rope, like a snake, lying across the surface of the mud. It didn't look like a turban, but she caught hold of it anyway.

'Now!' came the voice. 'Jump!'

She felt the cloth pulling at her hands, lifting her clear of the bottom. A wave of dizziness passed over her. She made a feeble effort to push against the relentless suction of the mud, but only floundered again.

A hand brushed against hers.

With a desperate effort Jo pushed forward, felt the warm flesh again, felt the fingers grip. Fighting for breath she hauled on the stranger's arm until she could get both of her hands free, then gripped him around the wrists. She could see him now: white eyes and white teeth, his body lying flat.

He smiled. 'We have got you half free,' he whispered. 'Come on. You can do it.'

It was only when he spoke the last phrase in English that she realized he had up till then been speaking in French.

He wriggled backwards, pulling her up. At first she tried to help, then realized it wasn't necessary and let her tired muscles relax until she was far enough clear of the mud to haul herself across the ground and collapse next to the young man.

When she had got her breath, she said, 'Thanks. I don't think I'd have lasted much longer in there.'

'Maybe, maybe not,' replied the young man, in French. 'But you were better off out of it, no?' Before she could reply, he added, 'And it's better if you whisper. The insects can't hear that, it seems.'

Jo frowned. 'Insects?'

The young man sat up, shrugged, began wrapping his muddy turban back around his head. 'They look like insects on the outside. And they have antennae.'

'True. But their eyes are like ours.'

The young man grinned again. 'We should discuss their natural history later, no? I'm Akram.' He extended a hand.

Jo took the hand, shook it. 'Jo Grant, from UNIT.' With her other hand, she tried to brush her hair back, discovered that it was full of mud. She looked down at herself, blushed. Mud, she decided, wasn't very becoming. 'I'm a bit of a mess, aren't I?' she said in English.

Akram grinned broadly. 'Come on,' he whispered. 'We must move from here.'

He got up and began to follow a weaving path under the mushrooms. Jo followed, taking care to place her feet where he did. There was a sudden swish of wings above her, and a bright light shone in her eyes. She ducked, flinched, almost cried out.

'They're harmless,' whispered Akram, touching her shoulder. 'At least, they haven't attacked me yet.'

'How long have you been here?' asked Jo.

'Almost three days. I was with Monsieur Benari's "special force". There were a thousand of us. He sent us to kill all the Gilteans of the FLNG, you know.' He stopped walking, leaned against the trunk of one of the mushrooms. ' "Top Secret", of course. As if it matters now. You are UN, you say?'

Jo nodded.

'Everybody hates the UN. But I like the UN. You do what you can for world peace. It is not easy.' He paused. 'You don't have a cigarette, I suppose?'

Jo shook her head. 'Sorry.' She grinned, gestured down

at her muddy clothes. 'And if I did it wouldn't be worth smoking, would it?' She paused. 'What happened to the other men?'

Akram looked away. 'You do not want to know.'

'I do want to know,' Jo insisted. She paused. 'I'm the scientific advisor to UNIT.' Well, she thought, his assistant; but it's better to sound impressive at this point. When the young man still didn't speak, she added, 'It was this place that we came to see. I need to find out all I can.'

Akram looked at her. He seemed to be weighing her up.

'Very well, I will show you,' he said at last.

He led the way across the forest. The light grew steadily brighter; in places, the fungi themselves seemed to be glowing. Finally they came to a downward slope of bare soil across which blew warm, sweet-scented air.

'It smells nice,' said Jo, but Akram shushed her with an upraised hand. Then he pointed down the slope.

The roof was low, making it difficult to see, but Jo could just make out a row of amber spheres. They were shaped like the Carvol capsules that her mother used to give her when she had a cold. It was hard to judge their size, but she reckoned that they must be at least six feet across.

Very cautiously, Akram slithered down the slope. Pieces of loose earth trickled down ahead of him, making tiny clattering sounds; every time this happened, he stopped. Jo followed, trying to make no sound at all.

They were about half-way down when she realized that the blobs had faces.

No: the remains of faces. Pieces of purplish skin, flayed out across the top, crudely delineating a mouth, a nose. Eyes, half-buried in the glistening amber flesh. Jo gasped, saw one pair of eyes turn to look at her. She covered her mouth to stifle any further sound, but the eyes lost interest, rolled slowly away.

Akram tugged at her arm but she ignored him, forced

herself to look in more detail. She realized that not all the honey-globes had been human: she could see patches of coarse camel-hair on one, whilst another, much smaller, globe sprouted a single, forlorn, black feather. Faint brown shadows within the amber must be the internal organs of the original human and animal bodies. Jo wondered why they were being kept alive like this.

Akram tugged at her arm again, pointed along the row of amber spheres. Jo saw a pair of waving antennae moving slowly towards them.

'They have heard us!' hissed Akram. 'We have to go!'

But Jo had seen something else: two pairs of raised mandibles behind the antennae. And a body being carried between them. A body dressed in a familiar cape, purple jacket and frilly magenta shirt.

'It's the Doctor!' Jo hissed. 'He's my friend! Akram, we've got to help him!'

'And how do you suggest we do that?' said the young man. 'If we go down there, we end up like my friends and yours.' His hand was still on her arm, tugging her upwards.

Jo could see the Doctor's face now. His eyes were closed, and what looked like a rime of ice had formed on his skin.

She looked round, gave Akram her best smile. 'Please. I've seen the Doctor like this before. That time he nearly died. We have to save him. We have to do *something*.'

Thirteen

The Brigadier looked at the bloodstained bandage on his arm. The *Sakir*'s aim had been precise: the bullet had nicked the flesh of his arm, covering it with red, human, blood. The old man had been satisfied after that, had apologized profusely and provided a bandage and some water.

Which was all very well, thought the Brigadier, but it wasn't going to mend the hole in his arm, or buy him a new uniform jacket.

The sound of voices raised in anger returned him to the present. He looked up, saw that the *Sakir* was arguing with his son again — the Brigadier couldn't follow the rapid, colloquial Arabic, but gathered that it was something to do with moving the encampment. The Brigadier didn't blame them for wanting to move. One look at the aliens' structure from ground level had been enough to convince him that UNIT should have investigated it earlier. Despite its apparently crude construction, the mound was larger and more impressive than, for example, the Axon spaceship — and that had caused enough trouble. He could understand the Arab's fears in the face of it. He had almost forgiven the *Sakir*'s rather drastic method of checking that he wasn't one of the aliens.

Almost, but not quite. Even after two hours, his arm hurt too much for that.

Around him, tents were being folded, guns loaded and checked, petrol drums and smaller plastic containers of water loaded on to jeeps, all to the accompaniment of much shouting and cursing. The Brigadier realized that they were definitely moving on. He pushed himself to his feet, took a few steps towards the *Sakir* and his son, who were talking about jeeps and petrol.

'Excuse me.'

The younger man looked round sharply, but the *Sakir* carried on talking.

The Brigadier remembered his diplomatic training and switched to Arabic. 'I don't think we should move from here yet.'

The *Sakir* broke off in mid-sentence, frowned. 'Why not?' he asked in English.

'The Doctor is in that – building, whatever it is. We need to find out what has happened to him. I can't order your people to stay of course, but I would greatly appreciate it if you could render some assistance *pro tem*, until I can contact my people in Rabat.'

The younger man, the one with the Omar Sharif moustache, shook his head violently. 'We have decided we must go. It is not safe here. Even I am convinced of that. You can come with us and share our water until your people come for you, but we can do no more than that.'

The Brigadier looked away for a moment, out across the jumbled rocks glaring in the late morning sun. He knew that he probably wouldn't even reach the alien installation if he tried to get there on his own, let alone get in. These people had weapons, fuel, water, knowledge of the desert. They would probably be almost as useful as a UNIT battalion – at least until they got in. Then it would probably be down to the Doctor.

Assuming the Doctor was actually in there.

He looked back at the young man. 'Look, I'll be frank. I'm not in a position to offer guarantees, but I do have some influence within the UN on account of my previous services. I could try to obtain a new hearing for your people –'

But the older Arab was shaking his head sadly. 'Listen,' he said in Arabic. 'If your friend is in that place, he is gone. He is dead — worse than dead. He is one of the dancers. If you see him again, it will be your time to die. Believe me: it is better that we all leave, and warn the world.'

The Brigadier shook his head. 'The Doctor always manages to survive when you'd least expect him to. I think we should –'

He was interrupted by a shout in Arabic. '*Sakir!* There is a helicopter!'

He looked round, saw someone pointing to the north, at the same time heard the faint sound of rotor blades.

'We have to take cover,' said the Brigadier, taking charge of the situation automatically. 'The chances are that those are alien aircraft, not helicopters at all.'

Tahir was staring at him. 'Are you mad?'

'It's not impossible,' said the *Sakir*. 'And anyway it doesn't make any difference. They are hardly likely to be friends of ours.' He started shouting instructions. Men with guns dived for cover. Others hurried towards the protective shadow of a ravine.

'Good strategy,' commented the Brigadier – but both the *Sakir* and Tahir had gone, running across the encampment towards the ravine. After a moment's hesitation, the Brigadier set off after them.

Behind him, the sound of the turning blades grew closer.

It was Akram who saw the gun first. He grabbed Jo's arm, pointed. Jo saw a machine-pistol lying half under one of the honey-globes. Akram whispered something in French which Jo didn't follow, and before she could question him began to slither down the slope.

Jo hesitated, then followed, but when she reached the bottom Akram had vanished. She stayed behind the first of the honey-globes, tried to get a look at the thing that was carrying the Doctor. She caught a glimpse of grey, shiny skin, with the Doctor's booted foot flapping against it. Before she could react, there was a burst of gunfire. Jo

136

jumped forward, saw the Doctor's body sliding down the side of the creature.

He hit the ground, flopped like a rag doll, landing on his back almost at Jo's feet. She crouched down, brushed the loose frost from the Doctor's face and put her hand an inch above his mouth. A slight movement of cold air told her that he was breathing.

'Doctor!' she said. 'Doctor, wake up!'

Another burst of gunfire rattled from somewhere in the chamber; Jo heard Akram's voice shouting, 'I am almost out of bullets! Quickly!'

Jo shook the Doctor violently. 'Wake up, Doctor! Please!'

The Doctor's eyes opened. 'Jo? What are you doing here?'

His voice was weak. With a frown, he dusted the remaining melting ice away from his face, then gingerly explored his ribcage with one hand.

'Not too bad,' he muttered, sitting up slowly.

Suddenly, Akram screamed.

'I've got to help him,' said Jo, springing up. She started to move away, but the Doctor reached out and put a restraining hand on her arm.

'It's too late for that, Jo,' he said solemnly.

Jo heard the sound of bones splintering, followed by a horrible, agonized gurgle that faded into silence. She felt the blood drain from her face. She stared in the direction of the sound.

'If I hadn't asked him to help —'

'I know,' said the Doctor quietly. 'Come on, or we might be next.'

He stood up, keeping his head down to avoid banging it on the low roof, then started to run along the row of honey-globes. His hand was still gripping Jo's arm: she didn't have much choice but to follow.

She looked over her shoulder, thought she saw the bottom of the slope where she and Akram had descended from the mushroom forest. 'Doctor, we're going the wrong way. Akram and I came from –'

'Yes, Jo, I know,' interrupted the Doctor. 'But we can't just run away. We have to find out –'

He was interrupted by a hollow booming noise, rather like a muted drum-roll. It went on and on, echoing from the walls of the chamber. Jo tried to cover her ears, but it didn't seem to make much difference.

'What is it?' she shouted.

'Alarm call, I should think,' said the Doctor. 'Don't worry, if I'm right this should be the main ventway.'

He gestured ahead. Jo saw a high-roofed tunnel leading down into darkness. 'But where does it go, Doctor?'

The Doctor turned to her and grinned. 'That's what we've got to find out.'

The Brigadier put his eye to the binoculars and watched as the gleaming spot with the fluttering rotor blades moved into the centre field. Still out of anti-aircraft range, he thought; but a clatter of gunfire along the gully told him that not everyone agreed.

The shells burst harmlessly, well short of the target. The thing carried on approaching, and suddenly the Brigadier realized that it wasn't one of the alien objects he'd seen last night. It was a perfectly normal human-made helicopter –

In fact, a very familiar helicopter –

In fact, *his* helicopter. He could even see the UNIT acronym emblazoned in large, friendly letters on the side.

'Yates!' he shouted. 'What the hell are you doing?'

He looked around for someone who might be able to give orders, but there was only an Arab boy with a light machine-gun, who was staring at the Brigadier as if he were mad.

How had Yates got out? thought the Brigadier, then decided it didn't matter. What mattered was that the Captain was up there in the UNIT helicopter and the Gilteans were about to shoot him out of the sky. He stood up, shouted down the length of the gully.

'That's my helicopter up there!' yelled the Brigadier. 'Cease fire!'

The Arab boy next to him continued to stare, and there was a rattle of light machine-gun fire from further down the path. The Brigadier set off at a run to the place where the *Sakir* and his son were stationed, his shoes slipping on the loose gravel.

It occurred to him that Yates had no way of knowing he was with the Gilteans. He would have flown to the last known position of the Superhawk; having seen the parachute canopies on the ground he'd have known they were in the area and now he was having a scout around to see if he could find them. But now that he'd been fired on, he would probably withdraw.

The Brigadier saw Tahir crouching in the shadows, cradling a machine-pistol.

There was another burst of gunfire from along the gully: fortunately, it all fell short. The Brigadier looked over his shoulder.

'For God's sake stop that!' The chopper had lurched upwards when the shells exploded. Now it was hovering at about a thousand feet. The sound of its engines echoed around the slopes, mixed with the fading rumble of the shell bursts.

The Brigadier heard the *Sakir*'s voice shouting something; he hoped it was an order for a cease-fire. He ran up out of the gully into the sun. He could still see the helicopter, but it was clearly moving away. He jumped up and down, waved his arms.

After a moment, the chopper began to swing around, circling the site but keeping a safe distance. The Brigadier imagined Yates or perhaps Benton trying to focus a pair of binoculars on him. He carried on waving his arms as the chopper completed two wide circles. At the end of the second, it came in, slowly, and high – for a quick get-away in case of trouble, no doubt.

He heard footsteps behind him, turned and saw Tahir Al-Naemi.

'You are leaving us, Brigadier?'

The Brigadier looked at the incoming helicopter again. 'I hope so.'

The Arab extended a hand. 'Good luck. I am sorry that my father shot you.'

The Brigadier shook, left-handed. 'So am I! – But it was an understandable mistake,' he added politely.

The helicopter was quite close now: the Brigadier turned and beckoned it in, pointing at a patch of level rock just beyond the parked jeeps.

'I hope you will tell them we are disciplined soldiers, not terrorists,' shouted Tahir suddenly over the growing racket of the engine.

The Brigadier frowned at him, then nodded. 'I'll try,' he said. 'But I can't guarantee that they'll listen.'

Tahir nodded, then ducked back down into the gully as the Brigadier ran towards the descending chopper. From the corner of his eye, the Brigadier noticed that the guns were still trained on the craft.

'Well, I hope you are disciplined soldiers,' he muttered to himself.

He didn't want to think about what was likely to happen if any of them weren't.

The chamber was bigger than any that Jo had yet seen: ahead, stumpy pillars of rock receded into the distance until they merged together into a dimly glowing mist. Huge, translucent eggs hung from the pillars and the walls, bunched like grapes, or sometimes in larger masses, like frogspawn. The nearer ones had distinct shadows inside them, shadows that looked disturbingly human.

She stopped, stared. 'Doctor –'

The Doctor looked over his shoulder. 'Come on, Jo. There's no time to lose.'

As if she'd needed a further reminder, chitinous rattling sounds became audible from the tunnel behind her. She jumped forward, grabbed the Doctor's hand. He strode on, leading the way through the maze of pillars as if he had a map of them. As they walked, the ground grew softer – not squelchy, but peaty and dark, like potting compost – and the air grew even more humid. Thin, waist-high plants with dark purple leaves sprouted in the clear spaces between the eggs; some of them were infested with a bluish fungus.

'Be careful not to go too near the eggs, Jo,' said the Doctor suddenly. 'They're quite close to hatching.'

Jo, who had in fact been avoiding the eggs as far as possible, glanced across at the nearest heap and saw that their skins were shrivelled and puckered, the human forms inside them quite clearly defined. She shuddered.

'Are they going to hatch into people?' she asked.

'Well, not exactly. Quasi-people would be a more accurate term, I should think.'

There was a movement somewhere ahead. A leg – an arm – a body came into view, dressed in combat fatigues. Slime trailed around it as it shuffled towards them. Blank eyes stared.

Jo took a breath as the Doctor steered her away.

'Doctor,' she whispered. 'That's one of Vincent's men. He was in the hospital. His name is – was –' She tried to remember.

'Don't say his name,' murmured the Doctor. 'He may recognize it. We don't want him following us.' He led her towards a darkened space between the pillars, thick with the purple vegetation.

'You mean –' said Jo, as they pushed their way between the leaves '– they can remember who they were?'

'Up to a point, I should think. There wouldn't be much point in making the copies otherwise.'

Jo shuddered again. 'But what are the copies for?'

'I wish I knew, Jo,' said the Doctor. 'To go to such lengths to produce humans in bulk when they already have fighters of their own doesn't make much sense.' He stopped for a moment, broke a leaf off one of the plants and examined it thoughtfully. Jo saw a small pod, like a butterfly chrysalis, hanging from the tip of the leaf.

'Unless of course that's only the first stage.'

'First stage of what, Doctor?'

But the Doctor didn't reply, merely set off again, but in a different direction. Jo glanced around her, shrugged, and followed him.

The vegetation had become quite dense. The thick stems of the plants pushed against her, and the leaves shed cold water on to her clothes. She saw smears of something dark on her arm, hoped it wasn't a parasitic fungus like the one that had infested her on Spiridon.

The Doctor stopped suddenly, turned to her. 'Shh!'

He crouched down, motioned Jo to do the same. Jo listened, heard the familiar chitinous rattling.

Getting closer.

She peered over the tops of the leaves, saw a tank-like shape moving between the pillars.

'Doctor –' she whispered

The tank-like object turned. There was the sound of leaves being pushed aside.

'Run!' shouted the Doctor.

Jo needed no encouragement. She sprang up, ran as fast as she could through the impeding stalks of the plants.

It wasn't fast enough. The rattling sounds grew louder. She could hear a constant, loud, hissing, like a steam engine in a station. She looked over her shoulder, saw open mandibles, the heavy, dark body tensed as if to spring –

'Jo! Over here!'

She jumped towards the sound of the Doctor's voice, heard the defender crash down in the space where she had been standing. The Doctor caught her hand, physically dragged her forward. She saw the brighter light, the shrivelled eggs, Vincent's soldier still standing, staring.

'This is the only place we'll be safe,' said the Doctor. 'The hatching zone. I think you'll find that the defenders are too big and too clumsy to be allowed to roam around in here.'

Jo looked around her. She saw that several more of the

eggs had hatched: dark-faced men in Army uniforms stood or crouched, silent and unmoving. She took a few steps forward, then saw the hatching egg in front of her and stopped.

The skin was slipping down, breaking up, revealing the body beneath, slime falling away from the familiar uniform, the familiar features –

She put a fist to her mouth, gasped. 'Doctor! It's Sergeant Osgood!'

The Doctor swung round, stared. 'You're right, Jo. But how on Earth did they get the material –'

He stepped forward, reached out a cautious hand and touched the inert body.

The eyes opened.

'Hello, Sergeant,' said the Doctor quietly. 'How's your fiancée? – Becky, isn't it? Nice girl, as I remember it. You met her at the folk festival, didn't you?'

The Sergeant's mouth opened and a golden, oily bubble formed between his lips. It burst, and the honey-like fluid ran down his chin.

'Come on, man, stand to attention,' said the Doctor, trying a different tack.

There was a hollow *snap* from behind them. Jo looked over her shoulder, saw the grey shapes of the defenders lined up behind the nearest pillars, less than ten yards away. In the brighter light of the hatching zone, their hunched, armoured bodies looked more like rhinos than giant insects, the stumpy legs and forward-sloping heads added to the impression. But from the front of their heads sprang metre-long mandibles, the gripping edges lined with hooked teeth. As she watched, one of the creatures jerked its head upwards and shut its mandibles with another audible *snap*.

Involuntarily, Jo took a step backwards. She turned to the Doctor, who was still speaking in a low voice to the copy of Sergeant Osgood.

And that was when she saw it.

From the corner of her eye: the immaculate uniform,

143

the brass buttons, the neatly trimmed black moustache. The brown eyes staring at her.

At her.

'Doctor,' she said quietly.

The Doctor looked up from Sergeant Osgood, followed the direction of her gaze.

The copy of the Brigadier glanced at him, then returned its attention to Jo. Slowly its hand moved towards the gun holster strapped to its waist.

Jo felt her stomach clench. 'This is where he shoots us, isn't it?' she whispered.

The Doctor said nothing. Slowly, the copy Brigadier's hand rose, with the gun in it. Jo felt her face, her hands, her feet go cold. The gun was pointed directly at her now.

– I'm going to die I'm going to die this is what we saw the Doctor was right there's nothing we can do I'm going to die –

The Brigadier's finger tightened on the trigger.

Fourteen

The Brigadier had a last glimpse of the Giltean encampment as Yates turned the helicopter towards the mountains. The guns were still trained on them. It was a disconcerting sight, even though the Brigadier knew that they were out of range.

'I took a gander at the alien installation, sir,' said Yates. 'Got a couple of pictures from the automatic camera.'

'You didn't see the Doctor?'

Yates shook his head. 'Just a lot of Kebirian Army men. They seemed to be held prisoner in a compound –'

'I know, I know. Al-Naemi told me about it. And some sort of fairy tale about "dancing the code".' He paused, decided he'd better ask. 'So how the blazes *did* you get here, Yates? And what are you doing in my helicopter?'

The Captain glanced sidelong at him. 'Apparently Benari's given in to UN pressure, sir. But we've got to be out of the country as soon as possible and –' Yates broke off for a moment. 'They want Miss Grant, sir. For murder.'

The Brigadier was so startled that for several seconds he couldn't think of anything to say. Finally he just repeated, blankly, 'Murder?'

Yates swallowed.

'She escaped from prison, with a journalist. Several of the prison guards were killed and they reckon Jo got one of them.'

'I don't believe it,' said the Brigadier. It was true: he didn't. He still remembered the occasion when Jo had told him off for using fly spray, and had shown him how to catch a fly with a teacup and a piece of paper so that you could let it out of the window alive. He could no more imagine her killing anyone than he could imagine –

He swallowed, forced himself to complete the thought.

Himself killing her. With a .38. And that cold expression on his face.

'I don't believe it either,' Yates was saying. 'But the Secretary-General's office have given us a direct order to hand her over if we find her.' He paused. 'Actually it was addressed to you, sir, but in the circumstances I felt I ought to open it.'

The Brigadier waved a hand at him to signify that it wasn't important. He looked down through the tinted glass of the helicopter's cockpit at the grey and black rocks of the desert drifting below. Ahead, the ground fell away and the Brigadier could see a brown plain dotted with thorn trees.

He cleared his throat.

'You have my authority to ignore that order, Yates. Tell your men. If we find Miss Grant, she goes back to England and we argue about it with the politicians later.'

Yates nodded, grinned. 'Yes, sir!'

The Brigadier gazed at the desert, and wondered how many more orders he was going to have to ignore before this operation was over.

When the gun went off, Jo fell to her knees, clutching her chest. She saw the Doctor rush forward, saw the fake Brigadier stagger backwards and fall against one of the eggs. But only when he pointed his ruined hand at the oncoming figure of the Doctor, only when she saw the shards of chitin spreading out from the end of his fingers, did Jo realize that she wasn't hit, that nothing had happened to her, that instead something had happened to the gun.

Dazedly, she removed her hands from her chest, saw only the drying film of mud over her T-shirt. She got to her feet, started towards the place where the fake Brigadier and the Doctor were grappling. The alien appeared to be getting the better of it. The Doctor was being pushed back towards the floor, his head twisted to one side. Jo looked around for something she could use as a weapon, saw nothing. She kicked out at the alien's leg, hoping to unbalance it, but her foot was jarred as if she were kicking stone and the alien didn't appear to react at all.

Before she could think of anything else to do, the fake Brigadier's body tumbled forward over the Doctor's shoulder, and landed on the ground with a hollow snapping sound. As Jo stared, horrified, huge cracks formed in the body, and a gelatinous fluid ran out, filling the air with a sickly-sweet smell. Slowly, the body literally fell apart, like a china doll filled with honey.

The Doctor stepped back. 'Shame about that,' he said. 'If I'd known the chitin was still that brittle I'd have been gentler with him. He might have been able to tell me something useful.'

'I think I prefer it dead, if it's all the same to you,' said Jo, still staring at the shattered body. Bubbles were rising through the fluid now; the left leg, which was intact, jerked repeatedly.

'Double contrapnuemainterfluidostatic action,' muttered the Doctor, stroking his chin. 'That's very interesting.' Then he glanced up at Jo. 'Sergeant Osgood wasn't with the team that went to Kebiria, was he?'

Jo shook her head.

'I didn't think so.' He paused, began pacing to and fro in the narrow space between two of the huge, luminous eggs. 'I just wish I knew where they got the material to make these copies.'

'Press photographs?' suggested Jo.

The Doctor shook his head. 'No, Jo. Look at the detail. You couldn't get that from a photograph.'

147

Jo examined the shattered face of the fake Brigadier. It was perfect, down to the individual hairs of the black moustache.

'I see what you mean,' she said doubtfully. 'But what else —'

The Doctor interrupted her. 'There has to be some guiding intelligence behind all this. Something that's been studying humanity for a while and knows who the key figures are.' He turned to Jo. 'Something that knows exactly what UNIT is and what it does, for example.'

Jo shuddered. 'But that means they could have copies of — well, anybody.'

'That's right, Jo. But if my theory's right —'

Before the Doctor could complete his reply, strong arms grabbed Jo around the stomach. She called out, struggled, but it was like fighting a living statue. She saw another figure take hold of the Doctor, saw it thrown to the floor and shattered: but two more replaced it, took an arm each.

'Doctor!' she shouted. But the Doctor was being dragged away into the darkness.

A hand was pressed over her face and a sweet, thick, syrupy scent filled her nose, clogged her throat.

Gingerbread men, she thought.

Then Aunt May kissed her and everything went black.

Catriona was several miles inside what was officially Algerian territory when she saw the jeep parked across the road ahead of her. She swore under her breath. The vehicle was only a few hundred yards from the white concrete hut that was the Algerian customs post, but she knew that the chances of it being Algerian were slim. One man sat behind the wheel; another had already got out and was walking up the track towards her, presumably having heard the sound of her approach. He had a light machine-gun slung casually over his shoulder.

Catriona stopped her Land Rover in front of him, saw the Kebirian flag stitched to the lapel of his khaki shirt.

Nervously she pulled out her passport.

With any luck they'll just let me through, she thought. They won't know I'm wanted in Kebir City. Nobody will have got around to telling them.

Please.

The man took her passport, examined it closely.

'Why do you wish to leave Kebiria?' he asked at last.

Catriona felt a huge wave of relief. Just an ordinary busybody patrol, then; probably hoping to pick up some of Vincent's people. 'I already have left Kebiria,' she pointed out dryly.

The man smiled thinly. His face was plump, for a soldier's, and beads of sweat clung to his moustache. 'Yes, but I do not think you went through customs,' he said. 'Not on this road.' He glanced up at the ridge of hills that lay between them and the site of Vincent's settlement.

The remains of Vincent's settlement, Catriona thought fiercely. Aloud she said: 'I didn't get a chance to go through customs. There were too many bombs exploding.'

The man didn't smile, and his brown eyes remained fixed on hers. 'Well, we will just have to inspect you now.'

Catriona didn't like the sound of it, or the look in the man's eyes. 'Look,' she said levelly. 'I'm a reporter. I work for the *Journal* newspaper in London. I will –' She broke off as she saw the change in the man's expression. Realized her mistake too late.

They might not recognize a name, a face, but they would remember that it was a Western reporter who –

The gun swung up to cover her face. 'You are the reporter, then? The reporter who kills Kebiriz?' He shouted in Arabic to the driver, who was still sitting behind the wheel of the jeep. Catriona heard her own name, hideously accented, then the word 'assassin'.

She wanted to say, I'm not an assassin, I'm innocent. But she knew she had lost that right. For ever.

'Get out of the car,' said the man, opening the door.

There was a quite new tone in his voice. 'And keep your hands above your head.'

'You're mixing me up with someone else,' said Catriona desperately. 'I don't know anything about it.' She was aware of how inadequate, how predictable, how pathetic, her lies sounded. And she could tell from the soldier's contemptuous expression that he was aware of it too.

It doesn't stop with the killing, she thought. It doesn't stop with the guilt. It goes on.

She got out of the Land Rover, felt the sun's heat hit her like a wave. The gun prodded into her back; she raised her hands above her head and walked towards the jeep. She could hear the driver on the radio, repeating her name. As she got to the jeep, he looked up, over her shoulder at his comrade.

'It's her,' he said in Arabic, then in French to Catriona, 'Miss Talliser, you are under arrest, on charges of murder and treason. Do you have anything to say?'

Catriona swallowed, shook her head. The other soldier opened the door. She got in and the man got in after her, prodded her in the neck with the gun.

'No trouble or I shoot you, straight away,' he said.

Catriona risked a sidelong glance at his face, saw that the sweat was running down it, dripping off his chin. She realized that he was afraid of her. She wondered what stories the Kebirians were telling, that made a soldier afraid of an unarmed woman. She also wondered if, in the unlikely event that she got a chance, she would kill these two in order to get away.

With a sensation of cold horror, she realized that she probably would.

– good good honey honey good good to be honey to be good good sweet honey to be good good honey to be sweet sweet –

'Find the key,' said Aunt May calmly, wiping the flour off her hands with a chequered towel. 'Find the key.'

The Doctor's got it, thought Jo. The Doctor's got the

key, he's bound to have, he's always got the key. He always knows.

She felt hard grit against her palms.

— *good good to be honey good good to be sweet to be honey good good* —

Someone was leaning over her. She could see the girl through her closed eyes. She was wearing a blue T-shirt and brown trousers. She was called Jo.

'I'm so sorry you have to die,' said the other Jo. 'But it's all right, you see, because I'll live. I'll be you, and I'll do lots of wonderful things.' She winked cheerfully and turned away.

'No!' shrieked Jo, 'Stop!' But no sound came out: her mouth wouldn't move. She tried to open her eyes, but, this time, she couldn't.

— *good good honey honey honey dancing good good dancing honey dancing to be sweet to be dancing the code dancing the code dancing the code* —

'Doctor,' she said, or tried to say, hoping he could hear her even though she wasn't breathing. 'Doctor, help me.'

But the Doctor wasn't there.

Fifteen

It had been a long drive from Algiers, and Marwan Hamwai was tired. He had that pulsing pain between his eyes again, the pain that made the dusty road beyond the windscreen of his truck lose its reality and become an abstraction of glaring white and heat-shimmer. Marwan wanted to turn it off, make it go away, so that he could go to sleep.

He glanced at his watch — real gold, 9 carats, all the way from Switzerland — and saw that it was already half-past ten.

No good. He had to have the load at Ibrahim's by twelve noon, and there were over a hundred kilometres to go. He couldn't stop. He would just have to stay awake, somehow.

He tried thinking about his wife, Nazira. Her bare wrists glimpsed under the cuffs of her chador as she walked across the kitchen. The smile in her eyes when he lifted her veil in the privacy of their room and kissed her. Her swelling belly under the bedclothes, proof that he was a man, that he could father a son.

Or a daughter. He might even prefer a daughter; it would be useful for the eldest to be a girl, she could help her mother with the other children when she was older. And she would have black hair and black eyes, lustrous like her mother's, and she would marry a rich man —

The truck jolted violently, the tyres screeched. Marwan grappled with the wheel, pulled the vehicle round the curve and back on to the metalled part of the road.

'You stupid bastard!' he muttered, pinching his right wrist, hard, with his left hand. 'You want the baby to be fatherless? You want Nazira to be a widow?' He thought again about stopping. Perhaps he could go back to Wadi Sul-Hatar. Deliver the load later in the afternoon. Ibrahim would be furious – but Marwan reckoned he would be better off bawled out than dead.

But then, Nazira would worry about him if he was late back, and if she worried too much when she was pregnant –

That was when he saw the hitchhikers. They were standing by the side of the road, there, in the middle of the desert, two Europeans: a blonde woman in a blue T-shirt, and a grey-haired man in what Marwan at first thought was a burnous with the hood folded down. As he drew closer he saw that it was an altogether stranger garment, a cape over a bright-coloured frilly shirt, like something out of the movies.

'Crazy gear,' he muttered. 'Must be hippies.'

Ordinarily Marwan wouldn't have stopped. He didn't like Westerners much, hippies even less. They were a nuisance; they got drunk in the streets; they encouraged the beggars. But a bit of company would keep him awake, keep his eyes on the road. He pulled up, wound down the window.

The man spoke, without waiting for a greeting. His French was fluent, Parisian, without the trace of an accent. 'Would you be so good as to take my assistant and I to Kebir City? We could pay you.' He reached into his pocket, pulled out a thousand-*sulfa* note.

Marwan stared: it was more than a week's wages. Still, Westerners didn't appreciate the value of money, that was well known.

For the sake of form, Marwan grinned dismissively, said, 'Five thousand, my friend.'

The man reached into his pocket again, pulled out four more notes and handed them over with a smile.

This is my lucky day, thought Marwan. I should have

asked for ten. He grinned at the Westerners, opened the passenger door. They got up: the man first, in his crazy costume, and then the girl.

'You in the movies?' asked Marwan as he put the truck into gear. He was feeling friendly now, with that money in his pocket; he was feeling like practising his French. And perhaps they would give him another tip when they got to Kebir City.

'No, we're not in the movies, I'm afraid,' said the man.

'Our work's classified,' said the girl. She smiled at Marwan, her brown eyes radiating an impossible sincerity.

He grinned back. 'The CIA?'

'We can't really talk about it, I'm afraid,' said the man. 'But it's extremely important that we get to Kebir City as soon as possible.'

Marwan nodded. They had to be having him on, they were hardly likely to be real spies in that get-up. But he didn't mind going along with them. After all, they were paying him well enough.

'Well, then,' he asked, looking at the girl. 'What do you think about Mr Nixon in America, and the Watergate scandal?'

'The water gate?' asked the girl. Her face was blank.

Marwan frowned. Surely *everyone* in the West had heard of the Watergate scandal. He glanced at the man, who frowned and said, 'That's impossible! Think about it, man. How can you make a gate out of water?'

Marwan looked away nervously, fixed his eyes on the dusty road. Obviously these people were quite mad. He wondered if he should stop and tell them to get off before it was too late. But then he noticed for the first time a sweet, cloying scent that came from them.

Of course. That was it. It wasn't like hashish, but he guessed it was one of those fancy Western drugs that some of his wilder friends talked about. He glanced at the couple again, saw that they were staring ahead, their faces blank, almost as if they were switched off.

154

Well, that explained it then. These people were stoned; there wasn't much point in trying to talk with them. Marwan shrugged inwardly, thought about the five thousand *sulfa* in his pocket, and gave his attention to the road ahead.

Catriona watched the hazy concrete towers of Kebir City rising ahead of her and tried not to think about how frightened she was.

She kept remembering the face of the woman interrogator. She kept half-dozing, and waking again, wincing from imaginary blows.

Perhaps there would be a trial, just for appearance's sake. Perhaps Mike Timms would start a campaign for her release, like the campaign she'd persuaded him to start for Vincent. Leo would raise the issue in parliament and Paul Vishnya would write to the Secretary-General, and meanwhile the Kebirians would execute her by firing squad, blood pouring from her chest as she fell to the concrete floor, and they would be right and Mike Timms would be wrong because *I killed her Jesus Christ I killed her* –

A violent jolt as the jeep ran over a pothole brought her back to the present. Catriona stared at the buildings around her in a distracted way, to her horror recognized the white concrete bulk of the police headquarters.

The jeep drew up with a screech of tyres, and the older of the two guards got out. Two men moved from the entrance of the building, grabbed him and bundled him inside.

It took a moment for Catriona to realize what had happened. Only when she saw two more men run towards the jeep, heard the driver shouting something in panicky Arabic, saw them grab hold of his arms and physically drag him out of his seat –

'What the hell's going on?' she shouted.

Then she smelled the roses and cloves. The sweet, alien, honey smell.

The driver was screaming, begging for mercy as they carried him away. Catriona shuffled sideways until she was against the door of the jeep, clambered over the back of the driver's seat. Her knee landed on something hard: a gun. She picked it up, aimed it towards the retreating backs of the policemen.

They're aliens, she told herself. You can do it now.

But before she could bring herself to squeeze the trigger, they had gone inside. Catriona started to run towards the entrance, then stopped.

– Jesus what am I doing I've got to get out of here get away from them –

But she couldn't leave the Arabs to the aliens. She knew she couldn't.

There were more 'policemen' issuing from the entrance, their feet clicking on the stone steps. 'What are you doing to them?' she shouted, raising the gun.

The aliens ignored her.

She tightened her finger on the trigger: nothing happened.

The aliens continued their advance. Catriona pushed at the trigger but it wouldn't move. She realized that the safety catch was on. She flicked it upwards. It didn't seem to move enough, but there was no time left; the aliens were almost within arm's reach. She aimed the gun, pulled the trigger.

The gun almost jumped out of her hand. The shot hit one of them in the chest. Cracks spread from the point of impact, as if the figure – clothes and all – were made of china. But it carried on walking.

Catriona stepped back, fired again – again – again. The last shot toppled one of the pair, but it carried on trying to walk lying down, slowly spinning round like a broken toy.

The other one kept advancing, though part of its face was missing.

Catriona turned and ran.

– I need to get a car I've got to get away from here NOW get

to the British Embassy or the airport or anywhere but I've got to get out of here —

She saw a woman in a chador and veil push herself against a wall, protecting her child with her body. On the other side of the wide pavement, a small, balding, middle-aged man was crouched down beside a parked car, his hands covering his face.

— of course the gun I've got a bloody gun in my hand —

She noticed that the car door was open.

She ran up to the man, shoved the gun against his throat.

'Your car?' she asked.

The man nodded, terror in his eyes.

'Give me the keys.'

The man handed her the keys. Catriona got into the car, pushed the key into the ignition.

The man shouted, 'Here! She is here!'

Catriona started the engine, looked across at the little man. She could see the 'policeman' only yards away on the pavement behind him, approaching slowly, with thick, brown fluid leaking from his damaged face.

'Here!' shouted the little man.

'Run away!' shouted Catriona. 'Run like hell, you fool!'

The man stared at her, backed away. The 'policeman' grabbed him from behind.

'No it isn't me it's her it's no-o-o-'

Catriona swallowed, looked through the windscreen and saw 'policemen' swarming out of the front of the headquarters building and along the wide pavement of the boulevard.

'Sorry,' she muttered, then stamped on the accelerator and pulled out into the traffic. She detested herself for leaving the little man behind, but she knew that she had no choice.

She steered the car through the traffic into the lane marked AEROPORT. *I've got to get out of this bloody country,* she thought. *Get to somewhere safe and tell*

157

everyone what's happening.

Before it's too late.

The Brigadier looked around the dusty tarmac for the last time, wiped at his face to remove the sweat and the ever-persistent grey flies. Everything was ready: the Hercules was fuelled up, Captain Yates and his men were on board. They had even managed to get a slot from Kebirian Air Traffic Control.

The Brigadier would have liked to delay their departure, but there was no arguing with the repeated direct order from the Secretary-General's office:

'Leave at once. We will make every possible effort to locate your Scientific Advisor, and pressure will be put on the Kebirians for leniency in the case of Miss Grant, but we repeat: for the present it is imperative that you leave at once.'

Yates waved from the top of the steps as the second engine fired, the huge blade spinning slowly and then speeding up. The Brigadier remembered the famous scene from the film *Casablanca* and, not for the first time, found himself wishing that real life was as straightforward as the movies.

It was no good. He was being *ordered* to leave.

'I'm sorry, Doctor,' he said aloud.

Then his eye caught a flurry of movement near the airport buildings, a few hundred yards away across the tarmac. He looked across, saw three of the local policemen and, standing between them, Jo and the Doctor. For a moment it seemed that they were all moving so fast that their limbs were blurred. An illusion caused by the shimmering heat-haze, no doubt, thought the Brigadier.

He started across towards them, wondering how he would manage to get Jo out of the hands of the local police. Perhaps he could bluff it, say that as a UNIT employee she had to be tried by an international court. It might work.

But even as he thought about it, he saw that the Doctor and Jo were walking towards him, clear of the police.

158

'Well done, Doctor,' he said as they approached. 'Did some fast talking again, did you?'

'You could say that, Brigadier,' said the Doctor.

The Brigadier turned to Jo. 'I have to say that I didn't believe it for one minute, Miss Grant. I know you would never kill anyone.'

Jo frowned. 'Believe what, Brigadier?'

'But surely you know!' He turned to the Doctor. 'Miss Grant's up for murder, according to the Kebirians.'

The Doctor smiled. 'Oh, don't worry about that, old chap. I think you'll find there's been a bit of a change of policy in Kebiria. Jo's perfectly all right.'

Nonplussed, the Brigadier looked from one to the other of them. He half-expected Jo to giggle, but she didn't: she just stared into the distance, as if contemplating the horizon.

There was something odd about that stare, thought the Brigadier. 'Are you all right, Miss Grant?' he asked quietly.

'Quite all right, thank you, Brigadier,' replied Jo. But her eyes stayed fixed on the horizon.

'Well, we have orders to leave at once,' said the Brigadier.

'Good!' said the Doctor, rubbing his hands together. 'We've a lot to be getting on with in England.'

He and Jo set off for the plane. As they passed, the Brigadier caught a whiff of perfume. Roses and cloves, it smelled like. Rich, cloying, expensive.

Funny. He wouldn't have thought Jo would have gone in for that kind of thing.

Catriona stared at the unmoving queue of traffic, at the blue-and-white striped barrier beyond it that marked the airport entrance, and clenched her fists in frustration. What was happening up there?

– if it's the aliens I'm finished it's too late I'm going to die like Deveraux did oh Jesus someone help me I've got to get out of here –

With difficulty she controlled her panic, took several deep breaths, wiped the sweat from her eyes. She looked across the metal barrier at the road which led to the goods entrance, at the slowly moving line of trucks.

But they were at least moving.

She couldn't get the car over there, but if she got out of the car, she could thumb a lift perhaps.

Or just run for it.

She switched the engine off, pushed open the door, clambered out and over the bonnet, over the metal barrier. Jumped down on to the rough stone at the edge of the carriageway.

A horn blared: she ignored it, started running towards the airport. Then the horn blared again, and Catriona heard the sound of breaking glass. She looked over her shoulder, saw a line of the 'policemen' advancing along the highway on the other side of the barrier, walking over the roofs of the stationary cars. She saw a man dragged from his car, heard his screams.

Then, before she could think, the aliens were crossing the metal barrier between the two highways, jumping like grasshoppers, their feet making chitinous clicks on the tarmac. Catriona aimed the gun at the nearest of them, pulled the trigger.

Nothing happened. She pulled the trigger again, heard a click. Obviously the magazine was empty. She swore, hurled the useless weapon at the aliens, ran out across the road, hoping to put the stream of moving trucks between her and them. A truck swerved, almost hit her. She heard a crunch as it ran over one of the police, a squeal of brakes as it stopped.

Don't stop my friend for God's sake don't stop –

But there was no time to turn, to warn the driver. She had reached the verge on the other side of the road by now: ahead was a concrete embankment, topped by a mesh fence that marked the boundary of the airport compound. She glanced over her shoulder, saw people struggling out of their cars and trucks, running, grey-

160

uniformed figures following them, making grasshopper-like leaps across the traffic to pin their victims down.

She scrambled up the embankment, hooked her fingers into the mesh fence at the top. Through the netting, she could see a big Hercules transport plane, its engines running, slowly turning away from the airport buildings.

Catriona stared at it for a moment, at the RAF roundels and the blue logo just visible above the loading door.

– *RAF thank Christ its got to be the UNIT plane Jo's people are on there I can tell them what's happening what happened to her and it's my only chance of getting out of this country alive I've just got to go for it –*

But the plane was taxiing away from her, towards the end of the runway. She knew that she had no hope of catching up with it.

There was only one thing she could do.

She clambered over the fence, catching her shirt on a jagged wire. She struggled free, jumped down and started running down the main runway. The plane, perhaps a mile ahead of her, was turning slowly, readying itself for take-off. Catriona wondered how much runway a Hercules used. It depended on the load, she supposed. She carried on running, her shoes clopping on the tarmac. Sweat was trickling down her face.

The plane completed its turn, hung there, shimmering in the heat haze.

She wondered if they could see her. Surely they must be able to. She waved her arms, pushed her hands forward palms first in a desperate parody of a 'stop' signal.

– *they've got to see me they've got to stop please they've just got to –*

She wondered what would happen if they didn't stop. If the wheels missed her, would she be sucked up in the airflow, then dropped to bash her brains out on the concrete?

No, she was probably too heavy for that.

But she realized that, if they didn't stop, she'd rather be killed here and now by the plane. Rather that than be caught by the aliens. She remembered Anton Deveraux's scratchy whisper: '– dancing the code –'. Remembered the contorted face, the ruptured skin.

– I don't want to die that way, any way but that –

The plane was moving, she realized. She could hear the roar of its engines as they throttled up.

– please they've got to stop please –

The plane was visibly bigger now, rumbling towards her. She ran faster, a head-down sprint of the kind she hadn't done since she was in school, keeping her eyes on the white guide line in the middle of the runway.

She wondered if she would feel the impact when the nose wheel hit her.

When the pilot put the brakes on, the Brigadier was almost thrown out of his straps. He glanced up at the Doctor.

'Looks like your change of policy didn't last very long.'

'Oh, I don't know, Brigadier. Perhaps the plane's got a flat tyre.'

But the Brigadier could tell that the man was worried. As the aircraft pulled to halt, he got out of his straps and strode towards the door. Jo followed him.

The door opened, letting a blaze of sunlight into the darkened interior of the plane. The Brigadier got up and walked to the door.

Outside a woman was shouting up at them. Her blonde hair was dirty, and her clothes were torn and bloodied.

'. . . *aliens!*' she shouted.

'What's she talking about, Doctor?' asked the Brigadier.

The Doctor looked round, an irritable expression on his face. 'Nothing, old chap. Just some mad woman.'

'Jo!' the woman was yelling. '. . . believe me! JO!'

Jo turned and pushed her way past the Brigadier back into the plane. 'I don't know who she is,' she said, then hurried away.

The Brigadier frowned. He could see several policemen running across the rough ground between the airport buildings and the runway.

'I think we ought to investigate the situation,' he said. He looked over his shoulder. 'Benton! Bring two of your men and –'

'No!' said the Doctor. 'Wait a minute, Brigadier! That doesn't make any sense. This woman has been infected by an alien virus. Her continued existence threatens the lives of everyone on Earth. The virus may make her act irrationally – dangerously. We have to leave at once.'

The Brigadier frowned. He wasn't sure that the Doctor was making any sense. One moment the woman was 'just a mad woman'; the next she was infected with a deadly virus. And surely it was UNIT's business to deal with alien infections?

But then, the Doctor quite frequently didn't make any sense.

'The local police are aware of the situation,' the Doctor went on, as if reading the Brigadier's concerns from his mind. 'It's fully under control. I've given them plentiful supplies of an antiviral preparation. We need to get to Headquarters as soon as possible to arrange for a worldwide immunization programme.'

The woman on the tarmac had noticed the approaching policemen now. She was glancing repeatedly over her shoulder, and almost screaming at them. 'Please! You've got to help! They'll kill me!'

'We'd better get down there, sir.'

It was Benton, looking over his shoulder. Captain Yates stood behind him, a frown on his face.

'No!' snapped the Doctor. 'If anyone goes down there without access to the antiviral preparation they will die.'

The policemen had reached the tarmac.

'THEY'LL KILL ME!'

'Far from killing her, Brigadier, they'll save her life – and ours, if I'm not mistaken. Now, please, we must leave at once.'

The Brigadier hesitated a moment longer. The policemen grabbed hold of the blonde woman, dragged her back across the tarmac. She screamed once, then struggled silently as they carried her away.

'You see?' said the Doctor. 'She's not dead.'

'I still think we ought to check –'

'Brigadier! They're immunized, you're not.'

The Brigadier looked at the policemen, now jogging back towards the airport building with the woman bundled onto their shoulders. He shook his head slowly, backed into the plane and let the Doctor shut the door.

'You'd better be right about this, Doctor,' he said.

The Doctor turned to him and smiled.

'Trust me, old chap,' he said. 'I know exactly what I'm doing.'

Sixteen

'Look, Doctor, are you all right?' asked the Brigadier.

The Doctor made his usual response to questions of that kind: in other words, he ignored it, and carried on with what he was doing. He had got the large retort down from its stand – the one the Brigadier had always imagined was in the UNIT lab purely for decoration, or possibly to give the cleaners something extra to dust. Now it was filled with a reddish-brown fluid, in which bobbed a brown object about the size of a ping-pong ball. The fluid was, in the true alchemical tradition, boiling, though the Brigadier could see no obvious source of heat. The lab smelled sweet, spicy, rather like that perfume Jo had been wearing on the flight.

He glanced across at Jo. 'Is he all right, Miss Grant? You haven't even told me what happened to you in Kebiria.'

'We didn't come to any harm, Brigadier,' said the Doctor without looking up. 'I can assure you of that.'

The Brigadier brushed his uniform down with his hands, looked at the floor for a moment. 'Good. I'm glad to hear it.' He hesitated. 'Look, we've got a bit of a problem with Kebiria and I think you might be able to help.'

'Problem?' The Doctor prodded at the retort, then looked up and smiled. 'Brigadier, Kebiria's problems are over. It's the rest of the world we have to worry about.' He returned his attention to his experiment.

'I'm afraid not, Doctor. We can't raise Kebir City on the radio or the telephone; the Foreign Office has apparently lost contact with its embassy staff there; the American embassy made a call for help about an hour ago, then lost contact.'

The Doctor looked up sharply. 'Are the Americans doing anything about it?'

'They're moving some ships into the area, but as for finding out what's going on — that's up to us. I've already been on to North Africa HQ in Rabat and they're providing some men.'

'Good, good. You take whatever steps you think are necessary, Brigadier. Keep me informed, won't you?'

'Frankly, Doctor, I was hoping you would have some suggestions.'

'The only suggestion I can make, Brigadier, is that you leave me to get on with this vitally important experiment *in peace*.' The Doctor returned his attention to the retort. The object floating inside it was noticeably bigger than it had been when the Brigadier had come in.

The Brigadier swallowed, glanced at Jo, hoping for sympathy; but the young woman didn't move, just stared at the Doctor's experiment. Suddenly she seemed to notice the Brigadier's gaze and jerked into life.

'That's right,' she said. 'The experiment has to be finished before we can do anything else.'

The Brigadier frowned, stared at his boots. Something was wrong. The Doctor's behaviour was no more irritating than usual: but Jo was acting — well, not like herself. She moved like Jo, she spoke like Jo, but she didn't behave like Jo. Jo would have been concerned about what was happening in Kebiria. Jo would have questioned the Doctor, asked why the experiment was so important. She wouldn't just have taken it for granted that he was right. It was almost as if —

An icy thought trickled into his brain. He remembered the cold, soldierly expression on his face when he had killed Jo. He would have to do that — he would have to kill both of them — if —

He swallowed again, hard. It was nonsense, he told

himself. Of course he wouldn't have to shoot them. Of course they hadn't been taken over by aliens. The Doctor was far too canny for that. No, he was just being his usual infuriating self: and Jo – well, perhaps she was feeling a bit off colour.

He decided to make one last try at communication. 'Is there anything that you need me to do? Shall I order up mass production facilities for this –' he gestured at the bubbling fluid in the retort '– this antidote, or whatever it is?'

'No, Brigadier, that won't be necessary,' said the Doctor. 'We have all we need here.' He was lifting the retort carefully off its stand, shaking it to and fro slowly. The liquid inside frothed and churned. 'Now if you'll excuse me, I really am very busy.'

The Brigadier shrugged his shoulders. That was a familiar enough line at least. 'All right, Doctor, have it your own way. I just hope you know what you're doing.'

'Of course I know what I'm doing, Brigadier. You can trust me.'

I hope so, thought the Brigadier as he left the lab. He was thinking of the locked drawer in his office, of the gun he had never thought he would use.

I really hope I can trust you, Doctor, he thought. I really do.

Private John Shoregood looked out of the sentry box at the grey forecourt of UNIT HQ and wondered if Kublai Khan III would win. If he did, Private Shoregood would be quids in – five quid, to be precise. Which would come in handy. Even with UNIT bonuses a private soldier's salary didn't come to much, and Jenny was nagging at him for a new washing machine.

Well, every little bit helps, he thought.

He looked at the black telephone on the wall of the sentry box and wondered if he dare use it to ring Ladbrooke's. It was four-forty now: the race should be on any minute.

But even as he was thinking about it, he saw the familiar figure of the Doctor running across the courtyard, his cape flying in the wind. He was shouting something, and the something was clearly aimed at Private Shoregood.

Cursing inwardly, Shoregood stepped out of the sentry box. 'What is it?'

'We need some help in the lab!' shouted the Doctor. 'An experiment has misfired rather badly, I'm afraid.'

Shoregood frowned. 'The lab, Doctor? But I'm on sentry duty. I mean, I can't just leave –'

'It really is extremely urgent. Miss Grant is in danger.'

'Jo?' Shoregood looked up at the main building, half expecting to see smoke coming out of the windows. But everything was quiet. 'What's the matter?'

'Quickly!' The Doctor seemed desperate.

Shoregood glanced at the road. It was quiet. He picked up his walkie-talkie, pressed the 'send' button.

'I'll have to get Ryman over to watch the gate,' he explained to the Doctor.

But the Doctor just shook his head. 'They've already got Ryman. Quickly, man!' He set off at a run for the main building: Shoregood followed, wondering who 'they' were.

Inside, everything was strangely quiet. The desk Sergeant was missing, there was no clicking of typewriters from the secretaries' offices.

'Doctor?' asked Shoregood. 'What's –'

But the Doctor was already running down the corridor that led to the lab. Once more Shoregood followed.

The lab door was open. Inside Shoregood saw a bench turned on its side, a uniformed figure lying across it with blood on his face.

A face that Shoregood recognized. 'Ryman?'

The Doctor was already inside the lab, leaning over the injured man. Shoregood raced in after him, saw something moving to his left. He looked up, saw Jo Grant.

Jo Grant, standing on a chair –

Jo Grant, with a hammer in her hands –

A hammer that was moving down towards his head, moving so fast that there was no hope of –

I don't believe it, thought Shoregood. It isn't possible.

And that was the last thought that Private Shoregood ever had.

I don't believe it, thought the Brigadier. It isn't possible.

The phone was ringing again.

The first opportunity he'd had to get some proper kip in almost two days and the phone was ringing. He wondered if he could get away with ignoring it.

No, it was too loud for that. And it wasn't going to stop.

He rolled off the bed, reached automatically for his trousers, realized he was already wearing them. And his green Army jersey. And his Army boots.

I must have been tired, he thought.

The phone was still ringing. Wearily, the Brigadier reached out and picked it up.

'Lethbridge-Stewart speaking.'

'Brigadier, old chap, we've got a problem in the lab.' The Doctor's voice. 'Jo's in danger. You'll have to come over straight away.'

Seventeen

Report, thought Catriona desperately. Observe. This is the story of a lifetime.

— the last story of my lifetime I'm never going to see the editorial office I'm never going to see London again —

Shut up, she told herself fiercely. Whining never got a reporter anywhere.

She parted her cracked lips, stared down at her swollen fingers.

'Catriona Talliser. Tape two.' There was no tape recorder, of course, but she could pretend, couldn't she?

— you can't pretend you're not dying you can't pretend you're not going to die like Deveraux —

SHUT UP!

'Tape two,' she said again. 'I'm in the — the nest, I suppose I have to call it, of an alien species, somewhere under the surface of Kebir City. There are perhaps a hundred of us in a dimly lit earth-lined chamber, and there must be many more people down here, judging by what I saw on the surface before I was kidnapped.' She broke off, thought about Jo, staring at her from the door of the Hercules, not recognizing her, denying her, betraying her. Why?

— honey honey sweet sweet —

She shook her head. No use thinking about that either. Now, where had she got to in her report?

She reached down to switch off her tape recorder and rewind it to find out, then remembered it wasn't really there. That she was really going to —

— die I'm going to die someone save me someone please —

170

— honey honey good good sweet sweet dancing to be good to be honey —

SHUT UP!

She swallowed, licked her cracked lips, remembered where she'd got to. 'I haven't seen enough to be sure, but it's entirely possible that the whole population of Kebir City has been captured. I don't know what they intend to do with us. I don't know —' She felt the panic rising again, tried to clench her fists, but her fingers were too swollen. 'We're all tied down — no, that's not quite right, we're attached to the walls — by rope-like tentacles. Most of the people here are unconscious, and the ones that aren't —' She swallowed, closed her eyes for a moment, then made herself carry on. 'I've tried to talk to the ones that are awake but they don't make much sense. They talk about —'

— honey honey sweet sweet —

'— honey and dancing, as if they were —' As if they were just like the insects, the mindless insects that had brought her down here.

— good to be honey to be sweet sweet dancing —

'It's as if their minds had been destroyed — no, that's too strong — as if their minds had been suborned. Changed. Made alien.' But on the other hand, she thought, it was comforting. It helped, when you knew you were dying, to be —

— sweet sweet honey dancing —

— it was so easy to believe and so much

— sweet sweet good good —

— sweeter than being a reporter —

— to be dancing to be honey to be good sweet —

'It's so much easier,' she said aloud. 'To be sweet to be honey dancing to be sweet sweet honey, to be dancing the code —'

— dancing the code —

'A whole city — a whole world —' It sounded wonderful, and yes so easy so *sweet sweet*, now that she didn't have to think any more.

– dancing the code dancing the code –
'*– sweet sweet honey observe report honey sweet –*'
– dancing the code dancing the code dancing the code –

The Brigadier stared at the locked door of the armoury and wondered why there wasn't anybody on duty. There wasn't anybody on duty anywhere in UNIT HQ. There wasn't a sentry on the gate; there wasn't a duty officer on the desk; and now there was no one in the armoury.

Something was wrong. Seriously wrong.

The Brigadier started to walk back along the cold, silent, neon-lit corridor towards his office, where he kept his own gun. But he had only taken a few steps when he remembered two things. Firstly, that he had locked the drawer where he kept the gun, and thrown away the key.

And secondly, why he had done it.

He hesitated, staring at his boots, feeling the chill of the corridor soak into him.

No use, he decided. It had to be done. He had to be armed.

Then he heard the footsteps.

He ran to the office door, which was slightly inset from the wall. Pressed himself against it, so that he was almost out of sight.

Waited.

The footsteps came closer, stopped. The Brigadier heard a sniffing sound, like a huge bloodhound catching the scent.

Then: 'Is that you, Brigadier?' The Doctor's voice.

The Brigadier didn't speak. After a moment, the sniffing sound was repeated. Then the Doctor stepped into view.

'Ah! There you are, Brigadier!' He smiled. 'We need to get to the lab as quickly as possible, to help Jo.' As he spoke, the Brigadier smelt the perfume on his breath: roses and cloves. He realized, now that he thought about it, that the smell had been around in the building since he'd first entered it.

No, thought the Brigadier. This isn't the Doctor. Or if it is there's something very wrong with him.

Aloud he said: 'I need to get my gun.'

'You won't need that, old chap, just come along with me.' The Doctor reached out a hand.

The Brigadier felt behind him for the lock, scrabbled with his keys.

'Jo!' shouted the Doctor. 'I might need a hand here!'

The Brigadier jumped past the Doctor suddenly, ran flat out down the corridor. He had to get to a phone, warn the Ministry, get some extra men –

Jo was ahead of him, running towards him.

'Help!' she screamed. 'Help me, Brigadier!'

No, he thought. She's not Jo, she doesn't need your help –

He swerved out of her path, just in time to avoid the arc of the hammer in her hand. He heard it crash into the wall behind him.

'Quickly!' The Doctor's voice.

The Brigadier passed the open door to the lab, saw a uniformed figure –

Private Shoregood –

Private Shoregood, with blood pooled around his head –

And a gun clutched in his outstretched hand.

The Brigadier heard the clatter of footsteps approaching in the corridor. They seemed to be running faster than was humanly possible.

He stepped into the lab, picked up Shoregood's gun. As he did so, he saw the other bodies, piled up carelessly against the benches. The insect-like things crawling over them.

His men. Dead. Food for some obscene aliens.

There was a sniffing sound behind him. The Brigadier turned, saw Jo in the door.

Not Jo. She had just tried to kill him.

He raised his gun. Fired.

She dropped, clutching her chest. Blood spurted out

through her hands, over her blue T-shirt.

Blood.

Human blood.

The Doctor appeared in the doorway as Jo dropped to the ground. He stepped over the body, looked at the Brigadier.

'Now, really old chap, that wasn't very sensible.'

Not the Doctor. The Doctor wouldn't speak like that. Wouldn't react like that.

And the Brigadier knew then.

Knew that he had to complete the prediction, or the Doctor would kill him.

He fired again, watched the Doctor drop to the ground, twitch and lie still.

Then he pushed the safety catch back on the gun and walked out of the laboratory with a cold expression on his face.

Book Three

Dance of Death

Eighteen

Tahir Al-Naemi didn't wake up straight away when Yamin shook his shoulder. For a moment he actually tried to turn over on his bedroll and ignore the intrusion.

Then, when he woke up properly, he was furious with himself. Even as he pulled on his boots, listened to Yamin's report of approaching jeeps, asked how many, heard the shouts outside, checked the clip of his Kalashnikov for ammunition – even then he was thinking, this is the second time in twenty-four hours that I've been caught napping.

Am I getting too old? he wondered. Is thirty-six past the age for fighting?

Outside, the night was not entirely dark: a half-moon gave enough light to give the desert shape and shadow, if no colour. I had been sleeping too long anyway, thought Tahir confusedly. He could see the vehicles approaching: plumes of dust to the east, half obscuring the yellow light of headlamps.

His father was standing outside the tent, looking through binoculars at the road.

'Well?' asked Tahir.

'Jeeps, Land Rovers,' said the old man. 'Eight of them.' He paused. 'There are women and a child I think. It's hard to tell.'

Tahir relaxed a little, went back into the tent and found his own binoculars. But when he came out again someone was shouting, 'GAF! It's the GAF!'

There was a clatter of metal as guns were readied. Tahir ignored it, sighted his binoculars. Sure enough, there was

177

the green-and-red flag of the Libyan-backed people, fluttering on the radio aerial of the lead jeep.

His father called the GAF traitors; but as far as Tahir could understand it their only treachery was to take foreign money, and to have started the fight earlier than his own people.

The convoy was slowing down now, spreading itself out on the dusty apron of rock below the encampment. Tahir could see the figures in the lead jeep well enough to pick out their faces in the reflected light of the headlamps. One of them looked like – probably was –

Al Tayid.

Tahir drew in a breath, strode forward across the sand. He took out his pistol, fired a shot into the air; several of his men did the same, and then they were all up, crowding forward, shooting skywards. A figure in one of the jeeps reached up and fired a shot, but was waved down by *Al Tayid.*

Tahir waved his own men down. 'They have women with them,' he shouted. 'And children. We should be careful.'

The shots stopped.

'I am not sure about this,' said his father's voice into the silence. 'Why should he bring any of his civilian people?'

Al Tayid got out of his jeep and ran across to Tahir and his father. He embraced the older man first, kissing him on both cheeks; then did the same to Tahir.

'My brothers in the desert!' he said. 'I am so glad to see you!'

'Why have you brought your women?' said the *Sakir* briskly. 'We cannot accommodate them.'

Al Tayid glanced at him sharply. 'You may have to,' he said. 'These are all of my people. All the Free Giltaz that remain, apart from those who are with you, and those abroad.'

'All?' Tahir looked at the figures disembarking from the jeeps, noticing for the first time the absence of any joy there. The dull, dejected looks on the faces of even the younger men. He looked back at Vincent Tayid.

'We were raided,' he said simply. 'First by Benari, then by his friends.'

Tahir frowned. 'The Moroccans?'

Vincent shook his head, looked at the *Sakir*. '*Al Harwaz*.' He paused. 'We were hoping that you could help us.'

The Brigadier watched as a loading truck manoeuvred its way across the crowded tarmac towards the waiting Hercules, its diesel engine grunting with every change of gear. In the brilliant floodlights, the vehicles and men scattered around the plane looked too sharp and clear to be real; it was as if they were plastic toys, moving around on clockwork motors. Even the plane itself seemed plastic, Airfix. It was hard to believe it could really fly. That it would really fly to Morocco.

Voices shouted orders, and a crate of ammunition was taken off the loading truck and carried up the ramp. The Brigadier did something he very rarely did, and allowed himself a fantasy: that the orders were being shouted by children, that the plastic-looking trucks and jeeps were really just toys, that the whole thing somehow wasn't his responsibility, his operation.

That he hadn't shot the Doctor and Jo.

But they hadn't been the real Doctor and Jo. He was sure that Jo hadn't been human any more. That the Doctor hadn't been – whatever he normally was. That they were different, alien, dangerous. He was *sure*.

Almost sure.

He remembered the red blood flowing through Jo's hands, staining her shirt.

Human blood.

'– report, sir?'

The Brigadier frowned, looked up and saw Sergeant Osgood. 'Medical report?' he asked. 'Yes, yes. Straight away. I've been waiting.'

179

'Sir?' Osgood looked puzzled. 'I don't know about a medical report, sir. I just wondered how often you'd like me to report from Rabat whilst you're in Kebiria.'

'Oh – ah, yes. Every –' The Brigadier stopped, shook his head, realizing that he had no idea how often he wanted Osgood to report. 'Use your own judgement, Osgood,' he said finally.

Osgood nodded. 'And the satellite radio unit? Can we take it?'

Again, the Brigadier couldn't think. There was the satellite radio unit. There were other things. They all had to be got on the plane. But it wasn't important, it just couldn't be as important as whether –

'Liaise with Johnson,' said the Brigadier wearily. 'He's in charge of loading.'

Osgood hesitated, saluted, set off at a trot towards the loading ramp of the plane. The Brigadier stared after him, knowing that he should have made a decision. He couldn't just stand here worrying all the time. He hadn't shot the Doctor and Jo. He couldn't have done. The real Doctor and Jo were still in Kebiria – weren't they? That was why he was going back out there. Wasn't it?

Or was he just trying to prove –

What?

Could he have shot to wound? No, there hadn't been time to think, to risk it.

There was time for the Doctor. He wasn't attacking you when you shot him.

But once I'd shot Jo I had to go through with it. Had to finish it. Dammit the Doctor's alien anyway –

So you don't trust him? You want him to be dead?

Suddenly the Brigadier couldn't stand any more of it. He bunched his fists, set off at a run for the airport building.

Yates was standing in the doorway, looking tired.

'Yates!' snapped the Brigadier. 'Take charge of the loading. I need to make a phone call.'

The Captain blinked. 'A phone call, sir?'

180

'The morgue. I need to find out — well, you know what I need to find out.'

Yates stared at him for a moment, then nodded. 'Of course, sir.' He stepped aside to let the Brigadier pass.

The Brigadier saw a phone on the desk, picked it up, began to dial. He wondered how significant it was that he knew the number of the UNIT morgue off by heart.

'What do you mean, you couldn't get their clothes off?' Dr Richard Moore stared fiercely at the mortuary assistant. He'd heard some lousy excuses in his time but this one beat them all. 'Look, I've just been woken up in the middle of the night and asked to do twenty autopsies in two hours; I've got Lethbridge-Stewart on the phone doing his nut because we haven't done his two civvies yet; and you're telling me you've put them on the slabs fully dressed? You'd better have a good reason —' he glared at the name tag on the man's white lab coat '— Timothy Witchell, or you'll be going on report.'

The assistant shook his head miserably. 'Try it for yourself, sir. It's impossible.'

Moore strode across the rubber-tiled floor of the morgue, pulled out the two drawers indicated by the bewildered man. A wave of cold air hit him in the face, scented with some kind of perfume. There lay the person that Lethbridge-Stewart called the Doctor, resplendent in his cape, pale green frilled shirt, trousers and boots; and in the drawer next to him Miss Grant, in her blue T-shirt and brown trousers.

Moore shook his head, bent down over the Doctor, pulled at the buttons of the shirt.

They wouldn't undo.

In fact, there was nothing for them to undo from; the buttons and the shirt seemed to be part of the same piece of material. And when he pulled at the collar of the shirt, the flesh of the Doctor's neck came with it.

Moore asked Witchell for a magnifying lens and took a closer look. He could see fibres running from the shirt into the skin, changing colour as they went. He shook his head.

'If they ever were human, something very strange has happened to them – something that didn't happen to the others.' He made a fist, tapped at the Doctor's forehead, shook his head again.

It didn't *feel* right.

He looked up at Witchell. 'Look, the Brigadier's still on the line out there. I'm going to tell him what I've found so far – you get this one on to a table for autopsy. Never mind about the clothes. Right?'

Witchell nodded. Moore strode out of the room, set off for the phone at a run.

When Moore had left the room, Tim Witchell went to the autopsy room, opened the door, switched the light on over the bare slab. Then he went back, rolled a stretcher trolley up to the Doctor's body and prepared to lift it.

He noticed that the Doctor's eyes were open.

He didn't like to think of a corpse being sawn apart with its eyes staring like that: it didn't seem right somehow. So he leaned over the Doctor's body, pushed the eyes closed again.

A hand reached up and grabbed his arm.

'I wouldn't do that if I were you, old chap. I need them to see with.'

Witchell started back, shouted, 'Dr Moore –'

But the Doctor's other hand shot up and blocked his mouth. Witchell tried to pull his head away, found that it was held tight by the hand that had been holding his arm. He punched at the 'corpse' with his arms, but it sat upright, pushed him back against the hard metal of the cold store.

Witchell felt a rich, cloying smell enter his nose and his throat.

A somehow soothing smell.

A smell to dream about.

He dreamed.

182

Nineteen

When Jo woke up she was walking. Or, more accurately, her feet were making walking motions but she was actually being dragged along, each arm clamped tightly by the china-hard hands of one of the alien copies. Ahead of her, two similar figures were holding the Doctor. Beyond him was one of the hippo-sized defenders, mandibles raised as if to strike.

Jo opened her mouth to shout a warning, then realized that the creature was walking backwards, keeping pace with them. Jo looked away, uneasily.

'Doctor?' she called.

'Jo! Are you all right?'

'I think so. How long have we been —' She abruptly remembered her dream, the other Jo winking and walking away, leaving her to die. Or had it been only a dream?

She shuddered.

'About twelve hours, I should think,' the Doctor was saying.

'Doctor, I remember someone who looked like me. She said I was dead.'

The Doctor looked over his shoulder, smiled. 'Well, you're not dead, I can assure you of that.'

Jo grinned, relaxed a little. If the Doctor was smiling, things couldn't be too bad. She looked around her. The passageway they were moving through was featureless, with walls of what looked like baked mud lined with slightly luminous fungi. More light came from somewhere ahead. Jo hoped it was daylight, but knew that it wasn't very likely.

'Where are we going?' she asked the Doctor.

'Well, we're moving in a south-westerly direction, at a slope of about ten degrees downwards. We have to be about four hundred feet below the surface of the desert by now. Apart from that –' he lowered his voice slightly '– I haven't the faintest idea.'

Jo turned her head slightly, looked into the perfect, expressionless face of one of her captors. 'Do *you* know where we're going?' she asked.

There was no response.

'They're not likely to be very talkative, I'm afraid,' called the Doctor. 'I think you'll find that they communicate largely by gesture and scent.'

'Like insects?' asked Jo, remembering her discussion with Akram.

'Yes, but also like fish, some reptiles, and quite a lot of mammals,' the Doctor said. 'Sophisticated aural communication is quite rare, evolutionarily speaking. The Venusians, I seem to remember, had a system of hand-signals which many of their cultures used almost exclusively for intimate conversation. The clan Dhallenidhall in particular thought it quite rude to speak aloud. Except in an emergency, of course. And then there are the Delphons, who communicate by means of eyebrow movements. If you think about it, sound isn't really a necessary part of intelligent communication, merely a convenient one.'

Jo wondered if being frog-marched down a dark corridor by unfriendly aliens to an uncertain destination was really the best time to engage in abstruse cultural and evolutionary speculations; but she knew the Doctor, and kept quiet. If they survived, and she managed to remember what he was saying, she might even find it interesting.

But before the Doctor could say anything more, the light ahead of them brightened and the passageway opened out into a space even larger than the brood chamber. Jo saw distant walls of what appeared to be concrete, hundreds of 'men' in Kebirian Army uniforms, and several of the defenders, stationed against the walls with their mandibles raised.

Straight ahead of her was a sausage-shaped object the size of a small cathedral, faced in something that looked like white plaster. As the defender walking ahead of the Doctor clumped off to one side, she saw that there was an entrance in the nearest wall of the cathedral-sized object. She saw a crude wooden door, roughly oval in shape; a flight of metal steps of the type used to board aircraft led up to it. The copies holding the Doctor pulled him towards the bottom of the steps, and Jo was forced to follow.

The Doctor looked over his shoulder, muttered, 'I think some of those Kebirians are originals.'

Jo frowned. 'Real people?'

The Doctor nodded.

'What does that mean?'

The Doctor grinned. 'I wish I knew. With luck it might mean we have some allies.'

They were marched up the steps. The door had swung open ahead of them, apparently of its own accord; the copies pushed and pulled them through. Beyond was a narrow passageway which sloped downwards. Jo's captors had to release her arms and let her walk by herself; but they stayed on guard, one ahead of her, one behind, as they followed the twists and turns of the passageway.

At last they came to another doorway, in which stood the figure of a little man with a round face and round spectacles, wearing a white lab coat.

When he spoke, Jo jumped, startled to realize that he was human.

'I am Sadeq Zalloua,' he said. 'Welcome to the control centre.'

He stood aside, gestured them through into a large room – or at least, Jo supposed it was a room. A mass of multicoloured tubing covered the walls and ceiling. Here and there knots of tubes bulged from the walls. In the middle of the room, looking totally out of place, was a large wooden desk. Behind the desk, his deeply lined face impassive, was Khalil Benari, Prime Minister of Kebiria.

'Well find out for certain, man, and report to me as soon as you can. I need to know.' Lethbridge-Stewart was practically shouting over the phone: Dr Moore opened his mouth to reply, was interrupted by a further barked instruction. 'And you'll have to contact me through Rabat control, the flight's ready to leave. Is that clear?'

'Yes, sir,' said Moore quickly.

'Very well.' The phone clicked and went dead.

Moore hurried back to the mortuary, the Brigadier's voice still ringing in his ears.

'Witchell?' he called.

There was no reply. Moore shrugged, strode into the room, ready to give the man an ear-bashing. If he hadn't done what he'd been told to do –

The two drawers had been closed, the light was on in the autopsy room. Dr Moore saw a figure in there.

'Witchell?' repeated Moore.

A figure stepped forward into the morgue: the Doctor.

The Doctor whom he'd last seen as a corpse. Who still had red blood staining his shirt.

'What –?' began Moore.

He never finished the question. True to the pattern of her original, the copy of Jo brought the corner of a heavy steel instrument tray down on his skull.

But unlike her original, she used killing force.

'You want us to help you?' asked the Doctor. He gave a sidelong glance at Jo, raised his eyebrows. Jo grinned back.

Behind the wooden desk, Khalil Benari remained impassive. 'We were hoping you could. That is why we had you woken and brought here. I am sorry for your –' he hesitated '– your treatment at the hands of the Xarax.

186

It seems we no longer fully control them.' He glanced at Zalloua, a flicker of anger in his eyes. 'You may be the only one who can stop what we have started,' he went on, 'or I should say, what Monsieur Zalloua has started.'

The Doctor looked from the Prime Minister to the man in the lab coat, who was standing beside the desk, twisting his hands together as if he were trying to tie knots in his fingers. 'Well,' said the Doctor. 'Perhaps Monsieur Zalloua had better explain what he's been doing. Then I might be able to help.'

Benari gestured at the scientist, who jerked his hand to his mouth, bit at a finger. 'There was a legend,' he said. 'A legend about a place in the desert where there were all-powerful demons. Demons who could imitate anything made by men, who could raze a city with the beating of their wings —' He broke off, laughed nervously. 'Of course I didn't believe that, but I had made a study of such things. Many such legends in fact originate with visits by extraterrestrials. From my contacts in the scientific world, I knew that there had been several such visits recently.

'It was significant, I thought, that the legend made no mention of the destruction of these "demons". So I searched the area of desert which seemed to correspond to the place described in the legend, using infra-red detectors, until I found an anomaly. Then I went and had a look.

'I found an insect-like creature, living underground like a huge termite. I —' He hesitated, twisted his hands together again.

Benari interrupted, said briskly, 'He found a way of using these "Xarax", as he calls them, in the service of our Revolution. He gave them a set of instructions using something called pheromones.' He pronounced the word slowly, carefully, glanced up at the Doctor as if for reassurance.

The Doctor nodded. 'Chemicals emitted by one animal to control the behaviour of another. Yes.' He sat down on the edge of Benari's desk, steepled his hands under his chin. 'Go on.'

'He said we could instruct the Xarax to destroy all the Giltean terrorists. He said they could do it on their own if we gave them the right instructions — we wouldn't have to fight at all.'

'But that's impossible!' said the Doctor. He looked from Benari to Zalloua and back again; Jo could see from his face that he was seriously alarmed. 'Even the most sophisticated pheromonal control systems only work in general terms — how on Earth did you expect the Xarax to know the difference between one human being and another?'

Zalloua hesitated, then said, 'If you allow the Xarax queen to —' he hesitated again '— to taste your pheromones, by licking your skin for instance, then she can link with you directly. She can see what you see, feel what you feel —'

'That's incredibly dangerous!' interrupted the Doctor. 'She might pick up any idea that's in your head! You could have programmed the Xarax to do anything at all!'

There was a long pause. Eventually Zalloua said in a small voice, 'But surely the fact that I consciously intended to let them fight the terrorists would make her choose that course of action over any other.'

'Of course not,' said the Doctor. 'Think about it, man. The Xarax aren't intelligent in themselves. How can they tell the difference between a conscious intention and anything else that might be in your head? All they'll have picked up is a general idea of what you wanted to do.'

Zalloua looked up sharply: suddenly he seemed very excited. 'You mean if the idea had been sufficiently general, they might have been able to carry it out?'

The Doctor nodded. 'Yes. But the idea you've tried to communicate is too complex. We'll have to find a way of simplifying —'

He broke off suddenly as the floor lurched beneath their feet. Benari jumped up, uttering a grunt of surprise and fear. Jo felt the floor lurch again, heard a hissing sound behind her. She spun round to make a run for the passageway they had used to enter the chamber. But as she watched, the entrance disappeared.

The Doctor ran across the rippling floor and pushed at the place where the entrance had been, but it wouldn't open. Benari ran across to him, stumbled, caught his elbow. 'What is happening?'

Behind him, Zalloua wailed, 'The control sequence is broken!' He dashed to the wall, began pulling at the complex tubing. 'If I can link –'

'Stop that!' shouted the Doctor. 'You haven't the first idea of what you're doing! If you let me –'

'Tell me, what is happening?' said Benari again.

The Doctor looked at him irritably. 'This room is reverting to its natural state – some kind of gland or digestive organ no doubt.'

The walls were starting to shift, colours bleeding out of the pipes and running like melted wax.

'What do we do now, Doctor?' asked Jo.

'Well, first of all, we get the system back under control.' He fished in his pockets for a moment, produced his sonic screwdriver.

But as he did so Jo saw a movement on the ceiling above him. She looked up, saw a drop of honey-like fluid bulge out from the white surface.

'Doctor!'

He too looked up, just as the droplet fell. Then he dropped to the floor, covering his eyes and rolling in agony.

'Doctor!' shrieked Jo.

The Doctor sat up slowly and removed his hand from his eyes, revealing a deep red welt over the skin around his eyelids. His eyes were tight shut. He pulled at the skin around them for a moment, then winced and shook his head.

'It's no good, Jo,' he said. 'You're going to have to help me. I'm blind.'

Twenty

Sergeant Dave Greene heard the commotion from the direction of the mortuary and frowned. These medical types, always horsing around – what was it this time? Greene shook his head, struggled to return his attention to the *Daily Mail* crossword spread out on the polished wooden desk in front of him.

'Famous novelist, six and six,' he muttered.

Then he heard the scream.

A man's scream, ending in a gurgling sound. Then a crash of metal.

Whatever was going on, it wasn't a joke.

Greene got up, ran down the corridor from the duty desk to the mortuary area. When he turned the corner, he saw the Doctor standing by the door of the mortuary, blood spattering his shirt.

But hadn't they said the Doc was –

'Sergeant Greene? We need a hand in here.'

The Sergeant drew his gun, stepped cautiously forward. The Doctor gestured him through the door.

Inside –

Inside was a scene from a nightmare. The corpses were on the floor –

– on the floor for Christ's sake all tangled up and those insects what the hell are those insects –

He raised his gun, then saw Jo Grant. She was standing on the back of a chair, holding a steel tray. The tray arced down towards him.

He jumped back, brought his gun up and fired.

Jo tottered on the chair, then looked down at the hole

190

in her stomach and grinned.

'Sorry, Dave,' she said. 'We've got used to that.'

The Doctor's hand went over his mouth, and Dave Greene smelled roses and cloves.

And started to dream.

The perfumed smoke of the fire gave an illusion of security inside the camel-wool tent, but Tahir knew it was only an illusion. He was used to the dangers of war; he was used to living with the thought that at any moment the tent might be blasted away, but this was worse. The story that Vincent Tayid had told him was like something out of an evil dream. It was hard to accept that it was real, that it had happened only yesterday.

But the look on the man's face was enough to assure him that this was the case.

'Didn't the guns have any effect on them?' he asked Vincent.

'Oh, the guns killed them all right, but we only had one battery left. The jets had taken care of the others.'

Vincent had a glass of tea in his hand, but it had long since grown cold. Mohammad had ordered every lamp extinguished: only the faint glow of the fire lit their faces in the tent.

'The jets were sent to "soften up" our defences,' said Vincent. 'That's how I know *Al Harwaz* and Benari are allies. It is too much to call it coincidence.'

'I agree,' said Mohammad from the darkness on the other side of the fire. '*Al Harwaz* were allied with bandits before. That is probably how the Caliphs were overthrown.'

'It doesn't say that in your legend,' said Tahir. 'It says they were allied with the Caliphs.'

'That's only because you persist in treating it as a legend, rather than as a record of something that really happened,' said his father irritably. 'If you think about it, what was that merchant Ibrahim up to? Why didn't he give the Caliph's men direct access to the powers of *Al*

Harwaz? Or, if he was really a merchant, why didn't he lie about the cost and make a big profit, in the way merchants always do?'

Vincent's fist thumped softly on the thick wool rug.

'We are not here to discuss legends!' he said. 'We need to take action now!'

'You propose to attack *Al Harwaz*?' said Tahir, letting the doubt show in his voice.

'What choice have we got? Should we sit here and wait for them to wipe us out? Or appeal to the United Nations, perhaps?'

'You are right,' said Mohammad. 'I think we should attack.'

Tahir glanced across at his father in surprise, but could see nothing except a shadow on the other side of the fire.

'How can we hope to succeed against these –' he nearly said, 'demons' '– alien beings, if they are invincible as you say?'

'I've told you, they're not invincible!' said Vincent. 'You have seen the base. It is only mud. Mud walls! And the creatures are only flesh. With enough men and enough weapons – and with the advantage of surprise – we can defeat them.'

'You have a plan?' asked Tahir.

Vincent smiled. 'Yes. I am famous for them, you know.' He paused. 'These *Al Harwaz*, they do not like fire, eh?'

'How did you know that?' asked the *Sakir*.

'By the way they burn.' Vincent was grinning now, enjoying the game. 'How many small canisters do you have, my friends? And how much petrol to put in them?'

Jo held the Doctor's hand, directing it and the sonic screwdriver it was holding along the maze of tubing on the wall. The screwdriver twittered softly, almost inaudible against the creaking, rumbling sound made by the undulating walls of the 'room'.

'We're looking for a resonance point,' said the Doctor.

'Quickly!' said Benari from behind them. 'It is burning me!'

'I'm going as quickly as I can, Prime Minister,' said the Doctor. Jo wondered how he could be so polite to the man: then remembered that he hadn't seen the wreckage of Vincent's camp after the government raid, hadn't seen the burning hospital, hadn't seen the little girl die.

She shook her head, forced herself to concentrate. 'Resonance point,' she said, repeating the Doctor's instruction.

'I don't know what that means —' Zalloua's voice. Jo decided to ignore him.

The floor jolted suddenly as the screwdriver passed over a point where two purple pipes crossed a single iridescent green one.

'That's it!' said the Doctor. 'Now find that spot again, Jo.'

Jo guided his hand back across the maze to what she hoped was the right point.

'Yes, that should do it,' muttered the Doctor. He adjusted the screwdriver: there was a brief, loud whirring sound.

The floor tilted, rolling Jo off her feet. She saw Zalloua with a hand clutching a bundle of broken piping, struggling to keep his balance. He shouted, 'This is worse! Reverse what you have done, Doctor.'

The Doctor took no notice. 'Close your eyes, all of you, and roll into a ball. It'll help.'

'What do you mean?' asked Benari, who was also struggling to stand. Parts of his jacket were slimy and smoking where the acid had burned them.

'I've made it think we're indigestible, so it's trying to excrete us,' said the Doctor. 'Make yourself as small and frictionless as you can, you'll make things easier for it.'

'But —' began Jo. Before she could complete the objection, a shower of cold, stinging fluid washed over her. She pushed her head between her knees, closed her eyes, felt herself sliding across the lurching floor. She banged against something, rebounded, skidded around, felt the skin of her face stinging. Instinctively she put her hands up to further protect her eyes.

Then she was falling, rolling down a long wet channel. She hit something hard, cried out; for a moment she was falling freely. Then she landed on a damp, soft surface. After a moment, she heard another body land beside her. She opened her eyes, saw the Doctor and, behind him, Benari hanging six feet above her on the lip of the jaws of – the jaws –

The jaws were at least thirty feet across, and above them towered a chitinous face the size of a large house. Antennae sprouted on top like small trees growing from a wall. The body behind it heaved up, cathedral-sized, under the dark roof of the nest chamber.

'Doctor!' shrieked Jo. 'It's enormous!'

The Doctor sat up, turned his sightless eyes in the direction of the huge face. 'Now steady on, Jo. It will be big. We were inside its body, remember, and only a small part of it at that.'

As he spoke, Zalloua appeared inside the huge mouth. He stood up, stared out past the Doctor and Jo. 'We have to regain control!' he shouted.

Jo looked over her shoulder, and saw why he was shouting. The nest defenders were advancing towards them from all sides, their jaws open.

Zalloua pulled out a gun, fired at one of the defenders. It didn't even stop.

Jo pulled the Doctor to his feet. 'Doctor! We've got to run!'

She led him away, ran into a phalanx of advancing defenders, turned –

Too late. She felt the long jaws close around her.

She smelled roses and cloves.

She screamed.

Twenty-One

'Greyhound to trap seventy-four. Greyhound to trap seventy-four. Come in, Rashid.'

The Brigadier tapped his swagger stick against the map on his knee, scanned the darkened landscape below.

Nothing.

He pushed the radio switch to 'receive', but heard only static. 'Where the hell are they?' he snapped.

Yates, piloting the helicopter, pointed down at the shadowy desert. A smudge of light moved slowly across the landscape; after a moment the Brigadier realized that it was a plume of dust, dimly illuminated by the light of the moon.

He glanced at his watch: six-thirty local time. About half an hour till dawn.

'Well, they'd better get a move on, or they're not going to get to the nest before it's light,' he said.

'I'm not sure it's them, sir,' said Yates.

'Eh?' But the Brigadier was instantly alert. True, he was expecting the enemy in the air more than on the ground; a squadron of Harriers were on watch around the nest, and Americans had carrier-based fighters on standby in the Gulf of Kebiria. But the Brigadier had insisted on Rabat sending ground support. He wanted to destroy the nest, but he wanted to do it carefully.

He wasn't going to risk killing the Doctor and Jo again.

If he hadn't already killed them, that was. He still hadn't heard from Moore.

He shook his head. No point in worrying about that

now. He got out his binoculars, tried to focus on the blur of dust. He thought he saw something that might have been a jeep; but on the other hand it might have been anything.

He opened the radio mike again. 'Greyhound to trap forty-one. Do you read?'

'Trap forty-one,' came the crackly response from the Harrier squadron leader. 'Are you seeing what I'm seeing?'

'Dust devil at –' the Brigadier looked at the map '– November hotel zero-six-five?'

'That's the one. Want me to go down and take a look?'

But before the Brigadier could reply, flickers of light burst out around the dust cloud.

Muzzle flashes.

'Or perhaps I'd better not,' said the voice of the Harrier pilot.

The Brigadier changed to the UNIT emergency frequency. 'Trap seventy-four! Rashid, do you read me?'

There was a loud explosion, and the helicopter slewed sideways.

'What the –?' said Yates. He yanked at the stick, pulling the chopper into a steep climb. 'I thought these fellows didn't have any anti-aircraft capability?'

There was another explosion, a little further away this time.

'They don't,' said the Brigadier. 'Or at least, they weren't supposed to.'

The helicopter lurched again, and the airframe began to shake in a way which the Brigadier knew probably meant trouble. Yates wrestled with the stick, cursed as the chopper went into a slow but accelerating descent. He glanced over his shoulder at the Brigadier.

'We've lost the fuel line, sir. Get ready for an emergency landing.'

A Superhawk and a helicopter in less than forty-eight hours, thought the Brigadier. If I get out of this alive, the

Minister's going to have my hide.

The radio crackled and bleeped: the Brigadier opened the switch.

It was Butler from the Harrier. 'Trap forty-one to Greyhound. You all right down there, sir?'

'We may be out of the game,' replied the Brigadier, watching the darkened desert rising towards him. He took a deep breath. If the aliens had anti-aircraft capability –

Then he was going to have to knock the nest out. Now. No questions.

Sorry, Doctor, he thought. If you're in there. If I haven't already killed you. And sorry, Jo.

The ground was getting closer. Fast. Too fast.

He glanced at Yates, who was still wrestling with the controls, but knew better than to break his concentration.

'Butler,' said the Brigadier at last. 'I want you to go for the alien construct – fire at will, flatten the thing if you can. Don't give them any chance to return fire.'

'Will do. Good luck, sir.'

'Thank you, Butler,' said the Brigadier. 'We're going to need it. Over and out.'

Tahir heard the helicopter's motor stop, and half a minute later the sound of the impact as the craft hit the ground. He looked up, struggled to find the crash site, but the moonlight wasn't bright enough for him to see clearly.

Suddenly there was an explosion of light. Tahir covered his eyes against the glare, but it was too late: the after-images on his retinas told him he'd lost a precious half-minute of night vision, maybe longer.

'We should go and help them out,' said Jamil, next to him. Jamil was one of Vincent's men: a keen, young, Libyan-trained killer. Vincent was ahead somewhere, with the first wave of men who were supposed to blow a hole in the nest wall. Tahir had a feeling that Jamil had been left back to keep an eye on him.

'The ones in the helicopter are beyond help, I should think,' he observed. He risked uncovering his eyes, saw only a dim flickering of flames. He reckoned that the site of the crash was at least half a mile away.

There was a distant stutter of gunfire.

'There are others!' said Jamil eagerly. 'They are still fighting!'

'We have no idea of the numbers and I'm not even sure which side is which,' said Tahir. 'If you think you can work it out, go ahead. I suggest we stick to our planned mission. Vincent won't be pleased if his back-up goes off chasing another battle.'

Before Jamil could reply, there was a brilliant flash from the direction of the alien tower, followed quickly by the roar of an explosion. The sequence was repeated three times; only when the echoes of the last explosion had died away did Tahir hear the sound of jets, see the three exhaust flares curving away against the dark sky.

He scowled. As soon as they'd heard the sounds of tanks and armoured personnel carriers moving across the desert, Tahir had argued that they pull out; but Vincent had insisted that they continue. 'We don't want the United Nations claiming credit for our victory, eh?' he'd said. But it was now becoming increasingly obvious that Vincent had made the wrong decision. Tahir knew that it wouldn't be the first time that had happened.

'Come on, then,' said Jamil. 'We follow *Al Tayid*.' He got up and climbed across the rough rocks, giving orders to his men as he passed them. They jogged towards the nest, the metal petrol canisters strapped to their waists making them look as if they were aliens themselves.

Tahir frowned. What was the GAF man doing? Did he think that those explosions had been Vincent's work? Surely it wasn't possible that he had failed to see the jets? It would be suicidal to take those men in. Ahead, the mound was a shadow against the mountains; in the half-darkness it was impossible to tell how much, or how little, the missile strikes had damaged it.

'Wait!' Tahir called. 'The planes might come back!' But he had left it far too late. Jamil was beyond hearing.

He stood up, gazed around him, tried to make a sensible assessment of the situation. But before he could think, bright yellow light flared above him. Tahir looked up, saw a cloud of burning fuel that, a few seconds before, must have been a jet aircraft.

The light from the explosion shone on the blue-black carapaces of hundreds of Xarax helicopters as they dropped out of the night sky towards him.

The Brigadier clutched at his ankle and wished he'd taken up the opportunity of a refresher course in helicopter emergency escape procedures. He'd always thought it was a case of 'if in doubt, jump'. But no doubt it mattered when you jumped, he thought.

He had a feeling he'd jumped a few feet too soon.

'Are you all right, sir?' came Yates's voice from somewhere in the darkness.

'I've sprained my ankle, cricked my back and I've got a hole in my arm which seems to have opened up again under the strain of impact,' said the Brigadier irritably. 'Otherwise I'm quite well, thank you.'

Yates appeared over the top of a rock, his face dimly lit by the flames from the wreck of the helicopter. The Brigadier struggled to get up, winced as he put his weight on his injured ankle.

Yates came down and helped him up. As he stood, he saw a flare of light from the direction of the nest.

'Looks like Butler's lot have got to work, sir,' observed Yates.

The Brigadier grunted, shook his head. 'I just hope that the Doctor and Jo aren't in there, that's all.'

'Jo?' asked Yates, glancing at the Brigadier sharply. 'I thought she'd escaped from prison. She could be anywhere.'

So could the Doctor, thought the Brigadier.

Best not to think about it, really. He had to do his job. People got killed.

A lot of people.

Definitely best not to think about it.

He could see a little now, well enough to make out the shadows of rocks all around him. 'Help me get up there, Yates,' he said, pointing at the highest of them. 'We'll see if there are any friendly forces around.'

'I'm not sure that's a good idea, sir,' said Yates. 'I'm fairly sure I saw some Kebirian troops west-south-west of here. We ought to keep –' He broke off, as white light flared behind him.

The Brigadier blinked a few times, then, as his eyes adjusted, he saw a young man in the uniform of a Kebirian Army sergeant pointing a machine-pistol at him. Behind him, someone held a powerful torch.

'We're so glad you're still alive,' said the young man.

'So are we,' said Yates. His hand was near the holster of his gun, but it moved away as more Kebirian soldiers appeared around them.

'We're sorry we had to shoot you down,' the Kebirian sergeant went on.

'That's all right,' said the Brigadier quickly. 'Orders are orders, I understand.'

The Sergeant started down the slope towards them. The Brigadier became aware of a strong smell of perfume. Now where had he smelled that before? – Oh, yes. The Doctor. And Jo.

The fakes.

Which meant –

The Sergeant was standing in front of them now, his gun levelled at the Brigadier. He smiled boyishly.

'You must come with us to the nest,' he said. 'You will make honey. You will be dancing the code.'

The Brigadier blinked. 'I beg your pardon?'

The young soldier repeated his statement, in exactly the same words, with the same boyish smile.

A smile of absolute conviction.

'Now look here,' said the Brigadier, trying to stifle a growing sense of unease. 'Under the terms of the Geneva Convention, we –'

'There is no more Geneva Convention,' said the soldier, still smiling. 'There is no more Law of War. There is only dancing the code.'

Dry soil falling on to her face woke Jo. She sat up quickly. Her body felt stiff, uncomfortable: her trousers pinched at the waist, her shoes felt several sizes too small. Before she could think about this, the floor jolted beneath her.

– *honey honey good good sweet sweet dancing honey dancing* –

Had she left the nest? Was she being taken somewhere in a truck? She couldn't see a thing.

The floor jolted again, and another rain of dry soil fell on her body. With a shock, she remembered something in her –

Dreams? Had they been dreams?

Zalloua and Benari – the room that tried to digest her – the Doctor –

The Doctor was blind.

– *honey honey sweet sweet to be UNDER ATTACK THE NEST IS UNDER ATTACK* –

The ground began shaking from side to side. There was still no light. Jo rolled against something soft: another prisoner? She prodded at the soft mass, felt the rough fabric of an Army uniform.

'We've got to get out of here,' she said in a low voice.

There was no response. Or if there had been, she might not have heard it anyway: a huge rumbling sound was slowly gathering force, as if the world were falling apart –

– *THE NEST IS BROKEN THE QUEEN IS DEAD THE NEST IS BROKEN THE QUEEN IS DEAD* –

Jo felt something break away from the back of her neck, something she hadn't even been aware was there. She put a hand up, felt a stickiness that might have been blood or honey.

There was a flare of light. Dimly she saw rows of honey globules, a flailing insect-like form, huge blocks of falling rock and chitin.

201

We've won, she thought. The Xarax are beaten. They're dead. All I have to do is –

Something hit her, hard, pinning her to the ground. Loose soil fell, covering her face, making it impossible to breathe. She tried to move her arms, but they were trapped by whatever had fallen on her. She tried desperately to breathe, started to choke on the dry soil.

– *I can't die now not now please not now not when we've won I only have to breathe and I can walk out of here to BREATHE PLEASE PLEASE NO* –

But the darkness came down anyway.

Twenty-Two

The men dug in around UNIT HQ looked almost as if they were there on an exercise, thought Sergeant Benton. They were chatting, passing fags and sandwiches and flasks of tea about, not even bothering to take proper cover.

Regular army, he thought. They probably think it's a bit of a joke, this alien lark. Well, they're wrong.

He picked up his binoculars and looked through them at the HQ building beyond the wire fence. It looked peaceful, bricks gleaming red against the clear blue morning sky. Only the broken window in the front office gave the impression of anything amiss.

Benton put the binoculars down, jogged across the muddy field to the army truck where Major Huffington had made his headquarters.

The Major was sitting on a canvas chair on the sunlit side of the cab, holding an unlit pipe in one hand and a plastic mug of tea in the other. He looked up when Benton approached, nodded a greeting by way of returning the Sergeant's salute.

'You're the UNIT fellow, aren't you?'

'Yes, sir.'

'Where're your men?'

'As far as I know, sir, they're on their way over from barracks.'

The Major grunted. 'Well, as soon as they get here they're going in, you understand?'

Benton blinked. 'Yes, sir. But –'

The Major turned a pair of cold grey eyes on Benton.

203

'But what, Sergeant?'

Benton looked at his boots. 'What are our orders, sir?'

'Well, flush the alien things out, of course!' He paused. 'Don't worry, Benton, you won't be on your own. We'll give you supporting fire. Small arms and mortar, and I've got a couple of artillery pieces if the worst comes to the worst. But you've got the knowledge – what it looks like in there, and so on. And how to fight these aliens. We don't know how to do it.'

We don't, either, mate, thought Benton. We just make it up as we go along.

He looked up at Huffington, who was lighting his pipe. 'Uh – sir, don't you reckon we should wait until the Brig gets back – uh, that is, Brigadier Lethbridge-Stewart, sir?'

The cold grey eyes looked at him again.

'Lethbridge-Stewart's helicopter went down over Kebiria about half an hour ago, Sergeant. Went up in smoke. We haven't heard anything further, so we have to assume he's bought it.' Unexpectedly, the Major's expression softened and he gave Benton a sympathetic smile. 'Sorry, old chap, but there it is.'

Benton suddenly felt sick. The Brig – and Mike Yates too, probably, if the chopper had gone down. He didn't dare ask. He knew he ought to feel grief, but what he mainly felt was confusion. So many men had been killed; but Captain Yates and the Brig had seemed to be immortal, invulnerable.

Like the Doctor.

And now they were all dead. Gone. Not able to help any more.

Benton swallowed, looked down at UNIT HQ.

'We'll just have to do the best we can, sir,' he said aloud, for something to say.

The Major's voice was still sympathetic. 'That's right, sergeant. Do the best you can.'

Someone was kissing Jo on the lips. If she didn't feel so ill

204

it would have been nice. As it was, she just wanted them to go away.

Then they did go away, and Jo became aware of something unexpected. She was breathing. Her lungs hurt, her throat hurt, and there was a line of pain across her midriff and more running around her shoulders. But she was breathing, and she was fairly sure that last time she'd thought about it she hadn't expected to do that ever again.

'Come on, Jo.' The Doctor's voice. 'All you have to do is keep breathing through your mouth, and you'll be fine.'

Jo opened her eyes, saw the kind, round face of the Doctor smiling down at her.

'Wha—' Jo croaked. She tried to clear her throat, nearly choked. Her lungs heaved.

She closed her eyes for a moment, then tried again. 'What happened, Doctor?'

'Well, you were dead — or, at least, your heart had stopped. Fortunately you hadn't been dead long enough to suffer permanent brain damage, so I was able to resuscitate you.' He paused. 'Do you feel strong enough to stand up yet?'

Jo tried to sit up, felt a wave of dizziness and pain. She clenched her fists, pushed them against the hard, stony floor.

'I'm okay,' she managed to say. Then she frowned, stared into his eyes.

His eyes.

'But Doctor, you were blind!'

The Doctor smiled. 'Fortunately Xarax macroproteins are fairly similar to my own, so I was able to use them to do some repair work. In fact I very nearly had the entire situation completely under my control — as opposed to Monsieur Zalloua's — before some idiot decided to blow the nest to pieces. You see the Xarax themselves are fundamentally —' He broke off as there was a clatter of falling soil from somewhere nearby.

Jo looked around, noticed her surroundings for the first time. She was on a sloping ramp of loose mud and pieces of rock. At the top of the slope were the remains of a mud wall, topped by a ragged patch of open sky. The sky was a deep dawn blue with wisps of rosy cloud.

'Have the Xarax been destroyed?' Jo remembered the message from the nest, the tendrils or whatever they had been disconnecting from her neck. She felt a surge of hope. Perhaps it was all over.

'Possibly,' said the Doctor, then looked down at her and beamed. 'If you've got your breath back now, I think we should go and take a look.'

Jo managed a smile and got up. The dizziness returned; for a few seconds she had to lean on the Doctor for support. She kept hold of his hand as they scrambled across the treacherous slope towards the mud wall. Jo could see an entrance in it now, half-blocked by fallen earth.

As she followed the Doctor towards the entrance, she realized that there was a figure sitting there, half-obscured by fragments.

She hesitated, but the Doctor pulled her forward. 'Don't worry,' he said. 'It's only Monsieur Benari.'

They drew up to the figure and Jo realized that the Doctor was right. But the Prime Minister was barely recognizable. His clothes were torn and stained with dirt. Jo almost felt sorry for him: almost, then she remembered the bombs, the little girl dying.

He lifted his face. To Jo's surprise it was streaked with tears. 'What have I done to my country?' he said. 'What have I done to the Revolution?'

Jo did feel sorry for him then. She looked at his grey and dishevelled hair, the deep lines in his face, and suddenly realized how much older he was than he seemed to be in the posters in Kebir City and the newspaper photographs. And after all, she reasoned, he might not have been the one who gave the order for the raid on Vincent's camp. He might have been down here, in the nest. She couldn't hold a grudge against him forever because the system he had created had gone mad.

She crouched down, took his hands in hers. 'Come on, Monsieur Benari, get up,' she said. 'We've got to help the Doctor.'

The Doctor was already on the far side of the entrance, standing at the top of a steep slope leading to a gully. When he saw Jo and Benari coming he nodded and started down; Jo followed, keeping a hand in Benari's.

Although it was steep, it wasn't as hard going as it looked: crude steps had been cut into the rock. They looked old — older than the nest, thought Jo, until she remembered how old Zalloua had said the nest might be. She wondered who had built the steps, and why.

She was about half way down when she saw the Doctor, already in the gully at the bottom. He looked both ways, his hands on his hips, then up at Jo. Then he started down the gully at a run. Jo hurried after him, followed by Benari. She almost collided with the Doctor at the end: he was standing, one hand raised, facing an open expanse of rock streaked with rust-coloured sunlight and dotted with the bizarre carcasses of the Xarax 'helicopters'. Jo took another step forward, saw several figures standing a few yards away in the shadow of a rock. They were wearing combat fatigues and carrying machine pistols.

'Ah — so these are your friends,' said an angry voice. 'I see that they include the man who ordered our people killed.'

'I think you're under a misapprehension —' began the Doctor, but the young man had raised his gun. As Jo watched in horror, he started firing at them.

The Doctor shouted 'Get down!' but Jo didn't need to be told. She dived for the cover of a rock, heard a bullet whistle past her ear as she scrambled for safety.

Then, abruptly, the firing stopped.

A voice shouted, 'Not the girl! She helped us at the camp! She is a nurse!'

The voice was familiar. Jo cautiously popped her head up, saw two of the men facing each other, another three running up across the rocks. Benari was lying flat on his face on the ground, his hands over his head. The Doctor was nowhere in sight.

Three guns swung to cover her. Jo ducked down again.

'Miss Grant! You can come out! We will not hurt you!' called the familiar voice.

This time Jo recognized it. She raised her head again. 'Vincent! How did you get here?'

Vincent grinned. 'Well, I didn't have a ride in a Martian helicopter,' he said. 'But I managed all the same.'

While he was speaking, Jo saw the Doctor's head appear behind a rock. 'Good morning, gentlemen. I think we should –'

A fusillade of automatic fire interrupted him. Jo shouted 'No!' The Doctor dived to the ground – or fell, Jo wasn't sure which. 'Don't shoot the Doctor!' she yelled, scrambling out into the open and waving her hands desperately. 'Please. He's not your enemy. He's my friend.'

The firing stopped once more.

'The Doctor's my friend!' repeated Jo into the silence.

'He is a doctor?' Vincent's voice again. 'He is unarmed? You can vouch for him?'

'He's a non–combatant,' she said carefully.

Vincent turned and whispered to one of his companions.

'Okay,' said the second man. 'We agree that he can come out. But with his hands up.'

Almost immediately the Doctor emerged, his hands in the air. He gave Jo a grateful glance. 'Now, what I think we should do is –' he began again.

'We give the instructions here!' interrupted Vincent. 'We are going into the nest. You will return with Jamil here and attend to our wounded.'

The one called Jamil gestured at the prone figure of

Khalil Benari and muttered something to Vincent, who nodded.

'Well, as far as the wounded are concerned,' the Doctor was saying, 'Jo and I will be happy to help as far as we can. But I really think the rest of you will be wasting your time going into the nest now. What you have to worry about straight away is whether –'

The Doctor broke off as Vincent shouted something, pointed his gun over Jo's shoulder. Jo looked round, saw that Benari had got up and was scrambling away across the rocks. Vincent fired a single shot and Benari stopped, slowly crumpled backwards and collapsed.

'No!' screamed Jo, far too late.

Vincent walked over to Benari, looked over his shoulder at the others. 'My honour, I think,' he said. He turned the man over with his foot, put the gun against his mouth.

Jo could see that he was still alive, his eyes terrified, staring at Vincent. 'No!' she screamed again.

'Wait a minute –' began the Doctor at the same moment.

But Vincent had pulled the trigger. Blood and pieces of flesh and bone spattered over the ground.

Jo felt her stomach heave and collapsed onto the cold stone. Somewhere through the ringing in her ears she heard the Doctor's voice. 'That wasn't really necessary, gentlemen.'

'It wasn't necessary,' said Vincent's voice, thick with some emotion that Jo didn't want to identify. 'But it was justified.'

209

Twenty-Three

The Brigadier looked around at the twitching bodies of the Kebirian soldiers. They were rolling on their backs, faces blank, limbs beating against their sides in what looked like a fruitless attempt to fly. One young man was persistently banging his head against a rock: blood pooled on the dry ground beneath him.

The Brigadier shook his head, looked up at Yates who was standing on a high rock, scanning the landscape with binoculars. 'Any sign of Rashid?'

'Nothing, sir,' said Yates. 'Just a lot of these Kebirian fellows.' He paused. 'All out of action by the look of it.'

The Brigadier sighed. 'Those shots must have come from somewhere.' He struggled to his feet, winced as he put his weight on his injured ankle. But it wasn't as bad as it had been ten minutes ago. He reckoned that he could walk, as long as he was careful. He cautiously climbed the incline to the base of the rock where Yates was standing.

There were two single shots in the distance, from the direction of the ruined nest. The Brigadier shielded his eyes from the low sun, stared, thought he saw some figures moving amongst the reddish rocks and slabs of fallen nest material.

'It's the Doctor!' said Yates suddenly, the binoculars still against his eyes. 'And Jo!'

They were alive!

The Brigadier felt as if a set of clamps had been removed from his head and chest. 'Are you sure?' he asked.

'Certain,' said Yates. 'Take a look.'

He handed over the binoculars. The Brigadier saw the

familiar figure in his cape and coloured shirt, Jo's head of blonde hair. There were some other people there – Arabs by the look of them. They seemed to be arguing.

'Better get over and say hello, I suppose,' he said to Yates.

The Captain nodded, started out at a run across the rocks. The Brigadier followed as fast as he could. As he got nearer, he saw the Doctor standing on a rock shouting something, heard the unmistakable sound of Jo's voice screaming.

Here we go, he thought. Never a peaceful moment.

He pulled his revolver from its holster and increased his pace to a trot, heedless of the pain from his ankle.

He almost collided with a man in combat fatigues and headscarf. The man pointed a machine pistol at him, then relaxed and laughed. 'Brigadier! So it was your people who destroyed *Al Harwaz* after all!'

The Brigadier recognized Tahir Al-Naemi, managed a tight smile. 'Never mind about that now. My scientific advisor and his assistant are being attacked –'

'More of a disagreement, Brigadier,' said a voice from somewhere behind Tahir.

The Brigadier saw the Doctor with his arm around a shocked-looking Jo. Both of them were covered in pieces of flaky mud. Three more Arabs in combat fatigues were jogging up behind them, guns in their hands.

Jo turned on them, shaking off the Doctor's arm. 'You killed him!' she shouted. 'You didn't need to kill him!'

'After what you saw yesterday you don't think that I had the right?' said one of the Arabs. The Brigadier recognized the face from somewhere.

'No!' Jo was shouting. 'It was horrible! You're –' She broke off as the Doctor put a warning hand on her arm.

The Brigadier stared at them. He was feeling increasingly bewildered and irritated. He wanted to say how glad he was that Jo and the Doctor were still alive. How happy he was to see them. How immensely relieved he felt that he hadn't shot his friends. But nobody was giving

211

him the chance. 'Look,' he said, 'Could somebody please tell me what's going on?'

'Monsieur Khalil Benari has been executed,' said one of the newcomers. 'In accordance with Revolutionary law.' He gestured at the Brigadier with his gun. 'Who is this person?'

Tahir told him who the Brigadier was, adding dryly, 'It was he who ordered the nest destroyed, so I think you can say he is on our side.'

Yates ran up from somewhere ahead of them, his hand on the holster of his gun. 'Everything all right, sir?' he gasped, looking around the little group. 'I thought that they were –' he gestured behind him.

'All under control, Yates,' said the Brigadier. 'Except that these people have just shot their Prime Minister; but that's not our problem.'

'It should be your problem,' said Jo. Her voice still quavered with shock. 'That's what the United Nations is for, isn't it? To stop the killing?'

The Doctor put his arm round her again. 'You can't expect the Brigadier to solve all the world's problems, Jo.' He looked up at the Brigadier. 'Talking of which, was it you that ordered the nest destroyed?'

The Brigadier looked at the ground. 'Yes,' he said slowly. 'Look, Doctor, I knew that you might be in there, but –'

'Really, Brigadier!' interrupted the Doctor. 'Why do you always shoot first and ask questions afterwards? I should tell you that I very nearly had everything under control when you –'

The Brigadier decided that it was his turn to interrupt. 'Under control! The Kebirians shot down my helicopter! They were going to turn Yates and I into – well, I suppose the same thing that they turned you into.'

'What do you mean, turned us into?'

The Brigadier looked at the ground again, then glanced at Yates. 'Well, Doctor, it's like this –' He told the Doctor everything that had happened since the false

212

Doctor and Jo had joined him at Kebir City airport.

The Doctor listened mostly in silence, nodding occasionally. Jo gasped a few times, and when the Brigadier told them how many UNIT men had been killed she sat down on the ground and started sobbing. Behind her, Tahir and his men were holding a whispered consultation of their own; of the Arabs, only the *Sakir* Mohammad appeared to be listening to the Brigadier's story. He nodded sagely from time to time.

'You *shot* us?' the Doctor asked finally.

The Brigadier turned away, took a few steps across the loose sand. The sun was already beginning to feel hot, though it was not yet far above the horizon.

'Sorry, Doctor,' he said finally. 'I thought I was doing the right thing.'

'But of course you weren't doing the right thing! Those things were third stage Xarax – perfect copies of human beings, in many ways. But I can assure you that it would take more than a gunshot wound to put them out of action for good. I don't suppose it occurred to you to have the bodies incinerated?'

The Brigadier turned and stared at the Doctor. 'Incinerated? Of course not! I didn't even know if – I mean –'

'Where are they now?' snapped the Doctor.

'Well – in the Army morgue. I asked Dr Moore there to give me an immediate autopsy report – by phone to Rabat if necessary.'

'And has he given you the report?'

The Brigadier shook his head.

'And this was – what, four hours ago? How long does it take to perform an autopsy?'

'Well, yes, I see what you mean, but there has been a war going on, you know, Doctor. I didn't think –'

'Right. You didn't think. Well, that's about par for the course, Brigadier.'

'Now look here, Doctor, I did my best –'

'Well I'm afraid it wasn't good enough!' snapped the

Doctor. 'You've endangered the whole of England by your actions – perhaps the whole of the world.'

There was a short silence. Then Jo said quietly, 'So what do we do now, Doctor?'

The Doctor put his hands on his hips, looked around him. 'The Xarax can grow very fast if they want to, given enough sources of food. They could be well advanced already. We need to return to England as soon as possible.'

The Brigadier nodded briskly. It made a change for the Doctor to give out instructions that could be understood, let alone ones that he thought were a good idea. 'Right,' he said. 'All we need to do is find Rashid's people and radio Rabat. They'll come and pick us up.'

'We might not need to find Rashid, sir,' said Yates, who was still holding his binoculars. 'I think one or two of the Harriers got away.' He pointed at two distant specks moving fast, close to the ground.

The Doctor turned and stared for a moment, then said, 'Those aren't Harriers, Captain. In fact, if I'm not mistaken –' he broke off, raised his voice. 'Quickly!' He turned to Tahir Al-Naemi. 'Have your people got any transport?'

Tahir hesitated, glanced at Vincent, then said, 'We have a dozen jeeps on the mountain road. But I don't think we'd get to them before –' He gestured at the moving specks, which were already visibly closer.

'Blue-black markings, sir,' said Yates suddenly. He had the binoculars to his eyes. 'I don't recognize the nationality.'

'That's because they haven't got a nationality, Captain,' said the Doctor. 'They're Xarax.' He paused, put a hand on Jo's arm. 'I suggest we make a run for it.'

Twenty-Four

Jo ran with the others, stumbling once or twice over the rough grey pebbles. Her body felt strange: her hands and feet were numb, as if she'd been given a local anaesthetic.

It must be the shock, she thought. Her stomach heaved again at the memory of what Vincent had done to Benari. She'd never seen anything so horrible. She still couldn't believe that Vincent had done it. He had never made any secret of being a killer; he had never made any secret of the fact that he was proud of it. But she hadn't expected him to just do it like that, just kill someone. Not even Khalil Benari.

They were almost at the road now. Jo glanced over her shoulder, saw the sunlit plain littered with the corpses of Xarax. Above it, the two jets were clearly visible now. She could see strange flanges and protrusions that belonged to no human aircraft design.

She reached the road, scrambled up the bank, saw the jeeps parked in the deep shadow of an overhang a couple of hundred metres away. The Doctor was already half-way there: he looked back at her, shouted something she couldn't hear over the whistle of the approaching jets. She glanced over her shoulder again, saw the two delta-winged shapes less than half a mile away. She realized that she wasn't going to make it.

An arm took hold of hers, pulled her forward, helped her to run. She smelled sweat and gun oil, saw the familiar dark, close-cropped hair. Vincent. Saving her life. She wondered if he enjoyed that as much as he enjoyed killing people.

There was an explosion ahead of her, and Vincent flung her to the ground. Rock scratched at her hands, but the pain was curiously muted, unreal. When she looked up, her blood oozed from her hands in long, sticky drops, brownish rather than red.

There was something wrong with that. But what?

'Jo! Come on!'

Something screamed overhead, deafening her, and she was on her feet again, running. She could see Vincent ahead, firing his gun at the receding jet. Beyond him the jet exploded, a huge ball of yellow fire.

'Someone needs to go to Kebir City,' the Doctor was saying. 'They've obviously got a nest there – that's where the jets are being controlled from. It's vitally important that it's disabled.'

'I'll go,' said Mike Yates, getting into one of the jeeps. Jo looked at him, realized that she hadn't said how pleased she was to see him, that she hadn't even said hello.

'I'll go with you,' she said. 'I've seen a bit of Kebir City. I might be able to help.' She got into the jeep after Mike, smiled at him. 'Hello, by the way.'

Mike grinned back at her, but said, 'I'm not sure you should be going with me. It's not going to be safe on that road. Besides, the Kebirian authorities want to arrest you for murder.'

'It's not safe anywhere,' said the Doctor. 'And I very much doubt the Kebirian authorities exist any more.' He was already getting into the jeep behind theirs, starting the engine. 'Look after her, Mike,' he called. The jeep sprang away in a clatter of small stones.

Vincent appeared from a cluster of his men, jumped into the back seat of their jeep.

'I will come with you. I know Kebir City; besides, it is my jeep, eh?'

Jo struggled to think of a reason why he shouldn't

come. She didn't want him to come. She didn't want to see him kill anyone. But before she could speak, there was an explosion of sound above them and the iridescent blue-black carapace of a Xarax jet flashed past. A gust of hot, dust-smelling air hit Jo in the face.

'Go, go, go!' yelled Vincent. Mike hit the starter, and the jeep was in motion, tyres grating against the rough surface of the road.

Jo frowned as they gathered speed. There was something she should have told the Doctor – something vitally important –

There was an explosion, a long way behind them. Jo looked round, saw a jeep plunge off the road and roll out of sight amongst the rocks.

Vincent swore: Mike hit the accelerator. The jeep lurched wildly as it headed down the track, throwing Jo from side to side. Grit stung her eyes. What was it she should have told the Doctor?

She looked at the brown blood oozing like honey from her swollen hands, and tried to remember.

The explosion rocked the jeep. The Brigadier heard a crash of metal, looked over his shoulder and saw the jeep at the tail of the convoy roll off the road. One of the others stopped; someone fired into the air, tracking the jet as it swept overhead.

There was an explosion of yellow fire as the jet disintegrated. Pieces of chitin arced through the air.

'Another hit, Doctor,' observed the Brigadier. 'Those things don't seem to be very bullet-proof.'

'Considering that they're using organic materials to travel at twice the speed of sound, Brigadier, it's a miracle they don't explode when you're not shooting at them.' He glanced over his shoulder at the wreckage and the thinning smoke. 'A shame really. It's a good idea, theoretically speaking.'

The Brigadier hastily turned his attention to the jeep's radio, before the Doctor could start getting technical.

'Trap seventy-four. Trap seventy-four. Come in, please.'

This time, when he pressed the receive key, there was a faint, crackly response. '. . . seventy . . . you, Lethbridge-Stewart?'

'Of course it's me, Rashid. What's your position? Over.'

'Ten kilometres north . . . target. We are surrounded. I . . . waiting, over.'

'Please repeat, seventy-four. What force is surrounding you?'

'. . . Kebirian Army! At least . . . brigades with . . .'

The Brigadier didn't quite believe it. 'You mean you've been sitting on your backsides for the last half-hour while we've been shot down, run around and bombed? Hadn't you noticed that the Kebirians have gone a bit quiet, man?'

'. . . but I don't understand,' replied the French-accented voice. There was a crackly pause and for a moment the Brigadier thought he'd lost the signal. Then it resumed with: '. . . your position and . . . meet us at . . .'

The Brigadier looked at the Doctor. 'Where are we, Doctor?'

'How should I know, Brigadier?' Infuriatingly enough, the Doctor seemed to be enjoying himself, steering the jeep at near impossible speeds along the twisting road, throwing clouds of dust and grit behind him. They seemed to have lost the others.

'Seventy-four, where will you pick us up? We're currently on the mountain road heading south.'

'. . . meet you at Al Gohi. Please repeat back, over.'

'Confirmed. Al Gohi. Over and out.' The Brigadier leaned back in his seat, heaved a sigh of relief. 'You can slow down a bit, Doctor. It looks like our problems are over for the time being.'

But the Doctor's face was serious. 'I don't think so, Brigadier,' he said. 'Look behind you.'

The Brigadier looked, and his heart sank as he saw the distant blue-black shapes of Xarax helicopters moving slowly across the plains behind them.

For a moment Jo thought the helicopters might be human-made, then she saw the legs folded beneath them, the scorpion tails, the shuttered Xarax eyes.

'Mike!' she shouted; but Yates had already seen them, and so had Vincent. He was standing in the back seat, sighting his gun on the nearest alien as it approached.

'Hang on, Vincent,' said Mike. 'They're not taking any notice of us.'

It was true: the Xarax flew past, keeping low, throwing up clouds of dust and grit.

'They're probably going to pick up the honey from the nest, so that it won't go to waste,' said Jo.

'How do you know that?' said Vincent, his gun still trained on the 'copter as it fell behind them.

Jo frowned. 'I'm not sure. I was — linked up to the nest while I was in there. I think I've sort of picked up the way the Xarax think.' She could hear it now, drumming away in the back of her brain: — *honey honey sweet sweet good to be honey to be sweet —*

She jumped violently as the cold metal of Vincent's gun touched the skin of her neck.

'You have become like them?'

'No!' said Jo.

Mike pushed the gun away. 'What are you playing at?' he snapped. 'Jo is —'

'It is possible for these aliens to imitate people,' said Vincent calmly. 'Jo could be an imitation, sent to trick us.'

'I'm not an imitation!' protested Jo. 'I'd know if I was!' But even as she spoke she remembered the dream image, the other Jo walking away. The Brigadier had said there'd been one copy of her. Could she be another? Was it possible? She looked at her hands again, at the sticky, brown, honey-like blood. It was just an infection, the

219

product of what the nest had been trying to do to her. Wasn't it? 'At least, I think I'm not,' she muttered aloud.

The cold metal of Vincent's gun touched her neck again. 'And I think we ought to make sure, eh?'

Jo felt her body begin to shake.

'Now wait a minute,' said Mike. 'I've already met the imitation Jo, and I can assure you that this one is the real thing.'

Vincent didn't move the gun. 'And what are the differences between the imitation and the real thing?'

Mike hesitated, then said, 'She didn't speak to me the way she usually does – she seemed to spend a lot of time staring at the horizon. And she wore a kind of perfume.'

Vincent leaned forward; Jo felt the gun track across her shoulder blades. Her skin crawled.

'A sweet perfume?' asked Vincent. He took Jo's shoulders and pushed her sideways, so that her body collided with Mike's. 'A perfume like this?'

Mike stamped on the brakes, throwing both Jo and Vincent forward. The jeep slewed across the road, came to a halt in a cloud of dust.

When the dust settled, Jo saw to her horror that Mike had drawn his gun.

'Now look here, Mr Vincent or whatever your name is, let's get one thing clear. I'm in charge here. I'm responsible to UNIT for Miss Grant's safety, and I would appreciate it if you would put that gun away now.'

Vincent said simply, 'No,' adding after a moment, 'And my name is *Al Tayid*.' His voice was cold and menacing.

Suddenly Jo had had enough. 'Stop it!' she said. 'Both of you stop it! There's nothing we can do but carry on. I – I don't know what's happening to me, but I'm quite human at the moment. I want to destroy the Xarax as much as you do.' – *sweet sweet honey honey sweet to be honey to be good honey* – 'More than you do.'

Vincent slowly lowered his gun, and Mike put his away. 'But we will keep an eye on you, eh?' he said.

Jo looked at her hands. They were swollen, she

220

realized; the knuckles were almost invisible beneath the stretched skin. 'If I start acting like one of them,' she said. 'Just kill me.' — *Benari, blood pumping from his head* — 'Just do it. And don't try to stop him, Mike, or they'll get both of you.'

Mike put a hand on her shoulder. 'It won't come to that, Jo, I'm sure.'

Vincent was silent.

Jo became aware that she was trembling violently, and that she badly needed to pee. She got out of the jeep, grinned at Mike. 'I need to disappear behind a rock.'

Mike grinned back, but Vincent was over the back door of the jeep, gun at the ready. 'I will cover you,' he said.

There was a deep gully by the side of the road which she decided in the circumstances would just have to be private enough. She kept expecting Vincent to appear on the side of the road above her, but he didn't. When she was finished, she walked along to the end of the gully, where the slope back up to the road looked as if it would be easier to climb.

She was just about to scramble up the slope when a hand grabbed her arm. She whirled round, found herself staring into the barrel of a revolver.

'Miss Grant!' said Sadeq Zalloua. 'I'm glad you're here. I don't think I could have travelled much further on my own.' He jabbed the revolver against her throat. 'Walk slowly, please.'

Twenty-Five

'You were being escorted by *terrorists*?' The Moroccan officer seemed incredulous. He gazed at the Brigadier in the dim light seeping in from the open turret of the tank. 'You know who *Al Tayid* is, don't you?'

'Yes,' said the Brigadier wearily, shifting his injured leg in a vain attempt to get comfortable in the cramped space. 'I know who he is.' He decided not to mention the fact that his erstwhile escort detail had just assassinated their Prime Minister. Rashid was technically on secondment to the UN; but he was still a Moroccan, and the Moroccans were friends of Khalil Benari's. If Rashid knew what had happened he was just as likely to follow his own agenda, and it might not include taking the Brigadier and the Doctor to Rabat. 'Look, we need to get out of here. The place is crawling with aliens and Kebirian Army, and it may not be possible to tell the difference between them.'

'Well – if you say so,' said Rashid. 'But I think it may be more useful to stay put. We can send for reinforcements. The aliens are, as you say, mostly out of action at the moment.'

'I'm afraid not,' said the Doctor from the driver's seat of the tank. He gestured at the blurry screen of the tank's battle radar. The Brigadier saw several fast-moving blips.

'What are they, Doctor?' he asked.

'I don't know, Brigadier, but judging by the rate they're going I'd say they're potentially dangerous.' The Doctor started the tank's engine. Lights flashed on the control board, and the whole body of the vehicle shuddered as it began to grind forward over the rough ground.

Rashid reached for the radio mike. 'Rashid to all units. Rashid to all units. We're moving out, repeat, moving out.' He flicked off the mike. 'I hope you realize, Doctor, that we will be more vulnerable to air attack when we are moving than if we stayed put and used our anti-aircraft defences.'

'These aren't exactly aircraft,' said the Doctor. 'Machine-guns should be enough to bring them down, if they're aimed properly.'

'I hope you're right, Doctor,' said Rashid.

'So do I,' said the Brigadier.

'Of course I'm right,' said the Doctor irritably. 'You saw what happened to the first two yourself. Really, Brigadier, I can't understand why you don't have more faith in me.'

He turned the wheel sharply, and the tank lurched onto the road.

Sergeant Benton crept across the gravel path, peered cautiously over the sill of the broken window.

He saw an empty office. A typewriter turned over on the floor. A broken vase.

He looked over his shoulder, beckoned to his men, then turned back and reached inside the broken pane to the handle. It turned; he carefully pulled the window open, then clambered in over the sill.

There was blood on the floor of the office, staining the carpet. He picked his way around it, past the map of the world on the wall, to the heavy door.

It wasn't locked. He checked behind him to make sure that his men were on their way in, then opened the door.

On the other side stood the Doctor, facing him. He smiled. 'Ah, there you are, old chap. We could do with a hand here, you know.'

Benton raised his gun, aimed it at the copy's head. He thought: this isn't the Doctor. I know it isn't. It's an alien and it's killed my mates. It's killed John Shoregood and Barry Ryman and it'll kill the rest of us if we let it.

223

'Now don't be foolish, sergeant,' said the copy, still smiling. 'You know that we need your help.'

It was then that Benton noticed the blood on the alien's hands.

Fresh blood.

He tightened his finger on the trigger.

— *I've got to fire I've got to kill it now before it kills me* —

But he couldn't do it.

There was a movement behind him, a sudden intake of breath. The copy flew forward, impossibly fast, pushed Benton over. He felt its hands close around his throat.

He saw one of his men stepping over them, heard a shot.

The copy jolted back, rolled across the carpet. Benton saw a hole in its head, leaking blood, but it didn't stop moving. Slowly it stood up again, casting around as if blind.

'Fire at will!' he yelled as he scrambled to his feet.

Guns clattered, but nobody actually opened fire. 'What's the —' Benton started to say.

Then he saw them, marching around the corner of the hallway. John Shoregood. Barry Ryman. The others. Their faces were blank, and their feet made chitinous clicks on the vinyl flooring as they advanced towards him.

Jo's head was full of ifs.

If she hadn't needed to go so badly. If she hadn't been so modest and had just gone by the side of the road whilst the men turned their backs. If there hadn't been that horrible argument that she'd needed to get away from.

'Sorry,' she said, as she returned to the jeep. 'I've messed it up.' Vincent and Mike turned to stare at her, saw Zalloua, drew their guns.

'Throw the weapons down,' said Zalloua. 'Or Miss Grant dies.'

'Now just a minute —' began Mike.

Vincent opened fire.

224

Bullets whizzed past Jo's ear; she heard Zalloua cry out, then the crack of the revolver.

'Get down, Jo!' shouted Mike.

But it was too late. Zalloua had hold of her again, an arm around her neck, the revolver against her skull.

Mike dropped his gun to the ground, put his hands up. She couldn't see Vincent.

'Good,' said Zalloua. 'Now get out of the jeep.'

Mike got out.

'Kick the gun across to me.'

Mike obeyed. Jo caught his eye, twisted her face into an expression of regret and sympathy. Mike managed the tiniest of shrugs.

Zalloua put his foot on the gun, reached down with his free arm. Jo saw blood running from it: thick, red blood. But he managed to pick up the gun, put it in the pocket of his tattered lab coat. Then he marched her towards the jeep, motioning Mike out of their path.

Then she saw Vincent.

He was lying in the back seat of the jeep. His mouth was open, with a thin trickle of blood running from it. There was a hole in his chest, bigger and messier than Jo would have thought possible from a single bullet. He was still breathing, and his open eyes stared at Jo.

'You!' shouted Zalloua, gesturing at Mike. 'Get him out of the jeep!'

Mike stepped forward, opened the rear door of the jeep, then reached in and took Vincent's legs.

'Touch the gun and I kill her!'

'I wasn't planning to touch it,' said Mike disgustedly. He pulled, and Vincent's body slid out of the car and on to the dry road, bashing Vincent's head brutally on the ground. He gave a little grunt of pain and fresh blood flowed from his mouth.

'You're killing him!' said Jo, struggling against Zalloua's grip.

'He is not a good man,' said Zalloua. 'And anyway, it is in the cause of peace. Get in the jeep.'

Jo got in, acutely conscious of the gun still against her head. She wondered if he would really fire it if she tried to escape.

But even as she thought about it, it was too late: Zalloua was in the jeep beside her.

'Start up the engine,' he said, then louder, for Mike's benefit. 'Try anything and she will be the first to die.' But Mike was out of sight, presumably trying to help Vincent.

Jo got the engine started; Zalloua prodded her with the revolver. 'Drive.'

Jo obeyed, driving as slowly as she dared. 'Where are we going?' she asked after a while.

Zalloua stared at her through his round spectacles. 'Kebir City, of course,' he said.

'But we were going there anyway! Why did you have to –'

'And no doubt your orders were to destroy the Xarax?'

Jo stared at him. 'The Doctor said –'

'Whatever the Doctor said was wrong,' interrupted Zalloua briskly. 'He is the one who hasn't the slightest idea of what he is doing. The Xarax must be allowed to carry out the program I gave them.'

'But your program won't work! The Doctor said –'

'That the Xarax can't tell one human from another? That's quite right. But the program I have given to the Xarax in Kebir City doesn't need them to be able to do that.' He paused, smiled. 'I wanted peace, you see. Not just between the Kebiriz and the Giltaz, but for the whole world. But given the nature of humanity, there is only one way to do that. Everything else has been tried.

'I have told the Xarax to make perfect copies of all humanity – and then to use the copies to replace us.' He smiled again. 'Don't you think it's a good idea?'

Twenty-Six

The tank slewed sideways, jolted violently. The Brigadier winced as his injured arm caught against a projecting piece of the gun sight. 'Doctor, do you think you could be –'

His comment was cut off by an extremely loud bang. The tank seemed to lift off the ground for a moment, then settled with another spine-jarring jolt.

'Missed!' said the Doctor, with some satisfaction.

The Brigadier looked at Rashid, who shrugged and passed him the radio mike. 'See if you can get Al-Bitar, he's got the ground-to-air missiles.'

The Brigadier looked at his list, found Al-Bitar's call sign. 'Greyhound to trap seventy-one, come in.'

Silence.

'Trap seventy-one, come in please.'

'Hello this is Lt Tanzi,' said a weak voice. 'Al-Bitar's had it, sir.'

There was another explosion, and the voice on the radio cried out.

The Brigadier came to a decision. 'I'm going up to take a look,' he said.

'Be careful, Brigadier,' said the Doctor and Rashid, almost simultaneously. The Brigadier grabbed a stanchion with his good arm, levered open the hatch and stepped up.

Heat, light and grit hit his face all at once. For a moment he was half-blinded, then he saw a blue sky streaked with smoke trails, the flash of a Xarax carapace in the sunlight. He looked back along the column, strung out along a rough trail which descended between high banks of red scree. He could see Al-Bitar's detachment dimly through a curtain of dust and smoke. Somebody was still firing something – a medium-calibre gun by the look of it – but at what, and with what degree of success, the Brigadier couldn't tell.

Abruptly the tank lurched sideways, and a wall of rock cut off the Brigadier's view of the action. He ducked down again, asked, 'Where are we going now?'

The Doctor didn't take his eyes from the forward scope. 'Short cut, Brigadier.' The tank lurched downwards, almost throwing the Brigadier off the ladder. The treads skidded for a moment on loose pebbles, then they got a grip. 'I suggest you get inside,' said the Doctor.

The Brigadier ignored him, looked out of the hatch again. Ahead there was something that looked perilously like a sheer drop.

'Doctor! I hope you know what you're doing!' he shouted.

'Of course I do, Brigadier!'

The tank nosed its way on to a ledge about a foot wider than it was, and started down the ravine at an angle the Brigadier didn't care to think about. He stayed just long enough to see the next tank in the column starting to follow them down. Then he got inside and slammed the hatch.

'How short, exactly, is this "short cut", Doctor?' he asked.

'It's only about ninety kilometres to the border from here. We should make it in a couple of hours.'

There was a loud thud from outside the tank, followed after a brief interval by the sound of a fair amount of rock clattering down on the armour.

'With a bit of luck, that is,' added the Doctor.

Benton wasn't sure how he'd reached the lawns. He remembered running, firing, a bullet shattering the plaster of a wall inches from his ear as he ran up the back steps.

Now he was in the clear. There was a rattle of gunfire still coming from the house; as he watched, two of the lads – Pepworth and Morgan – staggered up the steps and crossed the flagstoned path that ran around the rear of the HQ building.

Pepworth was hurt, red blood spreading over his combat jacket.

A first floor window shattered above them, gunfire sprayed down. Benton hit the grass, rolled into the cover of a hedge. He saw Pepworth and Morgan drop, saw their bodies jerk as the bullets hit them.

Swore.

The firing from above stopped abruptly. Glass shattered again, and a rain of fragments landed on the path, followed by something heavier.

A body.

No. The body of an alien. Benton could see the honey-like fluid flowing out of the cracks in the chest.

But the alien was still moving, bringing its gun to bear –

Benton rolled out of the way just in time, stood up, watched as the damaged creature went on firing into the hedge until the gun overheated and jammed.

He looked up, saw the face of Corporal Cranley in the window. The Corporal grinned, waved. Then frowned. Then fell forward through the remains of the window and pitched on to the stone path head first.

Benton raised his gun, waited until he saw something move. Then fired, a continuous burst.

A gun clattered down to the ground, with a hand still attached to it. The human form in the window continued to crouch and aim, the other hand crooked around the gun that was no longer there.

Benton ran up to Cranley, stopped when he saw the bullet hole in the back of the man's neck.

Swore again.

He stepped across to Pepworth and Morgan, saw Morgan sitting up, cradling his left arm. Bright arterial blood dripped from the cuff of his jacket.

Morgan looked at Benton, shook his head slowly; Benton looked down, saw the line of bullet holes in Pepworth's back. He reached down to turn the man over, stopped when he saw movement in the doorway at the bottom of the steps.

He raised his gun, then saw Corporal Marks's face.

'We seem to have got most of 'em, sergeant,' said Marks as he jogged up the steps. 'At any rate, they've gone.' Then he looked down at Pepworth. 'Oh, blimey.'

A crackle of gunfire from the building made them both jump around to face the doorway, but all they saw was the remainder of the platoon, following Marks out.

Then Benton heard the whistle and thud of a mortar shell and realized that the firing was coming not from within the building but from the other side of it. He glanced at Marks, who was tying a tourniquet around Morgan's injured arm.

'Best if we go round the front and take a look.'

Marks nodded; Morgan said, 'I can walk, sergeant.'

He got up, leaning on Marks. There was another whistle and thud, then Benton heard a scream of pain. He set off at a trot, rounded the side of the house, saw bodies scattered on the driveway.

Bodies in pieces. Bodies leaking a brownish fluid. Bodies that could only be aliens. He saw Huffington's men around the gate, heaved a sigh of relief. Round one to the humans.

Then the mortar thudded, a shell whistled overhead and exploded behind him. The blast almost knocked him off his feet. He glanced over his shoulder, saw the men rolling for cover.

He waved his rifle in the air, shouted, 'It's us! Sergeant Benton's squad!'

But the mortar thudded again, and a crackle of machine-gun fire started up. Benton dived, covered his head.

The explosion shook the ground, left him deafened.

He looked up, saw Huffington's men advancing.

No.

Not Huffington's men. They moved too quickly.

Too quickly to be human.

'Round one to the aliens, then,' he muttered aloud.

He looked over his shoulder, saw the men running, a body on the ground. He ran up: saw Morgan, his eyes glazed, his mouth slackly open, dribbling blood.

Benton looked back at the advancing aliens, heard the crump of the mortar again.

He ran.

The men were ahead of him, running in disorder across the rear lawn. The mortar shell exploded somewhere to the left of them: they dropped, then scrambled up again, heading for the narrow, one-man gate in the fence at the back of the compound.

The gate was locked. Benton saw them struggling with it, saw Marks take a shot at the lock.

The gate still didn't open.

'Cut the wire!' yelled Benton.

Someone produced a knife, began chopping at the wire of the fence next to the gate. Benton turned, saw the aliens approaching across the lawn, making grasshopper-like leaps. He fired into them, saw one spin out of control, land heavily and break into pieces.

The others kept coming.

'Okay, sarge!' shouted Marks from behind him. Benton turned, saw the men pushing their way through the fence. He took a grenade from his belt, pulled the pin, hurled it over his shoulder without bothering to look. Dived for the gap in the fence.

The grenade went off as he was struggling through. He heard an explosion of gunfire, saw Marks firing through the fence. Ran.

Marks ran with him. 'Where to, sarge?'

'Henley Wood,' said Benton, without hesitation.

Marks nodded. Henley Wood was their training ground; they'd fought more wars there than they were

231

ever likely to fight anywhere in real life. And there was plenty of cover. They should have a chance.

He hoped.

Benton looked over his shoulder, saw that the aliens had stopped, spread out against the fence. For a moment he thought that the barrier had confused them, that they wouldn't find the gap; then he saw the whole high structure topple forward. The aliens started their grassshopper-leap progress once more.

Ahead, the men were piling over the stile at the fringe of the woods. Benton sprinted to catch up with them.

Undergrowth, he thought. We need undergrowth. We need to *hide*. He scrambled over the stile, looked around him. A slope covered in scattered beech trees led away to a stream; on the far side of the stream was a green thicket of rhododendrons.

They would do.

'Down the slope!' he shouted.

Now he led the way, reaching the stream, splashing through it, diving for the cover of the thicket. His men crashed down around him. Benton heard gasping breath, smelled sweat, fear.

'Don't fire unless you have to,' he said. 'They don't seem too bright. They might not see us.'

As he finished speaking, the first of the aliens appeared. They stopped for a moment, twisting their heads around in a not-quite-human way.

Then they all turned at once to face the squad and began to run down the slope towards them.

Twenty-Seven

Mike Yates took Vincent's pulse again and slowly shook his head. The man wasn't going to make it. Even if by some miracle a helicopter turned up now, chock-full of paramedics, he doubted they would be able to save Vincent. He'd lost too much blood.

Yates stared out at the desert. The horizon was already beginning to shimmer in the heat. He was going to have to start to think about water soon, and about getting out of the sun. He supposed that some of the Kebirians they'd left twitching aimlessly near the ruins of the nest would have supplies, but going there would bring its own problems. A seemingly endless chain of Xarax helicopters flew to the nest and returned, as Jo had said they would, carrying glistening globes of honey. Since the first wave, none of them had come too near to the road, but Yates didn't want to risk attracting their attention.

A harsh whisper interrupted his thoughts: Vincent. He turned, saw the man's eyes roll to meet his. The whisper came again: 'Leave me.'

Yates bent down over the man, shook his head. 'No.'

'Not till I die, eh?' Vincent's lips twitched in the echo of a smile. 'Don't be –' The voice stopped. For a moment Yates thought Vincent was dead, but then his eyes rolled again and he said, 'No need.' Then, amazingly, he tried to push himself upright.

'Take it easy,' said Yates, but Vincent shook his head.

'Look out, father,' he said. 'The Israelis are coming.' Then he flopped back on the ground with a bubbling sigh.

Yates leaned forward once more, to see if he was still breathing, but then heard the faint sound of rotor blades behind him. He whirled, saw a Xarax helicopter approaching, legs flush against its body, tail raised to sting, tentacles trailing from its belly.

He reached for his revolver, cursed Zalloua when he remembered it wasn't there. He glanced at Vincent, still not sure if the man was alive or dead. Cursing again under his breath, he crouched down and lifted him over his shoulder. The body flopped limply.

He slid off the road, almost fell down the slope into the gully. Then he walked along until he found an overhang large enough to give him cover.

He heard the whickering sound of the Xarax helicopter, and a strange booming like a huge heart beating. A curtain of tentacles trailed past the overhang, missing his skin by inches.

The creature seemed to hover for hours. Twice it moved away from the overhang, only to return; Mike wondered if it could smell him.

At last it went away, the whickering rotors slowly fading into silence.

Mike looked down at Vincent, saw that his eyes had glazed over.

Dead.

Did I kill him by moving him? thought Mike; then shook his head. No point in worrying about that now. He closed Vincent's eyes, muttered, 'Rest in peace.'

Then he started wondering what he should do next.

The Brigadier stared in amazement over the sloping armour of the tank as they pulled up alongside the perimeter fence of the air base. The two UNIT Hercules transports were drawn up on the runway; American fighters moved between them. Moroccan soldiers were rushing forward, shouting and waving their arms.

'It's Al Haraf!' the Brigadier shouted down for Rashid's benefit. 'How the dickens did you get us here, Doctor?'

'Quite simple, Brigadier,' said the Doctor, climbing up beside him, 'I cut through the Wadi Mazami, across the Bor-el-Duba and down the side of the Al Gol hills. Just look at the map: it's perfectly clear.'

By now the tank was surrounded by soldiers, all cheering and clapping as if the brigade had returned from a major victory instead of having turned tail and run. Somewhere behind them the Brigadier was relieved to see the familiar English uniform of Sergeant Osgood.

He clambered down the side of the tank, pushed his way through the crush to the Sergeant. Osgood caught sight of him and saluted.

'Everything all right, Sergeant?' said the Brigadier, briskly returning the salute. But he could tell from the expression on the man's face that everything was far from all right.

'We've got a few problems, sir.' He paused as two of the American fighters thundered overhead. 'The Americans have put through a request for a nuclear strike on Kebir City. They seem to reckon its been taken over by aliens.' Osgood sounded doubtful, which the Brigadier himself would probably have been if he hadn't seen what he'd just seen in Kebiria. 'And it's the same with Rabat, sir. We can't reach them. There's something about dancing.' Osgood sounded even more doubtful.

'Dancing the code?' asked the Brigadier.

Osgood nodded. 'That's what's on the radio from Rabat, sir. But it doesn't make any sense.'

'Well, it won't, will it?' The Doctor's voice. 'And what was that about a nuclear strike?'

Osgood repeated his information.

'That's utter lunacy! It's the worst thing they could possibly do! – Brigadier, we've got to get in touch with the US government at once and put a stop to this. If they use nuclear weapons in these circumstances it could quite literally mean the end of the world.'

The Brigadier frowned, turned to the Doctor. 'I agree that it seems a bit drastic,' he said. 'But surely it would work – there wouldn't be much left of the Xarax after an H-bomb went off on their doorstep.'

'Oh, really Brigadier,' said the Doctor. 'That's a typical military attitude. Try to think, just for a change. We use helicopters – the Xarax imitate them. We use jets against the Xarax – the Xarax imitate them. What do you think will happen if we use nuclear weapons?'

The Brigadier thought for a moment.

'Well, I suppose they might –' He swallowed. 'Oh, I see.'

'Precisely, Brigadier. They only need to disable one warhead on its way in and they'll have the perfect model – and a supply of fissile material. Now get me a direct line to the President of the United States –' He broke off as two more of the American jets roared overhead. 'Before it's too late!'

'We're going to see the Queen,' said Sadeq Zalloua.

He'd said that several times, starting the moment when the concrete towers of Kebir City had first become visible through the heat shimmer on the horizon. He said it with a sure smile, a smile of such little-boy intensity that it scared Jo almost more than the gun pressed against the back of her neck.

They were well into the city now. The roads were littered with smashed cars, broken glass and other debris. Jo was having to pick her way between it all; twice they'd had to go back and take a different route. Zalloua wouldn't tell her where the Queen was: Jo wondered if he actually knew.

'What are we going to do when we get to the Queen?' she asked.

'I will take control of the Xarax. I will ensure that they carry out my program. They're not intelligent, you see.'

'Yes, the Doctor said that.' Jo stared out of the windscreen, slowed down as she saw the back of a truck projecting across the road. The front of the truck had smashed into a wall. As they drew closer, she could see a

236

thick trail of blood leading from the truck towards a low, red-brick building.

Jo thought she saw something move behind the door of the building.

'Are you sure they'll let you take control?' she asked Zalloua, steering the jeep onto the pavement away from the wreck. 'I mean, the Xarax might not need you any more.'

'They will know who I am.' Zalloua treated her to another of his unnerving smiles.

There was definitely something moving; a human figure. A figure in a uniform.

A policeman.

Jo heaved a sigh of relief. Being arrested she could cope with.

Unless of course –

She saw two more figures emerge from the building, begin to strut in line across the road. The way they moved was too regular, too clockwork for real people, even policemen. They had to be Xarax copies.

She steered back onto the road, heedless of the pieces of broken glass there. Stepped on the accelerator.

'Stop!' said Zalloua, jabbing the gun into Jo's neck. 'I have told you – they will know who I am. They will take us to the Queen.'

Jo drove on.

'STOP!' yelled Zalloua. 'I will kill you if you don't stop!'

Jo stopped the jeep, suddenly, with a screech of tyres. She became aware that her body was shaking.

'They won't know you, Monsieur Zalloua,' she said. 'They won't know anything. They're not intelligent. You said so yourself.'

The 'policemen' were only yards away now. Zalloua stood up in his seat, turned to them and said, 'I am Sadeq Zalloua.'

But the 'policemen' continued to advance. Jo, who had expected it, braced herself to run. Zalloua, who obviously hadn't, only repeated his statement, adding, 'I am your leader.' He was waving the gun around in the air, obviously no longer concerned with Jo.

She opened the door of the jeep, half jumped, half fell out. Zalloua, startled, shouted something and then fired his revolver. The bullet flew off the concrete surface somewhere near Jo's feet. She didn't stop running.

Then Zalloua screamed.

Jo didn't look over her shoulder to see why. She just ran on, blindly dodging cars, leaping over the trunk of a fallen palm tree. She ran until she couldn't run any more, until she collapsed against the side of a car, gasping, sweat pouring down her face. Only then did she look back.

The street was empty, except for the wreckage of cars. For a moment she thought that she saw movement at the limit of her vision; then she realized that it was just the heat shimmer over the concrete.

I must have lost them, she thought. She felt a wave of pure relief.

Then she realized that she was on her own, in a strange city controlled by aliens. She had no idea whether there were any other humans alive in the city, and if there were, she had no idea where they might be. The Doctor had talked about disabling the nest; she didn't know where the nest was, or where the Xarax queen might be, or how to disable it.

'What am I going to do now, Doctor?' she muttered aloud.

There was no reply.

'. . . honey honey good good sweet sweet honey dancing . . . code honey dancing . . .'

The voice on the radio went on and on, repeating its incomprehensible message. The words had an inflection that was robotic, repetitive, barely human.

'And that's Rabat, you say?' the Brigadier asked, wiping the sweat and the flies from his forehead. The

238

flies whirled up and away, began to orbit the slowly turning fan on the ceiling of the office.

Captain Oakley nodded. 'Even the Air Traffic control is out. Your pilot's going to have to fly by wire until you get across the Mediterranean.' The American Marine leaned forward, his hands pressing down onto the thick scatter of papers that covered the surface of his desk. 'Look, sir, I appreciate your position, and I am fully aware of the potential seriousness of the situation should we choose a nuclear option. But the facts are these. Kebir City is out. Rabat is out. Giltat is out. There's some kind of trouble in Algiers, and there's been an air raid in Malta. That's a radius of five hundred miles, Brigadier. They're getting more planes up all the time – and it's getting harder to shoot them down. They're learning.'

'But don't you see, that's precisely the problem!' interrupted the Doctor, whirling around from the back of the office where he had been apparently inspecting the notice board. 'I've explained to you –'

The Captain raised a hand. 'As I've said, Doctor, I understand your position. But I have my orders.'

'Then let me speak to the person who gave you the orders! Let me speak to the President!'

'I don't have a line to the President, sir. Only Admiral Carver on the *Eisenhower* has the authority to speak directly to the White House.'

'You're saying that you've been told what to do but you've got no means of –'

The Brigadier decided that it was time to stop this argument before any more time was wasted. He knew the Doctor well enough to know that he wouldn't give in; and he suspected that Captain Oakley wouldn't either. He stepped forward in front of the Doctor, held up his hand.

'How long can you give us, Captain?' he asked.

The Captain's blue eyes swung to focus on the Brigadier. Then glanced at the Doctor.

'He's safe,' said the Brigadier automatically.

'If the Xarax continue to improve their capability at the present rate, I'd say we have four hours before it becomes impossible to defend this base.'

'And then?'

'If we lose here, Admiral Carver will use the tactical nuclear capability on the *Eisenhower* to destroy the main Xarax bases.'

'Madness, sheer madness,' muttered the Doctor.

The Brigadier thought swiftly. If Rabat was out as Oakley had said, then the UNIT base there wasn't going to be any help. The best bet would be to get back to England. He could get in touch with the Ministry; he could contact New York and try to get the Secretary-General's support over the H-bomb business, and plan some kind of strategy. Perhaps the Doctor would think of something.

'Can you spare us a couple of fighters for escort?' he asked the American.

The man pursed his lips, said, 'Only as far as the coast. Then you're on your own.'

'Right.' The Brigadier glanced at his watch. 'Take off in ten minutes?'

The Marine shrugged. 'Whatever you think best, Brigadier.'

The Brigadier turned to go, but the Doctor stopped in the doorway and addressed the American. 'Captain, have you got any rosewater on the base?'

'Rosewater?' asked Oakley incredulously.

'Yes – and oil of cloves.'

'Well, we might have a little of that in the kitchen stores but I don't see –'

'Never mind.' The Doctor was already on his way out of the office. 'I dare say that they can get hold of some for us in England.'

'Doctor, what are you talking about?' asked the Brigadier.

'Brigadier,' said the Doctor impatiently. 'When we get back to England we're going to have barely more than an hour to get inside UNIT HQ and disable the Xarax that you so carelessly left to take charge there. And I can only think of one way that we're going to be able to do that.'

The Brigadier raised an eyebrow. 'Which is?'

'Protective camouflage, Brigadier.'

'But I don't see —'

'It's not a matter of seeing, Brigadier. It's a matter of smelling.' He smiled. 'To be exact, smelling of roses and cloves.'

Twenty-Eight

At the first sound, Sergeant Benton flung himself flat on to the damp earth. He didn't need to tell his men to do the same. Everything bigger than a squirrel that moved in the wood had been an alien, and each one had been more difficult to kill than the last. The squad had been forced back, step by step, from Henley Wood across the road to Marsh Wood; now, after perhaps a dozen encounters, they were almost in Marshstead, two miles from UNIT HQ.

Soon they were going to run out of ammunition.

This time it sounded like a large force. Benton could hear the regular, multiple tread of boots on gravel, growing louder by the minute. Obviously they were on the Marshstead bridleway.

He frowned. The aliens hadn't bothered much with using paths up till now; and they hadn't moved in large groups either.

Suddenly he heard a voice muttering, 'What d'you reckon the place is burned down when we get there?'

A human voice, speaking in a human way.

Benton glanced across at Marks, who nodded.

'I'm going to take a look,' said Benton. He thought: steady on, you can't be sure, that copy of the Doctor could speak.

He moved as silently as he could across the soil, up a shallow slope towards the hedge that bordered the path. The patrol on the other side was almost level with him now.

He peered through the hedge, saw movement.

Camouflage jackets. A glimpse of a grenade belt. A cape, a magenta shirt.

A cape –?

The Doctor!

Another copy, thought Benton. It had to be.

At the same moment, he smelt roses and cloves. He levelled his gun, took aim through a gap in the hedge.

Then he heard a voice: 'My missus, she says I ought to get out of the Army, like –'

Benton relaxed, grinned to himself. Aliens weren't likely to grumble like that! He stood up, saw the Doctor, the Brigadier, and a platoon of regulars.

Heads turned, guns were raised. The Brigadier looked round, raised an eyebrow. 'Benton!' he called. 'What the blazes are you doing?'

'Be careful, Brigadier.' The Doctor's voice. 'It might not be Benton at all.'

Benton turned, stared at the Doctor. 'Of course it's me –'

'Take your cap off, Sergeant,' said the Doctor quietly.

'My cap?' Benton was bewildered. Then he remembered the Xarax copies, their clothes cracking with the rest of their bodies as they fell.

He took off his cap, tossed it to the Doctor, who felt the cloth for a moment, then nodded.

'Okay, Brigadier.'

Only then did Benton turn to his commanding officer. He was just in time to see the Brigadier lowering his revolver and putting it back in its holster.

They stared at each other for a moment. After a while, Benton said, 'Good to see you alive again, sir.'

Jo peered into the windows of the café where Vincent's resistance movement had its headquarters. There was no movement, no sound. She pushed at the door, went inside. The red check tablecloths were spread across the tables, neat, clean. Salt and pepper shakers stood in the middle of the tables. Nothing stirred, except a few flies buzzing round the ceiling.

'Hello,' called Jo. 'Hello! I'm human! I need help!'

Silence.

'I come from Vincent Tayid! *Al Tayid!*'

A fly buzzed angrily against the window. Automatically, Jo began to look around for a cup and piece of paper so that she could catch it and set it free. She even went over to the counter, to see if she could see a teacup behind it.

Then she realized what she was doing, sat down and began to laugh hysterically.

When she'd laughed long enough, she stood up, put her hands on her hips, and muttered, 'I've got to do *something*.' She peered out into the empty street, almost hoping that someone or something would go past. She'd twice seen the Xarax 'police' since she'd started running; both times they'd seemed to ignore her. Either tracking down stray humans wasn't a high priority at the moment – which didn't seem likely, considering what had happened to Zalloua – or –

Jo looked at her swollen hands. They smelled of roses and cloves. Of Xarax. And her feet were swollen too: she could barely walk in her shoes, the prison officer's shoes that had once been almost too big for her.

– good good to be honey honey sweet sweet honey dancing to be honey to be sweet dancing the code –

It was there. She had to do something about it. The Doctor wasn't around to cure her. She was going to have to find the nest, somehow. Get to the queen, and control her, as Zalloua had hoped to do.

But how?

She sat down on one of the chairs, put her chin in her hands. There had to be a way.

Then she thought of it. If she smelled of Xarax, if she knew, or felt, what the Xarax were doing, then –

Except that it might not work. And if it didn't work, she was going to end up dead.

No – worse than dead.

— sweet sweet to be good good honey honey to be dancing —

She got up, walked out of the café, and sniffed the air.

— honey honey good good sweet to find honey dancing to find good good sweet sweet honey dancing —

After a few moments, she chose a direction and started down the street. She remembered what Vincent had said about her: 'You have the luck.'

Well, the luck had better not desert her now.

The Brigadier glanced over his shoulder to where Sergeant Osgood was spraying the last of Benton's men with the Xarax scent — on the move, because there was no time to stop. There were about forty-five minutes left before Captain Oakley's deadline; but the Brigadier knew that the Marine had been guessing. For all he knew Al Haraf might already have fallen and the Americans and the Xarax might be lobbing nuclear warheads around the Gulf of Kebiria.

It wasn't a pleasant thought.

He looked ahead to where the Doctor was strolling along, looking up at the crowns of the trees above him for all the world as if he was enjoying a quiet country walk.

'Ah, Brigadier,' he said, without turning round. 'Have you noticed any cows in the fields?'

The Brigadier frowned. 'I beg your pardon?'

'Cows — sheep — and there used to be some horses.' The Doctor pointed. 'Over there.' He turned and looked at the Brigadier, a serious expression on his face. 'It looks as if the nest has been growing more quickly than we thought.'

The Brigadier considered this for a moment, frowned. 'Are you quite sure we shouldn't call up that armoured brigade? I could have them here in five minutes —'

'Really, Brigadier. How many times do I have to explain it? If we use any kind of vehicle the Xarax will know straight away we're not from the nest and they'll attack us. Do you imagine they'll think diesel fumes are a nest pheromone? Believe me, this is the only way in. And

245

I need the nest intact, not blown to pieces by your men.'

The Brigadier shook his head. 'If you say so, Doctor.'

'Sir!' said Benton, pointing forward.

The Brigadier looked, saw UNIT HQ about half a mile away through a gap in the trees. Saw the ring of men – Xarax copies of men, he corrected himself – surrounding it.

'Doesn't look too promising,' he muttered.

But the Doctor smiled. 'Just carry on, Brigadier. Walk in as if you owned the place.'

The Brigadier thought about this for a moment. 'I do own the place,' he said. 'In a manner of speaking.'

'Well, then. Walk in like you usually do.'

The Brigadier marched a little faster and tried to put a confident expression on his face; then remembered the neutral faces of the Xarax copies and tried to copy that.

As the squad drew closer to the gate the Brigadier saw a man in a major's uniform sitting in a canvas chair with a pipe and a cup of tea.

'That's Huffington!' he muttered to the Doctor. 'I'd know him anywhere. Sandringham and –'

The Doctor shook his head. 'Sorry, Brigadier. Not Huffington any more.'

The Major had stood up, was staring at them with piercing grey eyes. As they drew closer, he saluted. The Brigadier automatically saluted in return, almost spoke aloud.

Then he remembered, set his face in a neutral expression and stepped forward between Huffington's 'men', walked through the open gate.

The aliens didn't move. He walked along the driveway towards the building, heard the footsteps of the squad as they followed him.

There was a guard at the front door. The Brigadier recognized the man, Private Shoregood. The Private saluted; again the Brigadier returned the salute. The Xarax copy stepped aside.

The Brigadier released a breath he hadn't realized he'd

been holding, then stepped through the door.

'Where to, Doctor?' he muttered.

'They'll be in the lab, I should think. That's where they set up first time, wasn't it?'

The Brigadier nodded, led the way through the maze of corridors to the Doctor's lab. The men followed, their boots thudding heavily on the lino.

The lab door was open. Inside was a white wall, about a yard from the door. The Brigadier stared for a moment, puzzled.

The Doctor appeared between the wall and the door, stared at him.

Not the Doctor.

The Brigadier drew his revolver, fired.

The copy, apparently unaffected by the shot, stepped forward.

'Brigadier, no!' The Doctor's voice. But which one?

The Doctor jumped forward, and suddenly the two Doctors, copy and original, were wrestling against the white wall in the laboratory.

The Brigadier stared. He really didn't know which was which.

A movement to his left: Jo.

Not Jo. But wearing Jo's blue T-shirt and brown slacks, smiling like Jo.

Someone pushed him aside: the Brigadier just had time to recognize Corporal Marks before he was half-deafened by automatic gunfire. The copy of Jo bent over, as if walking against a storm, then slowly crumpled back. There was no blood.

The gunfire stopped. The Brigadier saw cracks spreading across the skin and clothes of the copy-Jo, a honey-like fluid oozing out.

Obviously they'd had to remake themselves as less realistic copies in order to be less vulnerable to attack, thought the Brigadier. He stored the fact away in case it came in useful.

The two Doctors were still wrestling. One had pinned

247

the other against the white wall, a knee to his neck.

The pinned one's face slowly turned blue.

Vulnerable: therefore the original, thought the Brigadier. Got you.

'Marks! Benton!' he shouted. 'Get the one standing up!'

The standing Doctor whirled, shouted, 'No!' – but Benton had already opened fire. The figure crumpled back, bloodless, then slowly disintegrated.

When the firing had stopped, the real Doctor stood up. He rubbed his throat a couple of times, then said, 'You know, I wish you hadn't done that.'

'But Doctor –' began the Brigadier.

'But sir, he was killing –' began Benton at the same time.

'If you hadn't fired at him in the first place we might have been able to negotiate something! Now you'll have the whole nest on to us!'

'I'm sorry, Doctor, but I couldn't take the chance,' said the Brigadier. There was a clattering of chitin in the distance: a hollow, not-quite-human sound. 'Now get in there and do what you have to do. The men and I will hold them off.' He signalled to Benton to prepare a defensive position; the Sergeant nodded acknowledgement.

But the Doctor was still holding on to his arm. 'Look, Brigadier, what I had in mind depended on those two being alive. They were intelligent. I needed to talk to them.'

'Sir!' Benton's voice. The Brigadier looked up, saw the figures of Shoregood and others rushing down the corridor towards them. Benton fired, and his men joined in. The figures dropped. The Brigadier smiled to himself.

'Like shooting clay pigeons!' he said, turning to the Doctor.

But the Doctor was gone.

Reluctantly, the Brigadier stepped into the lab, over the broken, inhuman bodies of the false Doctor and Jo.

That was when he saw what the wall of white was.

At the far end of the lab, attached to the end of the 'wall' and crushed up against the TARDIS, was an insect head. It was about eight feet high; the antennae were pressed against the ceiling. The white wall was its body: now that the Brigadier had time to look, he saw the crushed remnants of lab benches and glassware under it.

He took a few steps forward in the narrow gap between the vast alien and the wall and saw the Doctor kneeling with his head quite literally between the huge jaws.

'Doctor?'

There was no reply. The Brigadier took a step closer, saw that the Doctor had his hands cupped in front of his mouth.

Beads of honey were falling from the creature, and the Doctor was catching them in his hands and eating them.

'Honey honey –' he murmured '– sweet sweet build nest honey good to build good to be dancing –'

So you're not the real one either, thought the Brigadier. He raised his revolver once more, took aim at the Doctor's head.

– *honey honey good to be sweet honey* –

Yes, thought Jo. Take me to it. Take me to the best –

– *honey sweet to be dancing* –

The best there is. The queen. Come on, you can do it.

A faint whiff of scent. Jo was fairly sure her human senses would never have noticed it, but the Xarax-attuned part of her picked it up, told her: turn left.

She turned the corner, found herself on a wide, three-lane highway. Crashed cars were everywhere. A metal sign on a post announced: 'Boulevard Abdul Gamal Nasser'. A little way down the road was a huge building that reminded Jo a little of the Brighton Pavilion. Huge, white onion-domes, gilded cupolas on flat roofs in between. She remembered it from the guide book she'd read at UNIT HQ: it was the People's Palace, the official residence of the Kebirian Prime Minister. The whiff of scent returned, and

Jo knew she had to go into it.

It's bound to be guarded, she thought.

She walked confidently across the highway, her arms hanging loosely by her side, the way she'd seen the Xarax copies walk.

Go in as if you owned the place, she thought. Don't talk to anyone. Don't even think anything except –

– honey honey sweet sweet good to be honey to be dancing sweet sweet good good –

There were no guards at the huge metal gate. Jo reached out, pushed. The gate swung silently back.

Inside the grounds Jo saw the first sign of activity: a huge heap of earth on one of the lawns, with the crudely carved beginnings of access tunnels.

The new nest.

– sweet to be honey dancing sweet build nest good to be honey dancing go nest build dancing –

With difficulty Jo tore herself away. She had to find the queen. Following instinct, she left the driveway, crossed the still-untouched east lawn towards the largest of the pearl-white onion-domes. There was a large ragged hole in the wall facing her. Loose brickwork was visible under the broken plaster and gilt.

This was the new entrance. It had to be. She walked up to it, feeling oddly secure. The same Xarax instinct that had guided her here told her that she was safe now, she was –

– honey dancing nest dancing good good dancing the code dancing the code –

Inside the nest, small, spider-like weaver units were slowly uncoiling the fabric of the building, turning it into something more suitable for the Xarax. Jo watched their intricate ballet for a moment, then shook her head as she remembered her mission.

The queen.

Down, said her instincts. She found a ragged hole in the floor with crude steps leading down, *down to sweet sweet honey honey down to be good good honey dancing to be sweet to*

250

be honey dancing and Jo was dancing down the steps. She was sure she was right. This was better than any feeling she'd had before, better than coming home.

Be careful, said Aunt May.

Jo felt a quiver of unease as she saw the amber globes of honey hanging from the ceiling, the others that still looked slightly human lying on the ground. The queen was here somewhere, wasn't it? Someone had told her that, surely? She hesitated at the side of the chamber, then saw something that made up her mind.

A little, bespectacled man in a lab coat, smiling at her.

Doctor Zalloua.

'Miss Grant! How wonderful that you could make it after all!' he said, putting an arm around her shoulders. 'I'm so sorry about all that business with the gun, I really am. It was so unnecessary. I see that now.' He paused, smiled broadly. 'I see everything now. I am reborn. As you will be, shortly.'

– reborn to be honey to be sweet sweet to be perfect to be good to be happy to be dancing the code dancing the code dancing the code –

Jo smiled, let the little man lead her to a vacant patch of soil between two of the half-made honey globes. The tendrils of the honey maker awaited her, twitching slightly in anticipation of the feast. Jo lay back, looked around her.

Saw a face she recognized next to her. A face stretched out of all proportion, above cracked skin leaking honey. A face topped by the tattered remains of blonde hair.

Catriona Talliser's face.

Jo stared, as Zalloua pushed her back towards the honey maker.

'No –' she muttered.

– honey to be good good sweet to be reborn to be perfect to be happy good good dancing honey dancing the code dancing the code –

Catriona's eyes rolled to meet hers, and one of them closed in a grotesque parody of a wink.

Jo screamed.

251

Twenty-Nine

'I wouldn't do that if I were you, Brigadier.'

The Doctor hadn't even looked round; his head was still between the jaws of the huge Xarax whose body filled the lab. The Brigadier held on to the gun, wondered if you could shoot a chap in the middle of arguing with him. Eventually he said, 'Why not, Doctor?'

'Because I think I'd find it rather difficult to work out the codon sequence for the pheromonal control system of the Xarax with a hole in my head.'

The Brigadier still didn't let go of the gun. There was another fusillade of shots from outside the lab, and one of the men shouted something.

'How do I know that's what you're doing?' asked the Brigadier. 'How do I know you're not working with them, like the other one?'

The Doctor stood up, slowly, turned to face the Brigadier. His fingers were sticky with honey; he wiped them on a handkerchief, then smiled. 'You don't,' he said. 'But in twenty minutes or so, if that American chap was right, it isn't going to make any difference. So I suggest you let me get on with it.'

The Brigadier thought about it for a while, then, very slowly, lowered the gun. 'Very well, Doctor,' he said. 'But what exactly is it you're trying to do?'

The Doctor had crouched down again, and was collecting more honey from the insect's jaws, this time into a lab beaker. 'It's a little difficult to explain. Basically I'm trying to persuade the Xarax queen here to help me reverse the primary command sequence in the

Xarax extracellular macroproteination pheromonal control system.' He broke off, found a pipette amidst the rubbish on the floor, opened a wall cupboard and took out a glass bottle filled with blue liquid. He filled the pipette and began mixing the liquid with the honey in the flask, one drop at a time. He stroked his chin in abstraction, muttered, 'There are only twenty million codon sequences involved. You'd think I could remember them.'

There was a huge thud from outside the lab, and the sound of a partition wall being torn apart, followed by a burst of gunfire. The Brigadier ran back to the door, saw a grey creature about the size of a hippopotamus with a pair of mandibles about three feet long attached to its face struggling out of the ruins of one of the offices and across the corridor. The men were firing at it; slowly it sank to the ground, leaking honey.

Then there was another thud, another tearing sound, and a second pair of jaws ripped through the wall in front of the Brigadier. He jumped back, fired at it.

Then a third pair of jaws ripped through the wall beyond him.

He backed into the lab, saw the Doctor standing in the one relatively untouched corner beyond the Xarax queen's jaws, stirring the honey mixture in the beaker.

'Doctor, I don't think we're going to have that twenty minutes,' he said. 'You'd better get a move on.'

Someone was screaming.

Catriona thought that it sounded familiar; but it was nearer than it ought to have been. Jo was on the plane, wasn't she?

But Jo was also lying there, staring at her. An ugly little man was pushing her back, back against the wall.

'Catriona! Help!'

He was going to rape her. Bloody hell.

– honey honey sweet sweet to be honey to be good good stay don't move the nest needs honey sweet sweet –

Shut up, thought Catriona. I'll see to the honey later. I'm not going to stand by and watch another woman being raped.

Her body didn't seem to want to move, though. It was only with a titanic effort that she managed to shift her legs. They seemed to be tied together. She tried to look down to see what was the matter, but her head wouldn't move either. Her eyes only showed a blurry view of an amber surface, rather like the *Probe 9* pictures of Mars. Above it, a dim, mud-walled chamber, and honey-globes –

– *honey honey sweet to be honey* –

Jo screamed again.

Catriona moved her legs a little more, half-stepped, half-fell sideways. She caught a brief glimpse of the little man, startled, falling under the amber surface, which seemed to have moved with her body for some reason. She heard a sickening crunch of bone. Hers?

No, she wasn't feeling any pain. Well, not any more than usual.

Usual? She wasn't in pain, was she? – *to be sweet to be good to be honey dancing* –

Then she realized what the amber surface was, and at the same time she felt the pain, the *utter unbearable agony in every limb every organ Jesus Christ this is what happened to Deveraux and now it's happening to me I'm going to die I'm going to die die die* –

And it was all Jo's fault.

With a mountainous effort, she half-turned, half-rolled her body to face the girl, reached out with her unbelievably swollen, agonized arms. She couldn't quite make her hands touch Jo's throat.

'You left me to them!' she tried to say, though she wasn't sure what sounds were coming out. 'You went on that plane and you left me and I'm dying you bitch bitch BITCH!' Her throat filled with something that tasted sweet and deadly: suddenly she couldn't breathe any more. Her lungs heaved, sending more waves of agony through her.

254

'It wasn't me!' Jo was shouting. Her voice sounded far away, as if there was a mountain of cotton wool in Catriona's ears. 'I don't even know what you're talking about!'

Catriona made a desperate effort to get her breath, failed. Her arms collapsed against the mass of disintegrating flesh that was her body.

Hands touched her skin, Jo's head moved somewhere beneath the range of her eyes. Something blocked her mouth –

– *Jesus Christ she's trying to kill me and I saved her from that bloody rapist –*

– but air was rushing in, Jo was breathing into her, using the pressure from her own strong lungs to clear the blockage and Catriona could breathe again Jesus she could breathe –

As the cool, sweet air of the room rushed into her lungs, Catriona had a sudden pin-sharp image of herself, hideous and broken, as good as dead, stinking of honey and rot and God knows what else, and Jo breathing life into her anyway.

'Thank you,' she managed to gasp. 'I owe you one.' She paused. 'But you'd better collect quickly, or you might not get the chance.' She found Jo's face, some way below her own, looking up with an expression of confusion that slowly gave way to a smile.

'I'll get you out,' said Jo. 'The Doctor will help you.'

I'm going to need more than a doctor, thought Catriona. I'm going to need a certifiable twenty-four carat gold five star miracle to get me out of this one.

But the thought made her feel better all the same.

She heard a sound behind her. Jo's face moved and her eyes widened with fear. Catriona tried to turn her head, couldn't.

'What is it, Jo?' But Jo just kept staring.

The sound grew louder: a scratchy, chitinous, alien noise. Wincing with the effort, Catriona turned her clumsy body around.

She saw three huge, dull grey creatures with pillar-like legs and scissor-like jaws. The jaws were open, and the creatures were advancing slowly towards them.

'We've got to do something,' said Jo. 'Quickly.'

If her face muscles could still have made the movements, Catriona would have smiled. She remembered the last time that Jo had insisted on doing something. The prison. The bucket. The –

Then she remembered what had happened when they'd escaped. The gun bucking in her hand, the guard dying, the thud as her body hit the ground.

Well, this time there was only one thing that could be done. And only she could do it.

It was time to pay.

'Fall back!' yelled the Brigadier, but it was too late for Corporal Marks. The long mandibles caught his arm, wrenched it off in a single movement.

Marks screamed.

The Brigadier put his one remaining bullet through the creature's head. It jolted sideways, but the grey body didn't pause in its advance. The partition wall between the corridor and one of the offices gave way with a crash. The legs trampled Marks's body; the Brigadier heard bones crush, and winced.

There was a shout from behind him. 'They're in the lab, sir!'

'Out of the way!' The Doctor's voice.

The Brigadier retreated from the advancing Xarax, looked into the lab. A huge Xarax head had broken through the corner wall where the Doctor was standing; the brickwork below it was bulging inwards where the body was trying to follow.

The Doctor was standing, staring at the thing, with the beaker of honey in his hands. Sergeant Osgood was retreating slowly along the narrow gap between the queen and the wall, his gun trained on the monster's head.

'Don't kill it,' said the Doctor. 'We just need to give it

some alternative instructions, that's all.'

There was gunfire behind the Brigadier, a shout, more firing. He glanced over his shoulder, saw that the Xarax in the corridor was down, but another was behind it, trying to climb over it. The ceiling bowed, creaked, then gave way. The creature slithered to the floor. There was an explosion of gunfire as the men opened fire on it.

Inside the lab, the Doctor was slowly advancing towards the head of the Xarax defender. 'Come and get it!' he said.

The wall gave way. The Xarax catapulted forward in a heap of bricks. The Doctor dodged nimbly, pushed the beaker underneath its jaws. There was a sound of breaking glass, and the Xarax stopped dead.

'Don't kill it,' repeated the Doctor to Osgood, who was standing transfixed, his gun almost touching the creature's head.

Slowly, the Xarax began to move again. It shuffled past the Doctor and Osgood, squeezed through the gap between its queen and the wall until it reached the Brigadier. Then it stopped.

'Get out of its way, Brigadier,' said the Doctor impatiently.

The Brigadier stepped back, and the creature stuck its head through the door. Then it stopped again, unable to turn its massive bulk any further in the confined space.

The Brigadier stared at the complex pattern of dark and light shading on the top of the creature's skull, only a couple of feet from him.

If the Doctor was wrong –

If it wasn't really the Doctor at all but one of the Xarax –

The Brigadier looked over his shoulder at the men, who were crouched in the corridor, guns at the ready. He waved them down, looked back at the creature. It had secreted a large blob of nearly clear honey, which dropped to the floor underneath it.

'Don't hang around,' said the Doctor. 'Give it to the other one.'

The Brigadier frowned, saw another Xarax defender outside trying to wriggle past the dead body of its comrade. Its mandibles were chopping at the air in a frantic effort to find something to grip. 'How the blazes am I meant to do that without getting my arms bitten off?' he asked.

'Use your imagination, man! Throw it if you have to!'

The Brigadier scooped up the sticky substance in his hands, attempted to throw it. A gobbet detached itself and landed on the floor near the flailing mandibles.

For a moment, all movement stopped. Then the creature dipped an antenna, tasted the stuff. Immediately it began wriggling backwards and fell to the floor with a crash. The creature in the lab was also backing away, returning the way it had come.

'That ought to take care of it,' said the Doctor. He literally clambered over the body of the Xarax defender to get to the door; it took no notice of him, but remained head down, drooling honey. The Doctor collected a little of it in a test tube, sealed it with a cork. Then he stood up, offered the Brigadier his handkerchief. 'Right, now I need an aircraft. Preferably a very fast one. I need to get back to Kebiria straight away.'

'An aircraft? Kebiria?' The Brigadier was bewildered. 'But you've just said that the problem's been taken care of!'

The Doctor looked up at him seriously. 'There's still the other nest in Kebiria, Brigadier. And I have to shut it down before our American friend starts throwing nuclear warheads at it.'

The Brigadier glanced at his watch, made a rapid calculation, swallowed heavily.

'If Captain Oakley's estimate of how long he could hold Al Haraf base was right, Doctor, that's in about ten minutes.'

* * *

When Catriona toppled onto her side and rolled towards the nest defenders, Jo almost screamed again.

Instead it was Catriona who wheezed, 'Run, Jo! Run! It's your only chance!'

'But —' began Jo. She looked around in desperation for a weapon, anything she could use against the aliens to get them away from her friend.

Then the scissor-like mandibles descended on Catriona's body.

She screamed.

Jo stared for another moment, her face crumpling, then she ran.

She would get to the queen. She would get to the queen and take control and stop them. She had to be quick.

Down, her instincts told her. *Down to queen to best honey dancing to help to queen to go down to honey honey —*

'Stop that!' she shouted aloud.

She was running blind now, her feet jarring on solid rock. How long had the Xarax been building here? she wondered.

The air grew cool, musty. Then an overpoweringly sweet smell hit her.

— queen to be dancing to be honey human to be peace dancing —

Light grew ahead, and chitinous rustlings. Jo saw a large chamber, nest defenders bustling about, and the stiff, quasi-human figures of the Xarax copies.

In the middle, as huge as a blue whale, was the queen. As Jo ran up, the huge jaws opened, and the long black cable of the tongue emerged, a drop of honey suspended on its tip.

This is it, she thought. This is what Zalloua meant by linking with the queen. Well here goes —

Jo knelt before the queen, felt the tongue touch the back of her neck.

Almost immediately she realized her mistake, but by then it was too late.

* * *

259

Captain James Oakley of the US Marines crouched in the shadow of the command bunker and watched the line of Xarax tanks rolling across the desert towards the Al Haraf base. Men were scattering in front of them, running towards the wire fence. Oakley could see that most of them weren't going to make it.

He picked up the handset of the field telephone and yelled into it. 'Kelly! Get me one of the first strike fighters!'

There was a crackle of static, then, 'None responding, sir. I think they're all –'

An explosion shook the ground; Oakley almost lost his grip on the phone. He glanced over his shoulder at the bunker, saw flames and smoke. Swore.

'Kelly!' he bawled into the phone.

Silence.

He cleared the line, dialled oh-one-oh.

The line crackled, buzzed.

Oakley waited. Ahead of him the tanks were rolling forward, sunlight gleaming off their chitinous armour. A section of fence a few hundred yards ahead of him exploded into flame: Oakley heard a man scream, saw him running, burning.

Napalm, he thought. Jesus H Christ, where did they get that idea?

The phone crackled, then a voice spoke. 'Carver here.' The line was surprisingly clear: Oakley imagined the white-uniformed man standing on the bridge of the *Eisenhower*. Imagined the key in his hand, the red box chained to the bridge controls.

There was another explosion of fire, near enough for Oakley to feel the heat on his face. He estimated the interval between the two impacts, the range of the weapon, the speed of the approaching tanks.

The next one would get him. There was no time to think about it – he just had to do it. To say it.

'It's Oakley, sir,' he said into the phone. 'The code is – Tripwire.'

'Tripwire,' said the calm voice. 'Confirmed.'

Then there was an explosion of flame and light and pain, and the phone was wrenched away from his hand.

Oakley's last thought before the darkness descended was quite simple: *we're going to get you for this.*

Thirty

'Brigadier, sometimes I think your grasp of practical temporal physics is somewhat limited. If we're all blown up by an H-bomb whilst I'm trying to repair the TARDIS navigational circuits, how can I possibly go back in time afterwards and stop it from happening? Besides which, the old girl's rarely on target at the best of times and I can't take the chance of anything going wrong. There's no way I'll ever repair the Prognosticator, you know.'

He made it sound as if this last was the Brigadier's own personal fault. The Brigadier decided to ignore the remark.

'If you say so, Doctor,' he said. He picked up the phone Osgood had wired to the remains of the lab circuits, dialled nine; jiggled the handset against the rest then put it to his ear. The line remained dead. 'But the fact remains that the telephone lines from this building are down, the radio room appears to have been eaten by our Xarax friends, and quite frankly the quickest way you're going to get a flight to Kebiria at the moment is to go to Heathrow and thumb a lift.'

The Doctor shook his head, glanced at the huge face of the Xarax queen. It twitched its antennae and dribbled a little honey onto the floor.

'Wait a minute!' He set off out of the lab at a run. The Brigadier shrugged to himself and followed.

He caught up with the Doctor in the car park, interrogating a bewildered Sergeant Benton. 'Are you quite sure you haven't seen any cars here?'

Benton shook his head. 'Not one, Doctor. We assumed —'

'Never mind what you assumed!' He turned swiftly. 'Brigadier! Have you checked the garages yet?'

'The garages? Not yet, but I'll —'

'Never mind,' said the Doctor again. He started across the tarmac at a run. Again, the Brigadier followed him, wondering what on Earth the Doctor wanted a car for. He could hardly drive to Kebiria.

He found the Doctor standing outside the open door of the concrete sheds where the troop transports were kept. Inside, instead of the usual canvas-covered trucks and trailers, was the sleek, gleaming black shape of a rocket plane.

'What the blazes is that doing in there, Doctor?' asked the Brigadier. 'It's meant to be a top secret —' He broke off, as he realized that the plane had eyes.

The Doctor advanced towards the plane. Its eyes examined him as he advanced, then the shutters clicked shut over them. A tiny pair of jaws unfolded and a proboscis reached down. The Doctor produced a beaker of honey, let the creature taste it. 'I *knew* that they had to be using the metal for something,' he muttered, apparently to himself.

A door opened in its side, grounded with a thud. The Doctor hastily clambered inside.

The Brigadier rushed up to him 'Hold on a minute, Doctor. You're not —'

'You can't come with me, Brigadier, there isn't room and there isn't enough fuel.'

The Brigadier looked inside, saw the Doctor crouched inside the — you couldn't really call it a cockpit, it was more like the creature's mouth, or even its stomach. Slimy green tentacles were wrapping themselves around the Doctor's neck.

The Brigadier remembered his earlier doubts. His hand moved towards the holster of his gun. 'Doctor, are you sure you're going to be in control of this — this thing?'

The Doctor glanced at him, smiled. 'I'm going to have to be, Brigadier. There isn't really any choice.' He paused. 'I suggest you take cover. Even though this is only a copy of a rocket, I suspect that lift-off will be pretty violent.'

Then the door flipped upwards, shutting the Doctor inside. The creature began a hissing sound, which gradually increased in pitch. The Brigadier ran to the side of the garage, crouched down behind a workbench.

A few seconds later the Xarax began to roll out of the garage. It had barely cleared the door when there was a deafening explosion. The Brigadier sprang up, ran through the clearing smoke.

He was just in time to see the black shape of the alien disappearing into the sky on a tail of flame.

'Well, Doctor,' he said. 'Good luck.'

He almost added, I hope you know what you're doing; but it was a bit late for that.

THE NEST IS UNDER ATTACK!

Jo struggled to respond to the situation. She wanted peace –

– *of course she wanted peace she wanted the nest to shut down that was what she was here for* –

– but there were missiles approaching.

ACT NOW!

She released the instructions to the rocket planes, and they steered towards the incoming missiles. She judged the distances from their radio and radar signals, realized that there was no hope of intercepting all of the missiles except by crashing into them.

You will have to die for the nest, she told the planes; and received their joyful acknowledgements.

– *this isn't right I'm supposed to stop all this I'm supposed to be here to* –

More missiles came from the west. More rocket planes needed to be despatched. Jo instructed them to send details of the missiles' construction, to disable one for analysis if possible.

Weapons must be met with equivalent weapons, until there was peace.

From the bridge of the USS *Eisenhower*, the Kebiriz coast was a smudge on the horizon, brown beyond the blue of the sea. The bow of the vessel pointed directly at the coast; the white painted lines on the flat grey deck seemed to be aimed at it, like sighting lines for an oversize gun.

Admiral Kent J. Carver of the US Navy stared at the scene for a moment, and wished it had been that easy. He shook his head, turned to the *Eisenhower*'s captain.

'Missile status?'

The captain didn't glance up from the radar screen. 'They've all gone, sir. Intercepted, every single one.'

'Anything coming in?'

'Plenty.' The captain glanced up for a moment. 'If they keep this up we aren't going to be able to hold them much longer. They'll be all over southern Europe by tonight.'

Carver looked away from the man's eyes. Looked out to sea for a few seconds.

It all looked so peaceful. So –

He saw the moving dots a second too late. They were skimming the surface of the sea, below the level of radar. He opened his mouth to speak, to warn the captain, but was beaten to it by a brilliant flash of light at the bows.

The blastproof glass held, just. Carver saw cracks in it, then focused on the ruined bows beyond, the buckled deck.

Every alarm on the panel shone a red light; somewhere, a klaxon started to sound. Next to him, the captain began bellowing orders into a microphone.

Carver walked away, across the deck that was already canting to one side. He knew that there was nothing to stop the aliens putting a nuclear warhead on their missiles next time. They'd been given a more than adequate supply.

There was only one course of action left.

265

But it wasn't up to him to decide on it.

He picked up a red telephone handset on one side of the bridge, ignoring the men racing round him, the shouts about firefighting crews and evacuation procedures. He took a key from his pocket, inserted it in the panel to which the handset was connected, put the handset to his ear.

The phone at the other end rang once, then a woman answered.

'Pentagon Navy five?'

'Carver here,' said the Admiral quietly. 'Put me through to the President. Now.'

Thirty-One

Jo's legs were cramped with constant kneeling and the skin of her face was crawling with sweat, but she couldn't let her concentration slip now.

She felt, rather than saw, the new missile coming in on its unusual trajectory over Europe. It was slower than the missiles from the ships, and there was something odd about its radio signals —

'— honey honey good good sweet sweet honey to be honey dancing to be sweet sweet —'

It was Xarax.

— that means the Doctor's lost or he never got there and the Xarax have taken over England as well it's all over all over unless I can persuade the defenders to destroy the missile —

— after all it might be dangerous —

— yes make the Xarax turn on themselves —

She issued the instructions: new missile is dangerous is fake Xarax will destroy nest destroy honey no dancing no honey no sweet sweet —

Jo watched as the defenders closed in on the missile. She could almost hear the Doctor's voice: 'This ought to confuse them.'

For the first time in hours, she smiled.

The phone on the Brigadier's desk made a few awkward, experimental tinkling noises. He snatched up the receiver, was immensely relieved to hear a dialling tone.

'Good old Osgood,' he muttered as he dialled the emergency MoD number.

The phone was answered at once.

'Who is this?' The Minister's voice.

'Brigadier Lethbridge-Stewart, Minister. We've got an emergency here –'

'I know we've got an emergency! Where on Earth have you been for the last twelve hours?'

'I'm sorry, Minister, I've been –'

'Well, it doesn't matter now,' interrupted the Minister. There was a pause: a phone rang, someone spoke, too quietly for the Brigadier to hear the words. Then the Minister's voice, muffled, 'Have the Russians been informed? And the Chinese?' A moment later he came back full volume: 'You'll have to get off the line, I'm afraid. We're about to go for a full strategic nuclear strike against these Xarax things. Wipe them out.'

'But Minister, with all due respect, that's not advisable! I've been told that –'

'I'm sorry, Brigadier, it's been agreed at the highest level. It's out of your hands now.'

The line went dead.

Jo couldn't believe the way the thing was dodging her defenders. It seemed to stop in mid-air, drop, or reverse direction with impossible speed. Once it disappeared altogether and reappeared in a completely different part of the sky.

It seemed to be playing with the Xarax.

It was then that she began to think it just might possibly be –

– but keep the thought to yourself or else –

The intruder was now too near the ground to be visible on radar, but Xarax all over the city saw it as it skimmed over the rooftops, swerving and dodging all the way, before finally skidding to a landing along the main boulevard outside the People's Palace.

A door opened in the side, and a familiar figure got out.

– Doctor! But what am I going to tell them how can I keep them from –

He was a Xarax copy. He had to be. The original Doctor was dead.

Jo bit her lip.

Watched as the eyes of the Xarax defenders showed the figure of the Doctor running across the lawns, into the Palace, put his hands on his hips and stare around him –

– *down, Doctor, down here–*

– the Doctor was heading for the hole in the ground which led to the honey chamber, but then he stopped, made as if to turn back –

– *no Doctor DOWN HERE –*

One of the nest defenders pushed its head through the hole: Jo saw the Doctor jump back, turn to run –

– *down the ventway –*

– and she could hear his footsteps ringing on the stone, and then his voice –

'Jo!'

She wrenched at the sticky tongue attached to her neck, felt it flick back in pain. She tried to stand, couldn't.

The Doctor reached her, put his arms around her.

'Doctor! I've been so scared I didn't know whether I was doing the right thing and Catriona's dead and Vincent's dead and I don't know what's happened to Mike and –'

'Steady on, Jo,' said the Doctor. 'First of all I've got to –'

There was a clatter of chitin on stone. The Doctor let her go, and Jo saw that several nest defenders were closing in on them, jaws wide.

Of course, she thought. Now I'm no longer in control they know the Doctor's not Xarax. They'll –

But the Doctor took a test-tube full of honey from his pocket and flung it into the queen's mouth. Almost immediately, her tongue flicked out and wrapped itself around the Doctor's neck.

'Doctor, be careful!' she shouted. 'They'll take you over!'

269

'Not now, Jo. That test-tube contained Xarax anti-pheromones. I've changed the programming of the queen, and she'll change the programming of the nest. Everything's under –' There was a pause. 'Oh. That might be a problem.' There was a longer pause. Jo saw the nest defenders crouch down, their mandibles twitching. They formed a ring around the queen.

'Doctor, what's the matter?'

'The fools!' exclaimed the Doctor. 'The absolute fools!' He rammed a fist into his palm.

'Doctor, what is it?' asked Jo.

The Doctor looked up, slowly shook his head. 'There's a missile strike coming in – this entire city will be destroyed in less than five minutes. And us with it, I'm afraid.'

'But Doctor, you can use the nest defences! I did it!'

The Doctor unravelled the black cable of the queen's tongue from his neck, shook his head slowly.

'No I can't, Jo.' He indicated the defenders, which were rocking to and fro on the floor, drooling honey. 'I've just immobilized them. Permanently.'

Thirty-Two

RADIO MESSAGE — GENERAL DISTRIBUTION

ALL FIELD UNITS US ARMY/NAVY/AIR FORCE IN VICINITY KEBIRIA

URGENT

THE PRESIDENT HAS AUTHORIZED FULL STRATEGIC NUCLEAR STRIKE REPEAT FULL STRATEGIC NUCLEAR STRIKE ON UNITS KNOWN AS XARAX. AIRBURSTS IN THE RANGE ONE TO FIVE MEGATONS EXPECTED KEBIR CITY AND DESERT AREAS TO SOUTH AND WEST WITHIN FIVE MINUTES OF THIS TRANSMISSION. ALL PERSONNEL ARE ADVISED TO TAKE APPROPRIATE PRECAUTIONS.

GOOD LUCK AND MAY GOD BE WITH YOU.

C-IN-C

'We've got to do *something*,' said Jo, struggling to her feet.

The Doctor was pacing to and fro in front of the immobilized defenders. At last he stopped, turned to Jo. 'Where are the radio units in the nest?' he asked.

'Radio units? What radio units?'

The Doctor stepped up to her. 'Jo, I'm not getting any information from the queen any longer. The antipheromones have broken the chain of command. I need you to tell me.'

271

'But Doctor, I don't know what you're talking about!' Jo felt her face flush with blood, felt pins and needles in her hands and feet.

'Think, Jo! Think! It must be somewhere – how else were you communicating with all those units in flight?'

Jo closed her eyes, struggled to think.

Radio.

Honey honey radio.

She opened her eyes, shook her head. 'It's gone, Doctor. I don't hear it any more.'

The Doctor took her shoulders, shook her gently. 'Yes, Jo. I know. The antipheromones will have worked on you too. But you can remember, can't you? You've got to try and remember.'

Jo blinked.

'Up,' she said suddenly, without quite knowing why. 'In the Palace.'

The Doctor let her go, turned and ran towards the tunnel that led to the surface. Jo ran after him. Their footsteps echoed on the stone.

When they reached the mud-walled chamber where the honey-globes were stored, Jo suddenly remembered Catriona. Catriona who'd given her life so that Jo could get away. She realized that she hadn't even thought of the woman since it had happened. Too much had been going on. She remembered Catriona in Vincent's truck, saying 'how is it possible to forget?'

'Don't worry, Catriona,' muttered Jo. 'Everyone does it.' She stopped, looked around at the broken faces of the honey-globes.

'Jo!' called the Doctor from the steps. 'Come on, we've got less than three minutes left!'

Jo sprinted after him, gazed around her.

'Which way, Jo?' asked the Doctor.

Jo saw a staircase, leading up to a landing. Gilded bannisters decorated its sides. 'Up there,' she said, then frowned. 'I think. Doctor, where are we?' But the Doctor was already sprinting up the stairs.

Jo hesitated at the bottom of the steps, tried to think. Radio. Where?

A room shaped like an egg, she thought suddenly. She could almost see it, and the signals pulsing out from it. But it was like the memory of a dream: it faded as soon as she tried to get a grip on it.

She shouted up after the Doctor: 'Like an egg! A room shaped like an egg!'

The Doctor looked down at her, smiled. 'Well done, Jo. I think I know where to go now.'

He set off at a run to the right. Jo sprinted up the stairs, followed him down a darkened corridor. At the end the Doctor had stopped short in front of a white-and-gilt door, with a human figure standing outside it.

'Excuse me,' said the Doctor, and pushed at the figure. It toppled to the floor, twitched its head once, then lay still.

The Doctor opened the door.

The room *was* egg-shaped – at least, it was oval, with a domed ceiling. A single, huge window with broken shutters let in a stripe of afternoon sunlight. The ceiling was broken open in places, revealing the bare ribs of curved joists; the floor was covered in pieces of fallen plaster and broken wood. In the middle of the room, on the crushed remnants of a bed, sat the strangest living thing that Jo had ever seen.

It was black, shiny, and resembled nothing so much as a huge, hexagonal nut. Where the bolt should have been a spindly cable rose through the broken ceiling and presumably out through the roof. Other cables sprouted from other sections and trailed around the room. Jo only knew the creature was alive at all because of a tiny shuttered eye, and a slightly larger pair of jaws, at the top of each section.

'Doctor, what is it?' she asked.

But the Doctor was already bending down over the nearest section. 'Copied the design from the Sontarans, by the look of it,' he muttered. 'They've been around, this lot.' He caught hold of the nearest chitinous face and pulled.

It came away with a sucking sound, revealed a tangle of coloured cables and pieces of what appeared to be metal. The Doctor reached in, started pulling at the wires. There was an electrical spitting sound.

'Reverse the polarity of the binary transmission decoder unit and link it to the reception unit –' muttered the Doctor.

You'd better hurry up, thought Jo. She wasn't sure how much time had passed since they'd left the brood chamber, but she knew that there couldn't possibly be much more than a minute left.

The Doctor took a step back from the creature, a cluster of wires in each hand. 'Well, Jo, here goes,' he said, and pushed the two clusters together.

There was a crackle, a shower of sparks, and then a very loud bang. The Doctor stood up, turned to Jo, his expression serious.

'It didn't work, did it?' she said quietly.

'It might have done,' said the Doctor. 'I put the whole of the residual voltage in that thing's batteries through the circuit in about three-fifths of a second. It should have been long enough.'

'Long enough to what?'

'Long enough to scramble the detonation mechanisms on the incoming missiles.'

'And if it wasn't?'

'Well, Jo,' said the Doctor slowly. 'If we're still alive after about thirty seconds, I think we can say it worked.'

Jo looked away, swallowed.

Thirty seconds.

She reached out and took the Doctor's hands, then let herself be hugged. She tried to imagine what it would be like, if the bomb went off. Would she feel anything? Or would she simply cease to exist?

Fifteen seconds, she thought. Fourteen. Thirteen.

No. They're too precious to count.

She stared over the blurry edge of the Doctor's jacket at the sunlight streaming in through the window. Felt the warmth of it.

The sun will still shine, she thought. Even if —

'Time's up, Jo,' said the Doctor's voice softly. 'I think we've won.'

Epilogue

A veil of smoke was still hanging over Kebir City, smoke that was scented of honey and roses and cloves. Jo stared through it at the low red disc of the sun setting over the distant domes of the People's Palace. Then she turned to the Doctor and Mike Yates, who were standing on the dry shingle beach, looking out over the Mediterranean.

The sea was smooth, oily; Jo could see grey shapes moving in the haze of smoke, hear the clatter of engines.

Helicopters: American helicopters, searching for bodies from the *Eisenhower*.

She shuddered.

'After Tahir picked me up we had a look for Vincent's body,' Mike was saying. 'We had a job on finding it; I thought it had been taken by the Xarax.'

'But you did find it?' Jo was surprised that she was so concerned. Vincent had been a murderer; but his death still touched her.

Mike nodded. 'We burned it, in case it was infected. The *Sakir* insisted.' He paused, turned to the Doctor. 'What did you do to the Xarax?'

'Well basically I told them to switch themselves off.' He looked at Jo, gave her a rueful smile. 'I don't think humanity's ready for such a tool yet, do you?'

Jo shook her head.

'Is that all they were?' asked Mike. 'A tool kit?'

The Doctor nodded. 'A biological tool kit, but a tool kit nonetheless. They just obey whatever program they're given. I imagine that originally they existed as very sophisticated symbiotes. Then some intelligent species discovered them, adapted them for their own ends, gave them control mechanisms that could be used by other species.' He paused. 'I realized that as soon as Zalloua told us how easily he could control the Xarax. Even though he said he was making mistakes, for him to be able to do it at all there had to be some pre-existing control mechanism.' He glanced at Jo. 'Of course, I should have realized that with a built-in control mechanism, it really wasn't very likely that Zalloua was having the problems he was claiming to have.'

'So how did they get to Earth?' asked Jo.

The Doctor shrugged. 'By accident, possibly. Or maybe they were dropped off deliberately; perhaps their masters thought they were doing humanity a favour. But of course they reckoned without humans like Monsieur Zalloua –'

He broke off as the *Sakir* Mohammad came into view, his head bowed.

'It is as you told us, Doctor,' he said. 'They are all gone.'

'Everyone in the city?' asked Mike.

The *Sakir* shrugged. 'Tahir and Jamil have checked all the districts. No-one answers them when they call. There may be a few that are hiding, but –' He broke off, shaking his head.

'Burrous Asi was empty when we came through it,' said Mike. 'Doctor, how far do you think the Xarax would have spread?'

The Doctor was staring out to sea. The helicopters were further away now, the sound of their engines fading. The smoke haze had thinned a little, revealing a gunmetal-grey horizon.

'Doctor?' asked Jo, when he didn't speak for a while.

'They wouldn't have bothered much with small population centres,' said the Doctor at last. 'Not when they were fighting for survival. The Kebiriz coastal towns should be all right, I think. And the Gilteans' desert oases, if they weren't too near the nest.'

There was a long silence.

'Kebiria was a country of six million people,' said the *Sakir* eventually.

There was another long silence. Mike slowly walked away, his hands in his pockets. After a while he picked up his binoculars and looked at the city through them, perhaps hoping to spot some sign of life.

'What will you do now, *Sakir*?' asked Jo.

The old man shook his head. 'I don't know. Start again, I suppose. But we will not call the country Kebiria any more.' He paused. 'And we will not call it Giltea either. I will think of a new name.'

Somewhere behind them, a man's voice began a soft recital, half-spoken, half-chanted. At some points, other voices joined in.

'I must join my people,' said the *Sakir*. He walked quickly up the shingle slope to the sea wall. Beyond it, Jo saw the jeeps drawn up in a circle in the middle of the wide concrete promenade, in front of the tourist hotels. Someone had put a camel-wool tent up; the voices appeared to be coming from inside it.

An encampment, thought Jo. A desert encampment in the middle of a city.

She turned back to the Doctor. 'They won't be able to bury any of them, will they? They'll have to burn them all.' She was thinking of Catriona. Catriona who had died saving her life.

The Doctor nodded. 'But they'll probably put up a memorial.'

'It's not much compensation.' Jo stared at the gunmetal horizon until her eyes watered. She thought about the Brigadier, shooting the copies of the Doctor and herself with that cold expression on his face. About the guard dying in the prison. About the little girl dying in Vincent's camp.

All the deaths.

'Perhaps I could be a reporter, like Catriona,' she said at

278

last. 'I could tell people what it's really like. How horrible it is.'

The Doctor smiled at her. 'Not everything's horrible, Jo. I know it seems that way sometimes, but –'

He broke off, looked up at the jeeps. Jo heard the sound of raised voices.

'– new state . . . Kebiriz welcome . . .' The *Sakir*'s voice.

'I would die first! After what the Kebiriz have done to us we can never allow them to be a part of our country. It must be *ours*!'

'The conflict must come to an end, and the only way is to let the Kebiriz take part –'

'We cannot! I will kill them first!'

Jo started up the shingle towards the makeshift encampment, but the Doctor caught her arm.

'It's better not to interfere, Jo. You don't know enough about this quarrel to decide –'

But Jo shook her head, and shook off his arm.

'We can't just let it start again, Doctor,' she said. 'We've got to do *something*.'

Available in the *Doctor Who – New Adventures* series:

The next Missing Adventure is *System Shock* by Justin Richards, featuring the fourth Doctor, Sarah and Harry.